Advance Praise

"This novel keeps alive not only the memory of my brother, but the vitality of his huge talent. I can hear his voice on every page – his quiet and sneaky wit, his wide-armed embrace of life's wobbliest characters, and his heartfelt fascination with why good people make the wildly improbable choices they do."

— Carl Hiaasen, best-selling author and brother of *Float Plan's* author

FLOAT PLAN

FLOAT PLAN

Rob Hiaasen

Apprentice
House Press
Loyola University Maryland

First Edition

Casebound ISBN: 978-1-62720-199-5
Paperback ISBN: 978-1-62720-200-8
Ebook ISBN: 978-1-62720-201-5

Printed in the United States of America

Design by Apprentice House Press
Edited by Carmen Machalek

Cover photo, titled "Sid Skiff," by Ingrid Taylar, licensed under the Creative Commons Attribution 2.0 Generic license: https://creativecommons.org/licenses/by/2.0/

Published by Apprentice House Press

Apprentice
House Press
Loyola University Maryland

Apprentice House Press
Loyola University Maryland
4501 N. Charles Street
Baltimore, MD 21210
410.617.5265 • 410.617.2198 (fax)
www.ApprenticeHouse.com
info@ApprenticeHouse.com

*"A float plan lets your family and friends know your whereabouts...
should a trip come to grief."*

— *BoatUS*

"The only joy in the world is to begin."

— *Cesare Pavese*

Foreword

I knew what my husband was up to.

We'd be decompressing from our work weeks, chatting over Friday night wine on the deck or in the family room. I'd lodge my latest complaint about the bureaucracy of public education, and suddenly he'd plant his glass and grab pen and paper (often a New Yorker cover or subscription post card tucked inside the magazine).

"Say that again," he'd say.

He'd flare his left eyebrow and scribble my line, then swing right back into our conversation. Another piece of string for his novel, *Float Plan*.

While this book fulfills one of Rob's lifelong dreams (he called it a pre-occupation that haunted him in a journal he kept for our then infant son Ben in 1989), Rob's wish with *Float Plan* was simple. He hoped to craft a touching yet comic story about a man who loses his footing in life when his wife up and leaves, a story that reflected the ambiance of Annapolis and conveyed truths about our common struggle to love and to adapt to disappointment and sudden change.

Of course, the task of writing such a book was not so simple. He spent nearly a decade drafting *Float Plan*, gathering string from observations at work and his private life, then revising and re-revising in hopes of producing something marketable. With a hellish weekday commute to Annapolis from our northern Baltimore County home, weekends proved to be essential writing opportunities.

Permit me to set the scene. Saturday mornings as I awoke to coffee and a short stack of high school English papers to grade in the kitchen, I'd hear Rob on his laptop in the living room, tapping out his narrative. We were a dining room apart yet together in spirit, attending to work that mattered to us, still mindful of the need for the restorative properties of a weekend together. Saturday morning independent work sessions typically yielded to some joint chore (trip to Lowe's for hydrangeas) followed by something more fun (biking on the NCR Trail at Gunpowder Falls State Park followed by dinner at his favorite rib joint). Sunday mornings, Rob would return to his writing, making the most of the solitude I generously provided him as I fed my weekly Wegmans addiction.

There's an imprint of our pattern in Rob's two main characters, Will Larkin and Parker Cool. But, I offer that level of domestic detail in hopes of explaining that while Rob pursued writing this novel passionately, he was not a workaholic. He never demanded time sequestered in separate writer's quarters. He valued our marriage and our family too much for that. Instead, he seized and used creative writing opportunities when and where he found them, filling moleskin notebooks with reporterly observations and writing whenever he could.

As one of Rob's close friends told me recently, "Rob had it all figured out. He knew what was important in life." It sounds a little pat, yet it rings true. Through decades of marriage, parenting, and career chasing, Rob believed people, relationships, and emotions mattered. The reporters and students he mentored saw it. I hope readers will see it here, particularly in the way Rob injects the value of poetry into this novel.

I should note that in typical Norwegian fashion, Rob was largely stoic and determined to achieve his goal of completing a successful work of fiction. But not always. He'd spend months not talking about the book, and then reveal the contents of a candid emailed critique he had solicited. A time or two, he even announced that he wanted to quit the book all together. Weeks or months would pass. Sure enough, I'd hear him back in that living room, tinkering with the portrayal of his protagonist, Will, the math teacher challenged to face the reality that not every problem can be solved by a tried and true formula.

"So, what makes Will Larkin happy?" asks Parker Cool, the woman he is drawn to after his wife ditches him.

"When life adds up."

"How's that been working out for you?"

"Not tops."

Indeed. Early on, Will's misguided (and farcical) reaction to his wife's rejection lands him in trouble with the local authorities (There's a chainsaw involved along with serious property damage.) Later, Will loses his classroom to a fledgling teacher and must "float" to the classes he teaches. Before long, his challenges include adjusting to life with his new girlfriend's child and his father's Alzheimer's disease.

Of course, nobody would take a chainsaw to a neighbor's property in frustration over a broken marriage. But isn't it tempting to laugh at such ridiculous options even as we pursue the sublime responses to life's vicissitudes? Rob – in touch with his inner child, and I have the silly emails to prove it – certainly thought so. No doubt, he adopted this attitude as he struggled with his own disappointments (toiling over a book that didn't seem to be going anywhere and losing his father as a teenager, to name a few).

I may be scaring you into thinking this is a dark or maudlin novel. Rob, practical optimist and avowed romantic, would never have written such a book. Two of his sayings come to mind as I reread *Float Plan*. One is, "Life is what happens to you while you're busy making other plans," which Rob probably remembered from John Lennon's song "Beautiful Boy" in 1980. Obviously, what I've described already qualifies Will as living proof of this maxim.

Another of Rob's favorite sayings is a line he repeated often during our 33 years together, one he wrote in the journal he kept for our youngest child, Hannah: "The purpose of life is to give birth to yourself." I believe Dickens' *David Copperfield* inspired that one, and I know Rob held it close to his heart. In the bedside notes for his novel, he actually wrote, "Will wants to succeed at being myself" (sic). The mistake in the reflexive pronoun is a telling one.

I surely hope Rob Hiaasen knew that *he* had succeeded at being himself. In person, in notes in emails and in Facebook messages, countless fellow journalists, friends, and family members have told me *they* knew he had.

That provides solace to Ben, Sam, Hannah, and me as this book reaches readers without Rob here to see that happen.

I began here by noting how Rob used observations of others (including me) to fuel *Float Plan*. But what I believe makes this book a fulfilling read is the fact that it is pure Rob, a creative attempt to expose and maybe even celebrate the state of being human. Again, I'll refer to something Rob included in one of our children's journals. It's a line Rob wrote to our daughter Sam, one she shared at his celebration of life. After describing toddler Sam's antics, he noted that he had mistakenly turned the journal upside down before he wrote that day.

"That's okay," he wrote. "*I'm* a little upside down."

Aren't we all?

— *Maria Hiaasen, August 2018*

Chapter 1

The masked algebra teacher was drunk to the point of embalmment, as the blood orange machine dented his lap. Will Larkin bought the chainsaw online ("Choose the Best Chainsaw for You!") and strummed its greasy fangs with his left index finger. A prick, ouch. He squeezed his finger to make blood, a drib. He drank again from a pitcher of mojitos infused with enough Myers's dark rum to stoke a beach bonfire. Raising his pollen mask before each gust of drinking, the fall allergy sufferer knew he needed a posse of mojitos when the time came to act.

Nursing his first injury involving lawn machinery, Will left the back deck of his rental townhouse and went inside for a Band-Aid, the baby ones. He hoped his wife left him that much when she moved out this morning, hoped Terri at least left him Band-Aids and the biblical "Complete Cartoons of The New Yorker." She left both – plus six coffee mugs from a fruitful litter of coffee mug parents. Baby bandaged, Will returned to his deck and mojitos. He needed an accomplice, but his network consisted of one dog, two friends, two parents, and Terri. He didn't know any new people.

He waited for the recessed light of dusk. A red-shouldered hawk snagged a chickadee off their backyard A-framed feeder – a puff of dusty gray feathers parachuted to the ground.

Will patted his Poulan 14-inch chainsaw.

In time, partner, all in good time.

• • •

Last Sunday, omens.

Will forgot to put on his watch, a major breach in his morning routine. And when he reached for his off-white, un-lettered coffee mug, he sideswiped the cupboard's corner and decapitated the ceramic handle. Will picked up the severed handle, light as a bird wing. Then, his Briggs & Stratton lawn mower that had never let him down wouldn't start. Will pulled and pulled the starter rope until the handle snapped out of his grasp and whipped his hand. There would be no mowing.

Will moped over to their back deck where Terri was reading *The New York Times*. Every Sunday they carved up the *Times* – Terri crab-picking out "Week in Review and Business". They believed themselves to be the only people under 30 who still got a newspaper. A couple of young-old souls, Will would say, gobbling up the sports section. He avoided the news, which made him antsy. News was always so *loud*.

"Don't you care about climate change? Stormwater run-off? Syria?"

"I care about you."

"I mean caring about something bigger than ourselves, bigger than us, Will."

"I care about mowing our yard."

"I'm being serious."

He stared out into their woodsy backyard as if it was an ocean's wobbly horizon. "Backyard watching" was his occasional Sunday morning pastime. The grandfatherly activity mystified Terri – that and how her husband waited, each year, for the return of a box turtle that once occupied the northern corner of the rental lot. The turtle never returned, a turtle he named Petey. Petey, the Non-Returning Turtle. Pining for a ghost turtle never struck Terri as something they both could enjoy.

"All right. Here's something I care about," Will said. "Maryland should have a law that makes air free at gas stations. No more paying four or five quarters for air."

Who isn't in favor of free air?

"You don't know what the problem is, do you?" she said.

Will studied his hands, which appeared to be sprouting age spots. He would be 30 next year.

"Are you still pissed about the lobsters?"

In a rare solo run to Wegmans, Will found himself distracted by the store's overhead train set and, in general, by the cavernous, cult-inducing Wegmanian vibe – but mainly by the awesome train. He wandered over to the seafood department where five, banded lobsters were stacked atop one another in a feature-less tank. He imagined a more exotic and natural existence for them. Could they survive in the creek way behind their townhouse? He had seen crayfish in Dan's Creek and what were they but practice lobsters? The jovial man behind the seafood counter was more than happy to bag up five, 2-pound lobsters from Maine. Will left Wegmans forgetting every item on his list (TP, milk, pulp-free OJ, some sort of spatula Terri wanted) and returned home with $110 worth of live lobsters. And Wegman's peach mango salsa. Never forget that.

While Terri took a rare Saturday afternoon nap, Will scurried down-slope to the creek bed with his special groceries. Lobsters, which are not prone to frolicking, hunkered down in the shallow slippery water and assumed their same docile positions in the bare fish tank at Wegmans. In a further disappointment, days later Will discovered the Freedom Crustaceans in no way adapted to life in the wild. They croaked. And the household still needed TP, milk, pulp-free OJ, and some sort of spatula.

"No, Will. This isn't about your lobsters."

"Then help me out here."

"The problem is," Terri said, "you're here, but you're not. You stare off into the back yard. You drift away. You've been drifting away, and I'm the only one who seems to notice or care. You don't even know when you're not here with me."

"I'm here, I'm here. What do you want, Terri? Tell me."

"I want a gazebo."

Two years ago, their neighbors built a redwood-stained gazebo. Buffered by blooming forsythia, a 30-foot wooden walkway led from the Dunhams' back door to the screened gazebo, which stood on five posts tucked into the woods both townhouses shared this side of Dan's Creek. Chestnut and live oaks nearly suffocated the back yards of the houses built here in 1975

– the last suburban parcel developed in Anderson Woods. On fall nights, the elderly Dunhams could be seen dancing in the gazebo. Show-offs.

"I think a gazebo would be a nice change," Terri said.

There was nothing wrong with their back yard. Plus, they had never talked about gazebos – especially on Sundays.

"Why do we need a gazebo?"

He heard the machine-gunning of a red-headed woodpecker drilling a tulip poplar. Chasing the morning sun, Will moved his deck chair. Clouds like shaving cream mounds slipped across the sky, as seashell chimes fluttered from a neighboring porch.

"A gazebo extends a home, creates a new room in the woods. Gives you a new perspective, a new place to be."

Had she enrolled in a continuing education course in architectural drafting? Studied the pros and cons of cedar vs. pine gazebos? Vinyl vs. aluminum? Octagon vs. rectangle? Did she want her gazebo screened or one gone commando?

"You want a place to go that's still your house but away from me," Will said.

"I didn't say that."

She was saying that.

"We're not getting a gazebo, are we?"

Will looked over at the neighbor's yard. The stilted gazebo looked like it might tear itself from the townhouse and raft through their woods. Someone should do something about that goddamn gazebo.

• • •

A week later, Will was sideways into mojitos, his lap heavy with chainsaw. He raised his pollen mask to drink to his crumbling marriage. Two years and eleven months, a 2.92-year marriage. Will never rounded off – math teachers rarely do. He met Terri at a soul-sucking faculty meeting (although he remembered her from high school; the opposite was not true). Teresa Morrow was Lakeview High's new English teacher and girls' lacrosse coach. They sniffed around each other for a few weeks – Terri hated the word *sniffed*. "We're not dogs!" – until they had coffee, a weekend lunch, three dinner dates. Soon Terri visited Will's two-bedroom apartment he shared with Mack, his best friend. That night, she wore what she called her ABC dress – ass barely covered. In the morning, she put it back on.

She had always wanted to be a teacher. He had wanted to be a teacher or maybe a journalist.

"Journalism is too risky. No job security. At least in teaching you know you can have a job for life."

"Well," Terri told him, lacing her fingers through his hand, "I think you're a great teacher."

Should you marry someone if you want to live off the air they were breathing at the moment you first kissed them? Will imagined he was the lone holder of Terri's air each time they kissed. He wasn't sure the thought rose to the level of romanticism, but it had to be in the ballpark.

Barb and Bill Larkin immediately liked Terri and wrangled her into the family even though she wasn't a Catholic. A year later, when the young people asked to get married in his parents' back yard and not at St. Mary's, Barb Larkin agreed and promptly set a dragnet for a suitable caterer. Her husband didn't care either way. Church. Back yard. Shopping mall. Delicatessen. It didn't matter where you started, only mattered where you wound up, as Bill Larkin told his son. It's about the history you make and hold together. Married people are each other's history holders, he told his son.

In the beginning, Terri was amused by Will's *ways*. His feet rubbed together at night; he claimed he suffered from Restless Leg Syndrome. Her quality of sleep was reduced, as she could only hope his legs would grow out of their restlessness. And this was a minor grievance, but Will refused to ride roller coasters. At the State Fair in Timonium one year – two years – Terri tried to lure Will onto a roller coaster, but he was not a roller-coaster person. People tried to make an early-riser out of him, too. But some people will never be early-risers or roller-coaster people.

Will loved Terri's *ways*. Her mistrust of exclamation points and the way she dog-eared the *bottom* of book pages signaling favored lines. Her devout preference for lawn seats at Merriweather Post Pavilion. How she hated green Bic pens and magic tricks – nothing more than a slick form of lying! How she liked his height – 6'3" – his shady blue eyes, the untamable cow-lick in what she called his pelt of chestnut hair ("It's just brown," he'd say, "I don't have a *pelt*"), even his elbow-sharp Adam's apple.

He did have grievances: the woman once wore a Red Sox sweatshirt to Camden Yards until a robust crowd reaction steered her toward different wardrobe choices at ensuing games. Less embarrassing was her refusal to throw her peanut shells on the ground during O's games. She was a neat, brand-challenged fan. Although she teased him about "minor infractions" (cramming the dishwasher; leaving his socks balled up in the laundry; snor-ing like a drunk Sasquatch), one growing complaint was Will could overdo his drinking, especially in social settings, which he tended to avoid so the issue didn't find initial traction.

They both agreed Thursday was the finest day of the week and Sunday the bluesiest. Terri didn't mind Will joy-riding on shopping carts in the Wegmans parking lot. He didn't mind the English books cramping their starter bookcases – multiple school copies of *Catcher in the Rye*, *The Grapes of Wrath*, *Fences*, *To Kill a Mockingbird*, *Johnny Tremain*, and a warehouse of anthologies. Terri made room for Will's favorite book, a raggedy paper-back of *Instant Replay: The Green Bay Diary of Jerry Kramer*. The book was from his grandfather, William Larkin Sr. (in a namesake firewall, his son was William Larkin Jr. and *his* son was William Larkin, no rank). From his grandfather, Will held loyalty to the Packers of old, Lombardi's Packers.

The novelty of each other lost its novelty. In the last frayed months, they hit rough patches until every day felt rough. Kissing was the first to go, followed by a sexual drought of Guinness Book proportions. Will thought it was a simple case of romantic remission. But things were said. He could be a cynical, young man who drank too much; she could be a nagger as if her mission was the overhaul and perfection of his character. Will obsessed over the *New Yorker* cartoon contest but didn't want to visit the city. Too many people, too nerve-wracking even thinking about getting around there. He even shied away from the neighbors' block parties. All that ho-humming around, all that smiling.

"You don't want to do anything or meet anyone new," Terri said.

"I have you," he said.

Until he didn't.

"A fucking gazebo," Will mumbled to Dean, their 9-year-old basset hound. The raising and lowering of his pollen mask was beyond the powers of his coordination, so Will kept the pollen mask on top of his head like a party hat. He faced Dean.

"Tell me, kind sir, do *you* want a gazebo?"

The dog was snoozing, his caramel-colored back leg bicycling. Will wondered what Dean would look like in a pollen mask. He would resist.

Under the cloak of night (9:15 p.m.), and with the Dunhams away, Will commanded Dean to stay on the deck, but the dog honored no commands. Will carried his weapon low on his left side, the chainsaw thumping against his leg. It was 45 yards to the gazebo. Earlier in the day, he had road-tested the tool. Terri hadn't taken all of her books yet, including several of her English textbooks. The chainsaw's single slice into *The Bedford Introduction to Literature* (Eighth edition) was thrifty and punishing; Will's hard target was the section "Approaches to Poetry" (p. 1067), which lay shredded in murdered verse on the garage floor. He considered cleaving *The Complete Poems of Emily Dickinson* when he remembered he bought Terri the anthology. Sorry, Emily. In multiple cuts, the chainsaw dismembered 1,775 of her poems, all her dashes dashed, her lyrical stanzas pulverized. Will viewed the episode as his only successful approach to poetry.

His feet crunching leaves, he walked past his rotted wood pile and found cover in his neighbor's yard in a cathedral of spring-green oaks, sprawling azaleas and finally, the Dunhams' hedgerow of forsythias. As Dean snuffled about, Will eyed the five posts. He remembered his father telling him the right way to saw. He hadn't listened.

Will assessed the wood pentagon above him and chose the gazebo's post farthest from the house. A lefty, Will struggled at first with the wrap handle, but true to its hype, the chainsaw started on the first pull, unlike his mower. Will cut a groove in the post, and the saw sharked into the wood, spitting out shavings. One post down, four to go. Then two. But the early work, coupled with massive amounts of rum, left him prematurely fatigued. Will sat down on his neighbor's grass, the chainsaw grumbling in neutral. He fought off early onset napping but granted himself a 20-minute restorative break. Then he rose to assault the deck's third post.

Dean was the first to detect the intruder.

"Excuse me, can you tell me what you're doing?"

Will looked up the slope. The Anne Arundel County sheriff's deputy looked eight feet tall. He appeared to have left his neck at home. The young deputy billy-goated down into the woods toward the wounded gazebo. Will thought he might have taught the kid a few years back.

"We've had complaints from two neighbors who say they saw someone under the house here." Will put the chainsaw down on the ground, nice and easy-like.

"Sir, do you want to shut it off?"

Will stipulated that, yes, he should turn the chainsaw off.

"The neighbors reported they saw someone sawing down this gazebo. Does that sound like something you would be doing out here?"

"Normally not. But today is different."

Yup. Had him three years ago. Billy Snyder. Did not excel in algebra. Caught the kid opening a back window to my classroom so he could have a smoke *while I was teaching*. Probably had the Herps.

"I taught you," Will said. "Algebra. Eleventh grade. Billy Snyder."

"Deputy Snyder."

"*Deputy* Snyder."

"Have you been drinking, sir?"

"In abundance."

While not technically a hobby, it was a decent starter crime. Will sawed two-fifths of a gazebo and, to his delight, the law was after him. Not something he and Terri could laugh about now, but they would laugh about this later.

"You gave me a D," Deputy Snyder said.

"I didn't give you a D. You gave yourself a D." Even in the throes of possible alcohol poisoning, a teacher has a code.

"Screwed up my college apps."

But look at you now – a cop, with a loaded weapon, and a genetically altered torso that did not require a neck. All coming back to him – the kid's dad came in for a teacher conference, raised macho hell, claimed his son *had* turned in all of his homework. The forensic evidence was absent, and Will told both son and father he did not change grades.

"I don't change my grades," Will muttered under the gazebo. Dean had placed his head on the deputy's black boot, as the man wrote a citation for William Philip Larkin, 29, of Anderson Woods, Annapolis. Trespassing. Malicious destruction of property. Public intoxication.

"Trespassing? I live next door," Will said, his twisted pollen mask covering one ear like a headphone.

"Please read the back of the complaint before signing. You will be agreeing to appear in the District Court of Maryland."

"Can't you change the charge?"

"Mr. Larkin, I don't change my reports," the deputy said. "Out of curiosity, what are you doing out here?

"Fighting back."

• • •

In the Anne Arundel School system, employees have 24 hours to the report to the Office of Investigations a charge, arrest or conviction for any offense. The school system, as Will learned after finally reading the employee handbook, took self-reporting very seriously. Depending on the severity of the offense, "administrative actions" could be taken, including a written reprimand, suspension or termination and loss of one's teaching certification. The laundry list of offenses did, in fact, cover Will's infractions: public intoxication, malicious destruction of property and trespassing. Twenty-one hours after his failed gazebo murder, Will turned himself in.

He contacted Lakeview's assistant principal, Mr. Thomas Hull, who seemed to run the school more than the principal, a sour, hairless bureaucrat just riding out his string until retirement. As part of his pre-punishment, the math teacher had to listen to Hull lecture him on the school system's ethical code. Hull said the superintendent would have to be notified, of course, and an internal investigation into the incident might result. Suspension or termination could result if a "nexus" existed between the charges against the employee and his "duties and responsibilities" with the school system, Hull said in closing.

"What do you mean by lexus?" Will asked. Given Hull's mild speech impediment, Will misheard and, reasonably, couldn't fathom why a luxury car was central to the deliberations. He clearly walked over to his neighbor's yard. He didn't roll over there in his Honda.

"*Nexus* – not Lexus," the assistant principal said.

Thomas Hull was unusually curt with the employee and before ending their conversation, informed Will that his self-report file will be removed if the courts confirm by receipt a ruling of not guilty or an expungement of his offense. Until then or until the Office of Investigations concluded its review, he would be allowed to continue teaching until further notice. If, however, there was another incident requiring "criminal sanctions," his teaching career could be irrevocably jeopardized.

"Goodbye, Will."

"Goodbye, Mr. Hull."

He had never been so happy to get off the phone with another human being.

Five weeks later, Will told his parents about the gazebo ambush but didn't say a word about Terri leaving. One wrecking ball at a time. They brought penne pasta with tomatoes and olives to his house for Sunday dinner.

"You were arrested?"

"Technically. I was summoned to appear in court on trespassing and destruction of property charges."

"This isn't like you."

Barb Larkin was mistress of the sublime, while Bill Larkin, retired attorney, was jungle hunter of trophy facts. His son did the best he could, given the humiliating circumstance, given he had been to court, admitted his guilt, fined $500 and handed 100 hours of community service.

"Judge give you a PBJ?" said his father.

"He did."

"What's that?" Barb Larkin said.

"Probation Before Judgment. I have to complete an anger management class and do community service at a soup kitchen, although I don't think they call them soup kitchens anymore. I'm not sure what they call them. Maybe they don't even serve soup."

"The experience might broaden your worldview," his mother ventured. Will was hoping his worldview had broadened enough lately.

Barb Larkin scooped out enough penne pasta for three dinner plates, a new, odd number. The Larkins sat around Will's dining room table – the table Terri had picked out. Dean lowered the boom of his muzzle on Will's foot. No one had much more to say about Will's criminal case.

"I didn't bring any dessert."

"That's OK, Mom."

"How's the other thing?" she said.

The Other Thing was code for his mother's private worry. She knew boys drank in college, a sloppy rite of passage, but she also knew or hoped boys grew out of all that drinking. She knew Will hadn't.

"That *thing* is under control, Worrier Queen."

"Were you drinking when you destroyed your neighbor's property? And I'm sorry but I do worry."

"Yes, I was drinking."

Will's rental townhouse seemed quieter with more people in it. He hoped they didn't notice two-thirds of the books were gone from the bookshelves – along with all of the artwork, most of the dishes, the finicky food processor, the hanging fuchsia on the front porch, and the smaller of the two flat screens. But how could they not? Terri had been his *girl,* and he had been her *guy.* Until today, their separation seemed like a mirage, as if she had simply gone for a long weekend with her girlfriends, some place out west like to a spa in Big Sur. Of course, his parents noticed her absence.

"Where's Terri?" Bill Larkin announced. His courtroom voice always carried more in private than his wife would have preferred.

"She doesn't live here anymore."

"What does that mean? What the hell did you do?" he said. Barb Larkin reached across the table and covered her husband's hand with hers. A step behind more than usual, he struggled to find a softer thought.

"Well, none of my business. You two will work it out."

They said their goodbyes out front on the driveway, with Will promising to call. He couldn't stand another minute in his home, so he walked around to the back deck where there were still two Adirondack chairs. Across the yard, the amputee gazebo was still standing and in between, a field of fireflies in synchronized spectacle. His wife left and he mowed down her literature and poetry books, tried to kill his neighbor's gazebo, and was headed for anger management and community service.

What the hell *did* he do?

Chapter 2

To fulfill his service hours, the court provided Will a list of area hot meal programs. He chose the Shepherd's Table on Simonton Street, which had served the homeless since 1976. Not one missed day of service; not one mistreated guest. He had never ventured into that part of Annapolis, the needy part.

Saturday's volunteers were students from Loyola High looking to earn service learning hours, a pod of insurance company office workers, and a math teacher from Lakeview High, who was more nervous than his first day of teaching. In early business, all the volunteers were given disposable hair nets. With netted hair, Will felt nostalgic for his pollen mask. He packed the front pockets of his green apron (name tag: "Will") with zip-lock bags and brown paper bags for the guests to carry leftovers.

"You won't be on the floor at first, Will. We need you on the line doing desserts," said Todd, the volunteer coordinator. "Each plate needs one dessert. No more than one. The dessert trays are over there." Stacked on a metal rolling shelf, the trays were elbow-to-elbow in cupcakes, pound cake, blueberry muffins, chocolate cake, pecan pie, marble cake, disowned wedding cake, star-shaped sprinkled cookies, and quaking wedges of lemon meringue pie.

In his first act of community service, Will was Dessert Guy.

At 10:30, the Shepherd's Table opened its weathered double doors. Seventy-five people took their seats and exchanged tokens for their only hot meal of the day. The 18 tables were set with tea and water pitchers on Easter-egg-colored placemats. Several guests said grace; others said nothing. The bread servers took orders, and each guest was entitled to up to seven pieces. The potato bread was always the first to go. The servers at each table began holding up five fingers to signal he needed five meals. On the line, volunteers began ladling out tuna casserole and green beans on the plates before Will loaded them with a dessert. Everyone knew their job. Will admired the logic and order of the operation – the soup kitchen ran like a classroom. But, better in a way. Here, instant results. You give a man a slab of marble cake, you have something to show for yourself. And people thank you! No one thanks an algebra teacher.

By noon, the orders came faster. Volunteers slid four, five plates at a rapid clip to Will for dessert placement. He rushed his work. Leaning towers of pound cake toppled into the tuna casserole, wedding cake slices lost their balance and went head first into the green beans. He manhandled slabs of pecan pie (not the pecan pie!) with such force they buckled. After emptying yet another tray, Will crossed the kitchen to retrieve a new tray. His fingers, exposed by torn gloves, were smeared with assorted frostings. This constant, intimate handling of sweets soon left Will with what he hoped was a temporary hostility toward desserts.

What happened next Will blamed on a slick spot on the kitchen floor. A more objective assessment might indicate a loss of concentration. In any case, Will dropped a tray of 45 desserts. Looking down at the carnage around and on his shoes, he had an epiphany: along with taste, desserts use their shapely form and appetizing presentations to attract. What he saw on the floor was not salvageable. Will had destroyed dessert for 45 homeless people of Annapolis.

"Do you have any potato bread?" a guest asked, startling the Dessert Guy.

Will was mopping up birthday cake from the tile floor. In the dining hall, someone was yodeling. While the homeless man was an able yodeler, the musical form quickly overstayed its welcome. Will's head was splitting.

"Excuse me, do you have any potato bread?"

Will looked up into the face a very tall homeless man.

"Sorry, I'm not the Bread Guy."

The older man wore too many coats for inside. He had a faded Orioles cap on – back when the bird looked duller, back when the team won a

World Series. Will sponged more cake off the floor before rising from his knees, his apron smudged with assorted frostings. Seven plates awaited dessert. Will's hairnet felt tighter on his head. His guest wanted potato bread.

"I can't help you."

"Pardon me?"

"Do you understand what I said? I said I can't help you. Now take your seat."

Will tried to make up for lost time but another volunteer stepped in to fill the dessert trays. Todd, the volunteer coordinator, asked Will to step aside and refill the iced tea pitchers. It was a blatant demotion; grade-school probationary rookies refilled the iced tea pitchers. Dessert Guy was the cool job.

When the shift ended, the Shepherd's Table had fed 412 guests, some of whom missed out on dessert. In the kitchen, volunteers stripped off their hairnets and threw their aprons in the laundry bin.

"Will, can I talk to you?" said Todd.

A soup kitchen does not have a principal's office, but the bread stock room worked in a pinch.

"Our mission is to help everyone who dines with us. One of our guests said you told him you couldn't help him."

"He wanted potato bread, and I didn't have any."

"The potato bread *is* popular," Todd said, which was understood.

"Did you tell our guest he needed to sit down?"

"It's a habit, I guess. I teach high school."

"I'm sure you're a fine teacher, but this isn't a classroom," Todd said. "If you treat a customer like that again, you won't be allowed back, and I will notify the court."

"But I was Dessert Guy..."

• • •

Maryland requires couples seeking a no-fault "Absolute Divorce" to stay separated 12 continuous months (buying a gun was far simpler). At such time, neighbors, friends, work colleagues can testify the couple in question has not strayed onto each other's orbit for one year. Easier ordered than done. Will and Terri couldn't help but run into each at school. Joint custody of Dean wasn't practical, so Will became the dog's sole caretaker.

One year:

Drunk dialing (six times) his legally-separated wife and spying on her coaching lacrosse (23 times) from the window in the teachers' lounge that overlooked Lakeview's ball fields.

Trying not to drink on school nights, but the need scratched at him from the inside when he got home from work. The loudness of his empty home. The rituals of his marriage inexplicably dissolved. No one to hold or kiss. No one's air to take when kissing.

Finishing his community service hours at the Shepherd's Table. Finishing a 10-hour, online anger management class and barely passing the final online exam on anger emotion, anger behavior, mental anger rehearsal and anger strategies – all of which agitated Will. The teacher had graduated from anger management school still trying to understand how *learning is changed behavior.* Crimes against poetry anthologies were not analyzed.

And one year of not looking twice at any other girl. One year to realize Terri Morrow, the first girl he ever loved, was not coming back.

The crisp business envelope arrived on a Tuesday – the week's dimmest day. Will never received business envelopes, except teacher union forms and updates he ignored. He opened this new, suspicious envelope and pulled out two pieces of paper from the Anne Arundel County Circuit Court. William P. Larkin and Teresa Morrow had been granted a no-fault divorce. No fault, no mess. No goodbye dinner or hug. The end.

Will showed the document to Dean, who expressed a startling lack of empathy. It was February and the dog was late for his rabies vaccination. Reminder postcards (2) had come in the mail. Beyond any tardy vaccinations, something was up with Dean. He had lost interest in eating, had become listless and snappish. Plus, he had this nagging cough. Will hoped it was just the dog missing Terri. Hell, he was listless and snappish, too.

On Saturday Will drove to the Annapolis Animal Hospital and took the parking space farthest from the front door and closest to the evaporated

creek bed where Dean took his pre-visit leak. Dean was on
back of Will's silver Honda. He reached back to stroke Dean's .
nearly bit. He left him on his blanket and went inside. In the wai
a mother and son sat on the plastic-covered couch under the pet a
notices. At the boy's feet, a Lab pup tried wiggling out of his leash.
mother showed her son how to pick up and hold the dog. The boy us
both hands.

Will loped over to the counter where they kept the Heartgard, dog beef
jerky, surplus business cards and second-string leashes with pharmaceutical
names.

"I'll be with you in a moment," said a veterinary technician, whose name
tag said "Parker." As in Parker Posey or Mary Louise Parker, Will thought,
conjuring his two favorite actresses spliced into one Parkeresque being. He
felt guilty for noticing her – guilty and excited, those two adorable first
cousins.

Will picked up a business card then put it back where he found it. On a
hook under the counter, the leashes looked artificially red and green. Dean
didn't need a leash anymore. He stopped walking three days ago, and earlier
this morning Will dabbed water on Dean's muzzle, but the dog wouldn't
drink.

The vet tech finished running a Visa card.

"I called about Dean. He's out in my car. Can you help me?"

Parker Cool got up from her swivel chair and disappeared into one of
those mysterious vet hallways and came out the other end through Exam
Room 2. Together they walked to the parking lot. Will pointed to the silver
Honda and walked back inside the office. Parker peered in the backseat.

"Hi, baby," she said. "I'm going to pick you up nice and slow. You can
stay right in your blanket."

She planted her feet, leaned into the backseat, and lifted the dog out.
Inside, Will played with the dog leashes, anything to distract him. Parker
came in with the dog and asked Will if he wanted to say his goodbyes.

"That's not my dog."

"What?"

"That's not my dog."

"You said the silver Honda," Parker said.

"I did say that, but that's not my dog."

They walked to the window, parted the cheap curtain, and counted two, no three silver Hondas in the parking lot. On the other end of the horseshoe-shaped counter, a middle-aged woman with an unnatural tan and chest approached the stunned vet technician holding a dog that was not Will's.

"Why are you holding my dog? I came in to buy heartworm medicine. There's not a thing wrong with my Buddy." Buddy, another basset hound.

Parker handed the dog over. A slew of professional apologies appeared to pacify the pet owner. With an escort this time, Parker went to the parking lot and found the correct silver Honda. Dean still hadn't moved. Will leaned in and kissed his dog on what he always believed was Dean's forehead, a bony peak book-ended by quilted ears. Still a beautiful coat. Still didn't look that sick. Parker waited until Will was ready. She carried Dean in his towel into the animal hospital.

Five minutes later, Parker found Will outside by his car.

"I'm so sorry about that. That's never happened to me."

"We all get distracted."

Parker Cool prided herself on *never* getting distracted.

"My theory is the world has too many silver Hondas," Will said.

"Do you want to see Dean? There's time."

"What do you mean there's time?"

"Didn't someone..."

"No. No one has said anything to me. I don't know anything other than you picked up the wrong dog. What's wrong with Dean?"

Parker raced back into the office and returned with Dean's vet, Dr. Branham. Dean had a sudden blockage of blood flow in his heart, something called caval syndrome that will lead to his heart's collapse, the vet explained. There is nothing we can do to help him, he told Will. It's your decision but the sooner the better.

Parker handed Will the dog collar. Will took off the circular tag and ied it onto his key ring. *My name is Dean. I belong to Will & Terri...*

"Are you going to be all right?"

Will's eyes were damp.

"I'll call you to let you know," she said.

Will walked out of the office and sat on the hood of his car, leaned back and felt the windshield wiper jab his back. At the corner of Randall and State streets, Wishing Well Liquors was open. Will could stand in the parking lot and try to stop crying or sprint across the street to Wishing Well Liquors. The sprinting would be a problem, though. He had not sprinted since middle school when his gym teacher required participation in the depraved event known as the 50-yard dash. Will had always been a lousy dasher, could not dash, so he walked (briskly) across the street to buy beer. Back in his car, he twisted open a Yuengling and stared at the bald eagle on the label. He drank two Yuenglings in his car before driving home.

At home, there was no hound dog bark or tail-thwapping against the back screen porch like the sound of jazz drum brushes. No clickity-clacking, as Dean tacked upstairs to the master bedroom, step by step hacking into gravity's pull. Dean was only 9. He should be at least 12 or some crazy age like 17. When he was a boy, Will begged his parents for a dog but instead, they bought him a gecko named Andrew, which moved three times during the calendar year. A few years later, Barb and Bill Larkin adopted a cat, but within three months it died of an intestinal ailment. Will forgot the cat's and ailment's names.

He remembered driving to Pennsylvania to pick up Dean. Across the state line, Interstate 83 turned rough and washed out. Will found the farm or maybe it was a ranch – no, probably a farm because there were free-roaming chickens and four, five goats staring at nothing. The dog breeder, a sour man of dubious commerce, sold the basset hound pup for $200. Insisted on cash. Will wanted to get the hell out of there. He put his new dog in the front passenger seat on a blanket, where the basset hound snoozed for most of the ride home...

"It's the Annapolis Animal Hospital. I wanted to let you know," Parker said on the phone.

Dean, with the bad breath and caval syndrome, had been put down. His foreleg had been shaved, his fur wetted to expose the vein, then the overdose of dark green anesthetic, the involuntary muscle twitching, the stillness.

"Were you with him?"

"Yes," she said.

Had they disposed of Dean's body? Was there a special box or bag for him? Maybe a company came around every Tuesday to collect the special boxes or bags out behind the building where pet owners couldn't see. Some people buried their pets in the back yard, but there must be county ordinances against that. God forbid flooding.

Will declined to take Dean's remains. The collar was enough.

"Hello?"

"I'm still here."

"Are you all right?"

"No."

He thanked the vet technician for calling then dragged Dean's green bed out of his bedroom and into the mud room where he folded the bed like an omelet. Dean's water dish was emptied, dried, and stowed in a supermarket bag along with Heartgard chewables, dog brush (used twice) and plastic tick remover. The dog's Christmas-red collar was hung on a peg in the mud room; the collar smelled of grass, dirt, and neck. Copper rabies tags matted together on the leash ring. Dean was finally up to date on his shots.

That night, Will drank five beers and called his wife.

• • •

Seven miles away in Terri's new apartment, the telltale number announced itself.

"Will?"

"It's me."

˃ hadn't heard his voice in a year. For a split second, she considered ˅p, but he wouldn't be calling if it wasn't important. It better be – her day had been lousy and dispiriting enough.

Terri discovered her sophomores had never heard of Frederick Douglass, the abolitionist, statesman, author, and native of Maryland's Eastern Shore. So, she threw together an impromptu lesson on Douglass and his escape from slavery in Fells Point, where he had worked as a shipyard caulker. This prompted a side-discussion not on slavery (her intended subject) but on what a shipyard was and what was meant by the word *caulker*. It sounded dirty, several students hypothesized.

"I'm sorry but I had to call," Will said.

"I'm listening."

"Dean got sick."

"Sick? How sick? Can I see him? I can come by tomorrow."

How he wished.

"He stopped eating, walking and even drinking water, Terri. You should have heard him cough."

No sound on the phone from her end or the sound of someone trying not to cry or scream.

"I had to do it."

"Do what?"

"I had to, Terri."

She said she couldn't talk anymore and hung up. Will turned off the light over his ill-fitting queen-sized bed. The alarm clock read 12:15 in red, double-jointed numbers. He wedged a pillow between his feet to stop the cricketing. A stale glass of water stood stagnant guard on his night table. At 2:43, he buried the alarm clock in the top drawer. Rogue sleeplessness filled the time with brutal self-evaluations before quicksand dreams of falling, and in one water dream, capsizing. Someone yanks him up hard by the arm, a man in a black robe. The man looks like Fred Gwynn. In a seamless segue, Will is in a courtroom decorated in marble ancient columns, and Fred Gwynn is reading charges brought against William P. Larkin. *For the crime of selfishness, how do you plead?* Guilty, your honor. *For the crime of immaturity, how do you plead?* Guilty. *I hereby sentence you to Life.*

Will was especially relieved to have to get out of bed and go to work.

• • •

At Lakeview High, he waited four years for Mrs. Howell to retire before they gave him her classroom. Will had been a "floater" – teachers unassigned a room who rolled a metal, warped-wheeled cart of their school belongings from classroom to classroom for six periods. For the dozen floating teachers, home base was a suite of cubicles aptly nicknamed "Dilbert." There, the floaters parked their carts until it was time again to haul their educational wares. Some teachers claimed to *like* floating, but they were also the ones who perpetuated the Secret Santa gift-swapping ritual. Real team players.

Will did his hard time and last year, finally, Room 215 was his. The classroom was closest to the men's room and the main stairway leading to the office, where moody gatekeepers issued paychecks, schedules and contested chaperone duties. Room 215 featured slender windows providing a cheap view of the football field. In the back of the classroom – where Will smartly stationed his desk and microwave – he could monitor his yearly crop of teens.

This year's menu of bureaucratic bullshit included the following edicts from the Hopewell County School Superintendent's Office: No student will receive a 0 grade; no accepting late work anymore ("Not even in July?" Will asked snarkily during a poorly-attended department meeting); homework grades are not to be applied to a student's academic record, and failing a student was essentially not an option. These new practices coupled fretfully with an "epidemic" of students leaving school grounds daily to dine at the nearby Chipotle and Chick-fil-A. Lunching off-campus was against the rules for liability issues, but students remained determined to take their appetites elsewhere. Once, Will interrupted one of his student's cell phone conversations with her Uber driver who apparently was charging too much to get the girl to Chipotle. He felt nostalgic for last year's cheating epidemic.

Still, for every front office cluster fuck, behavioral epidemic, debasing parent-teacher conference and further demolition of student accountability, Will's Honda was always 38 paces from his classroom. So what if his classroom was too cold in the winter and too hot in late spring. So what if the janitorial staff used a leaf blower to sweep out his room, which accounted for backpack flotsam clinging to the ceiling's cobwebs. So what if he taught house-unbroken pups of freshmen every year. Room 215 was *his*.

Will was not expecting calamitous news when he was summoned to the main office on Monday. He had faithfully reported the gazebo incident and received an officious warning, as noted in his personnel file. What was the worst thing Hull could do? Give him all Standards next year? Fine with him. Fewer college recommendations to write; fewer parents to e-mail-stalk him. Will preferred the Standard kids. He had been a Standard kid.

"Have a seat," said assistant principal Hull, who always struck Will as more of a loud oil painting than a human (and that croaking, glottal voice, that classic vocal fry). The administrator sat at his Office Depot desk and on the cinder-blocked wall behind him a laminated inspirational poster: "I'm a School Administrator. What's Your Superpower?" Two framed photographs of the Family Hull were turned outward on his desk for visiting staff and teachers to appraise. The Hull children looked cretinous. The Hull woman looked like she could drown the lot of them. Cut the brakes and roll their minivan into a lake with the doors locked. Staged press conferences. Fake tears. The whole show.

"As you know, we're getting a new math teacher. This is her first year, and I'm not going to have her float. She's going to be lost enough as it is. I need you to be the team player that I know you are," Hull said, scraping out his words.

"You're taking my classroom?"

"I'm hoping it's only for the remainder of the year, Will."

"I was a floater for four years before I got my classroom. Then I floated again this year. Now, I have to float *again?* Is this because of the gazebo? That was a year ago. I reported that immediately. I haven't had an issue, *any* issue since. And now you're giving my room to a new teacher?"

Hull had lost confidence in his algebra teacher and suspected Will of faking a cough on the phone last month so he could skip school for the first time in four years. Not to mention Will terrorizing his neighbor's property last year. The man might be cracking up, a man who had never once changed his daily lesson plan, never once asked for a different classroom or schedule. Hull feared the teacher might be capable of entering school grounds after hours and taking a chainsaw to his Ikea desk, family photographs or his inspirational poster!

"You're a team player, Will. And I know you will continue to be a team player."

Will walked out of assistant principal Hull's office and passed Pete Wilson rolling his cart to Ms. Emmart's room to teach his U.S. history. Pete was only five years older than Will, but Pete looked 65 and broken down like a junkyard microwave. The wheels of the metal cart wobbled and squealed. Pete took the corner with his cart and math books toppled onto the ground. Will felt sick to his stomach.

He was a floater again.

Chapter 3

In Annapolis, the weather-proofing shrink wrap comes off the boats in spring, as another season de-cocoons. The kid-friendly pirate ship *Sea Gypsy* gets back to work, as do the twin schooners, *Woodwind*. Polo-shirted marina employees strip wrap off the Sea Rays, Silvertons, Carvers, and Chris-Crafts. Other big boats come north from Florida and Bermuda. At the town's City Dock, the inlet is nicknamed Ego Alley for the throaty cigarette boats and yachts that idle through the small waterway between April and October. At the end of the inlet is a landing for tenders and dinghies. If you didn't have a boat, you could kayak or rent an inflatable Zodiac and zip around the creeks.

Will walked along City Dock by the statue of Alex Haley, whose "Roots" monument marks the spot where Kunte Kinte landed and was sold into slavery. Tourists stopped to skim the plaque's inspirational quotes. Will saw a private school girl (white shirt untucked) drop a solid scoop of black walnut ice cream onto the crotch of Haley. There were tears. "I want my ice cream!" the girl cried. Her mother attempted to delicately scoop the black walnut by using napkins from the ice cream shop, but she was overmatched. Witnesses saw the girl's mother resort to using her bare hands to swab the novelist's lap. Many had to look away.

Across the street at Starbucks, Will considered buying a smoothie, but smoothies were never as good as he hoped. He got coffee, either a Venti or Trenta, and took his confusion and brew to the seawall. Midshipmen from the neighboring Naval Academy grounds jogged by faster than most humans sprint. Gulls henpecked a muffin on the gum-pocked sidewalk (in the field of nature sightings, Will preferred starlings buck-shooting from a tree line). A Sea Ray yacht, maybe 50 feet of her, threaded the needle of the narrow waterway before ever so slowly spinning to offer a view of the boat's backside with its over-the-side attached grill and Poinsettia-themed throw rug. A golden retriever in a red bandana was curled up onboard. Dean had never stepped foot on a boat. He was more of a sit-by-the-window-and-pine-for-squirrels kind of dog. If he hadn't been a great dog, he would have made a good cat.

The coffee was either too Venti or Trenta, so Will emptied it in a trash can and walked to the end of the dock. In the red brick square, Will took a seat on a bench by a yellow life ring attached to one of the pier's pilings. It was a clear day, so the spans of the Bay Bridge were in focus. The water, which rarely looked blue, was tea colored. A bench away, a young woman in shorts and wearing a "Naptown" hoodie was cradling a book. She looked familiar.

"Hello?"

The woman looked up and blocked the sun with the back of her hand. Will saw evidence of minor scars.

"Parker?"

"Oh, hi. I remember you. You brought in Dean."

"In *my* silver Honda."

"Don't remind me."

"I never thanked you for helping me."

"You're welcome," Parker said. "It wasn't my finest moment, but I rebounded. Dean was such a sweetie."

Will sat on the bench next to her. She didn't leave or recoil in horror, although Will thought she stiffened a bit. He surreptitiously inched to the farthest edge of his side.

"What are you reading?"

"A poem by a man named Shapiro." She had bought *A Geography of Poets,* which she snagged for $3 at the Baltimore Book Fair.

"What's the poem about?" He had never uttered that question.

"I've read it only twice. You really should read a poem several times," she said. "But it's about being on the lookout for a 'great illumining' even among the desks and chairs of the office 'should it come between nine and five.' I like that part about the desks and chairs."

Will wondered what a great illumining feels like and whether every woman he was to meet on the planet had a thing for poetry.

"I'm Will Larkin."

"Nice to meet you again. I'm Parker Cool."

Parker's hair looked like it still wanted to be blonde but was losing the fight. Dimple on her right cheek. The most unusual eyes (Will wished he had a name for her eyes). An air of – what? – fabric softener about her? So kind when her job called for kindness. Hardly ever made small talk at the vet counter. He noticed she wasn't always checking her phone. He liked that. No ring, either. He still wore his but more on account his fingers somehow gained weight.

"What do you do for a living, Will Larkin?"

"I teach high school algebra."

"Ah, a left-brainer."

"It's my best side."

"I bet you didn't know you have a famous poet's name," she said, cracking her knuckles. Will hadn't heard anyone crack their knuckles since middle school. "Ever read Philip Larkin?"

"That's my middle name. Philip."

"You're a Philip Larkin! This could be my lucky day. Have you ever read your namesake?"

"I was named after my father and grandfather, none of them poets," Will said. Poems never added up. "I wonder if poets understand poetry."

Parker's chin clenched.

"Poems are temples; poems keep you company. Walt Whitman said that. Surely you've read Whitman. I mean everybody has read Whitman, right? I sing the body electric? O Captain, My Captain?"

"Is that where Whitman's Samples come from?"

Parker looked aggrieved. This Will Larkin was *such* a math teacher. She withheld disclosing her respect for slant rhymes.

"My ex-wife liked poetry," Will said. "I sort of took a chainsaw to her poetry books." For the first time since that night, he felt regret – not for the gazebo but for shredding poor beautiful Emily Dickinson.

"Sort of?"

"I *did* not take a chainsaw to her poetry books." Dumb, some really dumb shit that.

"I so want to ask why," Parker said.

"She left me. That's the best answer I got for now."

"Do you still love her?"

"I don't want to talk about love."

Will eyed a wobbly umbrella. Three months ago at a Starbucks, the wind lifted an outdoor umbrella from its concrete table and sent it rocketing toward Will's car. The umbrella's tip impaled the windshield, creating many little windshields. Starbucks paid for the damage and threw in a McCartney CD, but Will was shaken. Someone should write a poem about flying umbrellas and windshields – maybe it was a metaphor. This Parker Cool would know something about the metaphor business.

"What do you think of blogs?"

"I don't read them. Are they interesting?" Will said.

"Mine is."

Not that it was any of Will's business, she continued, but her blog was devoted to the dogs she had cared for at the Annapolis Animal Hospital. Parker posted entries on 165 dogs and wondered if her blog might make a book one day. Dean was post No. 162, and it featured the case of the mistaken basset hound.

"Did you write about my dog?"

"If I did, I'm sure it wasn't interesting."

This wasn't going swimmingly. Will felt safer at school explaining to 151 students that he didn't round off 89.2 to an A. He felt safer in a faculty meeting faced with a plate of lumpy mayonnaise passing for shrimp salad.

A Harbor shuttle, with its blue canopy and twin outboards, cruised by carrying four wide-eyed tourists and one focused boat captain with too much tan.

Speaking of poetry. "Dean had the biggest, eh, equipment, we ever saw in our office," Parker said, recalling the dog's most glaring attribute.

"He was remarkable that way."

This Parker Cool was pretty in a cute way. Something else, though, something bewitching – although Will never called anything or anyone bewitching. How did that word barge into his head? He was loping along, ran into a vet tech, and found himself talking about Dean's balls, dog blogs and some poetry dude named Philip Larkin.

By 6 p.m., the wind off the water was bracing. The sky turned sloppy, and the bay water turned gunpowder gray. Will couldn't think of another thing he could lose.

"I bet you haven't heard this classic before, but can I have your number?"

Parker frowned.

"Do you have anything to write on?"

A copy of the local newspaper *The Capital* had been left on the bench. Will borrowed a pen from Parker and wrote her number on the paper.

"Ah, left-handed, too," she said.

"You, too?"

"No, I am one of God's normal people."

"Benjamin Franklin, Julius Caesar, Paul McCartney, David Letterman, Julia Roberts, Bart Simpson, a bunch of cool presidents. All left-handed."

"All lies."

They were enjoying themselves despite their usual instincts for flight. Two old souls, Will hoped.

"I bet I write my name better right-handed than you write your name left-handed."

"Prove it, math man."

Will handed Parker the Arundel section, and he took Sports. Taking turns with the Bic, Parker and Will scrupulously wrote their names opposite-handed. They kept their backs turned as they worked.

Parker Cool.

Will Larkin.

Each claimed victory, but it was hard to objectively declare Will a winner given Parker's wedding-invitations-like penmanship. The girl must practice at home. They agreed to a second round but this time they wrote each other's names.

Will Larkin.

Parker Cool.

Both samples were a train wreck, but what surprisingly intimate business this writing each other's names with the wrong hand.

"We should do this again to check our progress," Will said.

"How could your handwriting show its face again?"

"We should have a rematch."

Parker got up to leave. Shaking hands would feel ridiculous, so they nodded to each other, which was exponentially more ridiculous. He wanted to kiss her. Taste her air.

"I'll call you," Will said.

"Better let me call you."

"Really?"

"It's complicated."

The last thing Will wanted was anything else complicated. Maybe this Parker person was *too* quirky.

"So, you'll call me," Will said. "Before you go, what's your favorite line from Walt Whitman?"

"You really want to know?"

"I do."

"This isn't the full quote, but it's what people remember. *We were together. I forget the rest.*"

They nodded goodbye, and he watched her walk for a few stirring steps until he turned toward Dock Street to visit his favorite ice cream shop. But Storm Brothers was out of Butter Pecan, and Will had never developed a second-favorite flavor. Quite normal not to like any other ice cream flavor, not quirky at all. Denied his ice cream, Will wondered if people actually sang the body electric or whether that was just one of those poetry things. He wondered about the girl with the dog blog.

Parker Elaine Cool was raised in a dust bowl.

The white dust from nearby quarried marble embedded itself in the floorboards of the front porches in her childhood neighborhood. Dust on the cars, on the bushes, dust in their hair when anyone played outside, dust on the dog. Children wrote their names in the dust on the back windshields of neighborhood cars. For decades, the Lone Star Quarry in Baltimore County blasted into benches of limestone and marble to make and truck asphalt, riprap, concrete, and bunker sand. The blasts rattled the windows and tipped pictures across the CSX railroad tracks from Parker's childhood home. For the dozen or so families who lived there, nothing else curious or interesting ever happened on Church Lane.

Some neighborhoods had state parks, baseball stadiums or prisons in their backyard; others had 500-foot rock pits. Cockeysville Marble was famous, though. It was used to build the Washington Monument – an ever-green fact school groups and Cub Scout troops learned on field trips to the quarry off tree-lined Interstate 83. "The Rumble," as the short noontime detonations were nicknamed, was a geological and sonic novelty for visitors to Baltimore County. Throughout the workday, processions of apple red Caterpillar dump trucks hauled away the crushed asphalt and aggregate as the dust flew. The quarry was never a playground. One day, though, it could make a great swimming hole.

"They should fill it in NOW," 8-year-old Parker told her parents. Her 10-year-old brother Steve concurred. Fill it in and plant grass and trees and have a playground with tall swings and not those lousy skimpy swings at elementary school. And don't skimp on the water fountains or have ones that shoot a mile over your head or dribble out so you have to put your lips on it to get some water.

"There should be a dog park. All dogs allowed," Parker said. "A fence, too, so they don't need leashes. Not a skimpy fence, either!"

"All right, Miss Skimpy. I'll call the quarry people and tell them your plan," her father said.

"Will you really?"

"I said I would."

"Will they listen to you?"

"Of course. I'm Parker Cool's father!"

On the afternoon of June 6, Parker's last day of third grade, a Caterpillar truck loaded with riprap approached its usual right turn out of the Lone Star Quarry. The Mack taxied as slow as any boy's hand-driven Tonka truck changed into necessary gears, and turned onto Beaver Dam Road across the tracks from Church Lane. At the top of the street, Parker was off the school bus and running the three blocks home. *I'm a fourth-grader! A FOURTH-GRADER!* She'd have to tell Brownie, her 5-year-old Beagle Lab mix. Brownie had elevated disobedience to an art form; he honored no commands and respected no leash. He was often seen traipsing down the CSX tracks or crossing Beaver Dam Road to inspect the rock pit – the Taj Mahal of fire hydrants. *You better keep him on his leash,* Parker's mother would harp. *Or keep the dog inside.* Must have said it a hundred times.

Parker, out of breath, stood on her dusty front porch and opened the door. Brownie bolted out but didn't stop to hear her exciting news. Didn't stop to bathe her cheeks in doggie kisses, didn't even stop to nudge her hand for ear rubbing.

The dog hadn't peed for five hours.

"You go take care of your business," Parker said. "I'll wait here."

She expected Brownie to do his number on the tracks and race back. Even if she wanted to, there was no time to put on his leash. Parker imagined not being able to pee for five hours. Not fun, no, no. Her second-grade teacher, Mrs. Howell, once made her wait a whole hour to pee. She was a meanie *and* wore stupid dresses.

Parker saw Brownie, her first pet, dash across the CSX tracks toward the quarry. The loaded truck pulled out from the gravel parking lot. There was no noise except for the sound of howling brakes. Moments later, the driver told the Cools he had a daughter himself about Parker's age and she had a dog, too, so he understood, and he was sorry he couldn't stop in time and, well, he was very sorry. Parker's parents said it wasn't his fault. It wasn't anybody's fault, they told their fourth-grader.

Parker's father brought an old Disney beach blanket to Beaver Dam Road. With cars stopped on either direction, he took his time scooping up the broken animal. He wasn't sure exactly how to pick the dog up, where to touch him, just do it quick. Mr. Cool was grateful for the lack of blood.

"Maybe he needs an operation, Daddy. Let's take Brownie to the vet."

All of them were off the road, walking up Church Lane to their home. A few neighbors and local business folks (two brothers who ran a car shop; a dog grooming lady tearing up) asked if there was anything they could do. More trucks rolled out of the Lone Star Quarry, more dusty business.

"Sweetie, our vet can't help Brownie."

There were options: the veterinarian's office could dispose of the cremated remains; several companies offered special Beagle Dog Urns and laser engraved urns created by photographs of the deceased pet.

Parker wanted Brownie's ashes thrown into the quarry. Her parents said no. So, she kept the boxed ashes in the third drawer of her night table and looked at it only a few times.

On September 4, the first day of fourth grade, she walked home from the bus stop and announced that her new teacher's breath smelled like pepperoni and her shoes were dumb. At dinner that night, Parker reminded her father to call the quarry people. *You said you would.* Time to fill in the rock pit and build a dog park with a fence.

"Not a skimpy one, either," his daughter said. "Also, I've decided what I want to be for the rest of life. A veterinarian technician."

"Well, that sounds very important."

"It is."

"What happened to becoming a novelist or poet?" he said.

"I'm still evolving."

"Sounds like you have a solid plan, sweetie. Maybe when you're a veterinary *technician* an abandoned dog will be brought into the office. People will ask if anyone wants to adopt it, and maybe you'll be the one."

"I *will* be the one," Parker said.

"And you can name it Brownie."

"No! There is only one Brownie!"

33

That night the Cool family all agreed there was only one Brownie.

• • •

Parker checked the balance on her humble Visa. She had enough to cover dinner for three at the Corner Stable, a neighborhood rib joint traditionally reserved for Cool family occasions. The booths were full, so Parker and her parents huddled up at the bar. It was no one's birthday, wasn't her parents' wedding anniversary – Richard Cool was *almost* sure as he noticed Steve hadn't been invited. What was Parker up to now?

For starters, she bought them a round of beer.

"I have some news," she said, staring into her reflection in one of the three flat screens over the bar that happened to be on the fritz. She saw herself looking back at herself in the black screen – a fish-bowled rattled version of herself. Parker imagined this moment would be joyful and celebratory with champagne toasts and giddy plan-making. But life often goes off-road even on quiet, dusty Church Lane. Parker broke from her self-stare-down.

"I'm going to be a mom."

It came out like a press release, but at least it came out. She had told them about meeting a man named Alex. Left it at that, filled in no further details. So, Parker has met a man, Richard, and Grace Cool had discussed briefly before branching off the subject. She was always meeting men or they were always meeting *her*. None of them got any traction, none of them were serious.

"What?" her father said.

"I'm going to be a mom. Alex and I are going to be parents." Parker faced herself again in the darkened flat screen.

"Well, this is exciting news," her mother tried. "Ed, looks like we're going to be grandparents."

An alert waiter named Mike – they had him before – leaned in to ask if they were ready to order. They were not, and he didn't force it.

"Who's Alex?" Richard Cool asked in a voice that struck Parker as spooky neutral.

His wife refreshed his memory on the scant details offered them upon Alex's arrival in their daughter's romantic orbit. They had never met him, of course. Didn't know his last name. Job? Prison record? Republican? Richard Cool pushed his Yuengling away.

"Are you going to marry him?"

"Honey, that's a personal question, don't you think?"

"Hell yes, it's a personal question, Grace. All of this is personal. This whole night has been pretty goddamn personal if you ask me."

Waiter Mike thought about leaning back in to take their order but veered off to the other end of the bar.

"Dad, it's 2010. Plenty of people live together, have a baby, and raise it together." Parker doubted listing the year would mitigate the shock, but it was a worth a try.

"You're living with him?" her mother said.

Since last month, Parker said. That was the other news she planned to tell them. She wished they would order: her dad getting his usual full rack of back ribs; her mother a crab cake with a half a rack; coleslaw and stable fries all around. Multiple adult beverages.

"I'll be OK. I promise. Please don't worry about me. I have a partner, and we'll raise our baby together."

Her mother reached out and patted Parker's hand. She never liked her mother or anyone patting her hand or shoulder or anything, always felt a little creepy this patting business. But tonight the touch of her mother's hand unexpectedly charged her with love, acceptance and the promise of another partnership.

"Please, Dad. Say something."

"I just don't want…" he said, "… I don't want you to be alone."

Parker reached over and patted her father's shoulders.

"I won't be alone. I won't be."

Mike the alert waiter swooped by just as nice as he could, and he interrupted everything for which the Cools were grateful.

"Y'all ready to order?"

• • •

35

"You have coffee dragon breath. Since when did you start drinking coffee?" said Alex Cavanaugh, former high school wrestler and current manager at the Gold's Gym on Richie Highway. The boyfriend and father of 5-year-old Dailey Grace Cavanaugh.

They had been living together for five years in Eastport over the Spa Creek Bridge from downtown Annapolis. Eastport was more Cape Cod and Key West than downtown Annapolis maritime proper. With its pocket parks and pubs, the town was Parker's speed. Named after the city in Maine, the town was walkable, drinkable and generally unaffordable for 28-year-olds. Two incomes barely covered the essentials.

Alex rolled over and took three-fourths of the buttermilk-colored comforter. Parker clung to her side of the queen bed in their two-story on Chester Street. Her feet were cold, but they were always cold (no one's fault there). Multiple layers of socks were ineffective; wader socks made from caribou hide could not have cut the chill. Her boyfriend took the good head pillow, of course he did.

If he would only fall asleep, she could reclaim the comforter and pillow she brought into the relationship. As if entombed, Parker did not speak or move on her side of the bed. She wondered if they left the outdoor floods on or was it the moon. A walk in all this light would be wonderful. It would be easy to slip out and walk by the marina across the street, hear the sailboat masts clank. Listen for restless dogs or chittering raccoons. Please start snoring, Alex.

"Who did you have coffee with, Park?"

"I had coffee with a girlfriend. I like coffee. I have liked coffee for many years."

"What girlfriend?"

"My secret lesbian lover, Alex. The one I'm going to leave you for. What do you mean what girlfriend? Paige from work, OK? Paige, a woman, not a guy, not even a lesbian, as far as I know. Hell, I wish she was. Call her up tomorrow if you don't believe me."

"Why wouldn't I believe you?"

"You are driving me fucking crazy, you know that?"

Parker flung off the sheet. He heard her slip into her jeans and cozy her feet into her running shoes. She didn't bother lacing up. She always wanted to stomp out on somebody. She hoped she didn't wake Dailey in the smaller of their two bedrooms. But the girl was a notorious deep sleeper, always was.

"Where are you going?"

"For a walk. By myself."

The night was chillier than she figured, but 4 a.m. was always chilly. She didn't feel like hopping the fence at nearby Mears Marina to creep up on silent sailboats. Parker walked up Chester Street and the three long blocks up Sixth Street toward the drawbridge at Spa Creek. The Royal Farms was open. Piping hot coffee called to her in whale song, but she kept walking.

They met in junior year of high school, a dull mess of a year. The only bright spot was Parker's English teacher, Mrs. Chisholm, who believed students should read good poems and books. Not only read them but talk about them, dissect them, argue for their very goodness. And Mrs. Chisholm had saved the best for last. At the start of the fourth quarter, Parker was assigned "The Grapes of Wrath." Each student would be required to read a key passage in front of the class. Three weeks later, Parker knew exactly what page she would perform.

On the book's last page, Rose of Sharon's intimate act of compassion culminates Steinbeck's epic. To save the life of starving man, a poor dying stranger in need of milk, Rose of Sharon...

...*loosened one side of the towel and bared her breast,* Parker recited. She knew she never could have paraphrased Steinbeck's final words. Somebody in class would have snickered at the mere mention of "breast," and that scene certainly wasn't in the movie. She stuck to the script:

"...*You got to," she said. She squirmed closer and pulled his head close..."*

Parker's voice steadied. There was no snickering, not even from the boys. Not even from Alex Cavanaugh, the cocky, brawny wrestler sitting in the front row closest to the speaker. Parker felt his panther eyes on her – like he was hanging on her every word. She suddenly became very aware of the clingy top she had on. Could people see...

"...There!" she said. "There." Her hand moved behind his head and supported it. Her fingers moved gently in his hair."

Parker felt twitchy. She swore she could hear Alex's panting. She imagined, if for a second, the feel of his hot breath...

"...She looked up and across the barn, and her lips came together and smiled mysteriously."

In that moment, Parker Cool smiled mysteriously, Alex told her the next week but she swore it didn't happen. But she had smiled mysteriously. And four years later, Lucinda Williams – not Rose of Sharon – was the culprit. If it hadn't been for Lucinda playing the Ram's Head Tavern, Parker would not have bumped into Alex again. He came over and offered her a beer she had never heard of – Flying Fish, Flying Dog, Flying Beer, something. After the concert and a scorching version of "Righteously," the two walked up West Street. Parker liked his aggressive smile – not mean or nasty but *aggressive*. Everything he said or did, every expression, seemed to clear a path for her. That night they hopped the fence at Mears Marina at 2 a.m. and stretched out on the clay tennis court. She nestled her knees and hands into the clay and heard wind chimes from somebody's boat, and as she rocked even his breathing was *aggressive*. Alex didn't have any stop in him. The boy was all engine.

Then, within a year, living together then Dailey, an accident, although Parker could never say that word out loud or to herself. How could her baby girl ever be an *accident?* If anything was an accident, it was that damn Rose of Sharon and Lucinda Williams.

Alone in the parking lot of the Boston Whaler dealership, Parker pulled out her iPhone. Her older brother answered on the sixth ring.

"Wake up, dear one."

"Please go away. I was in the middle of a sex dream. Brad Pitt was my dentist and he was taking out my wisdom teeth and I had like 60 of them so he was in my mouth all day."

"Visual achieved."

Steve didn't ask why his sister was calling at 4:00 a.m. and why, judging by the faint sound of road, wind, and water, she was calling from an undisclosed maritime location. He knew her well enough to know the reason would be forthcoming in baby steps. Steve sat up in bed. He heard wind chimes coming from her cell. Was she on the bridge at Weems Creek?

"Parker?"

She had started walking back until she was a block from her home.

"I'm here."

Parker reached Chester Street and looked up at Alex's bedroom window. She prayed he was still snoring.

"My living arrangement is less than satisfying."

"That's a start," Steve said.

"Can Dailey and I come over to stay for a few days?"

"I'll turn the lights on for you."

The call dropped out.

At the house, Parker took off her shoes on the front porch, squeaked open the front door, and walked upstairs in sock feet. At the bedroom door, she squeezed the knob counterclockwise. Nothing was ever accomplished quietly at night. Parker dodged the bedposts at the front of the bed, the knobbed masts that often were her foil in daylight. Alex wasn't snoring, but he was breathing deeply. If she lifted the comforter, he might feel a sudden wave of cool air and awaken. Parker lowered herself on top of the covers and lay still as a dead sparrow. Cold outside her covers. Not even the flat pillow on her side.

"Have a nice walk?"

Alex turned on the light over his head, one of those fancy reading lamps he used when pretending to read. She sat up, looked ahead to a point outside the window where purple, pink and lavender streaked Maryland's sky. Alex got out of his bed and walked to the window. Parker wrapped herself in the buttermilk comforter, a graduation gift from her parents after she became a veterinary technician.

"I'm leaving."

She walked to the dresser to get her key ring and handbag. She counted her bills and double-checked for her Visa card. Folding the comforter was cumbersome, but Parker managed to tuck the bundle under her arms. Then she went into their daughter's room, collected as much of her clothes under her arm as she could before gently hoisting Dailey from her bed.

"Mommy, where are we going?" said the groggy girl in her Disney "Frozen Elsa" pajamas bought from Kohl's.

"We're going to a sleepover at Uncle Steve's."

Alex's brain, which often lagged behind real-time events, finally snapped to attention as he watched Parker's ensuing hour-long packing of her Samsonite three-piece set, a high school graduation present from her parents. He followed his girlfriend and daughter out to her car.

"This is crazy, Park. You're acting crazy."

Parker closed the hatchback with a good shove. In her back seat, she kept a spare hula hoop for whenever the urge to emergency hoop overcame her. The rest of her stuff was still in the house: DVD player, ottoman, Wegmans cookware and a *Waiting for Guffman* movie poster. She jetted back into the house and snatched the poster off the wall. In the front yard, she uprooted her shepherd's hook and packed it, the bird feeder, and squirrel baffle into her car.

"Get in the house. *Now*," Alex said to the reversing car. Once out of the driveway, the compact stopped on Chester Street. She rolled down her window and waved him toward her.

"Alex?"

"What?"

"Goodbye."

Parker was so tired she barely remembered her brother steering her and Dailey to his guest bedroom where they collapsed in two lumps of exhaustion. In the morning, she remembered her dream, and she *never* remembered her dreams.

She was putting on a pair of Picasso's pants. The pants were cubed and hippie yellow, and she spent the dream (a time-bending, filmic vision) walking alone on a vibrant purple beach. The shore birds were tilted and still. The surf was also frozen in still life – waiting for someone to paint the waves free. Parker walked the still-life purple coast, looking for anything that would and *should* be moving. But only she was moving, only she was going somewhere in Picasso's pants. She wasn't part of the still life. Not in her dream.

Chapter 4

The afternoon bell was set to ring in 13 minutes.

Don't think about her.

Her name.

Her mackerel eyes.

Her scars.

But Will thought about her name, her scars and mackerel eyes – a phrase from an old James Taylor song he heard at his Dad's. He failed on numerous Google missions to unearth a definition of mackerel eyes. Parker had them, though, whatever they were.

Will sat at his metal cart doubling as his desk. On the bottom of the floater's cart was a framed photo of Dean gnawing on a poppy-seed bagel. Also, a broken stapler that worked as a decoy when kids asked to borrow his stapler. His freshmen had jammed or broken five of his staplers, so he hid the good one in a file cabinet back in the "Dilbert Suite." One positive had emerged again from floating: When Will had a sleeper, he rammed the kid's desk with his cart. The behavioral modification was consistently successful.

The teacher's focus was diverted to the back row where an Asian student named Min was slightly chopping the back of own his neck with his finger-tips. (Along with Min Zhang, Will also had a Cindy Yang and Alan Gaeng. Zhang. Yang. Gaeng. Tricky to remember was all.) Classmates turned to watch Min's self-flagellation.

"Min, what are you doing?" Will said.

"Acupressure. It helps relieve eye strain."

Denting a shopworn stereotype, Min did not excel at academics by any standardized measure.

"But eye strain would suggest time spent on school work, yes?"

The question handcuffed Min, as his teacher studied the moon-faced clock on the wall. School clocks were notoriously off. One minute until the bell. Maybe.

"I smoke more dope that Dracula," a kid named Justin interjected. The school was teeming with Justins and Joshs and Jordans this year. School administrators believed it was Justin who burned his copy of *Crime and Punishment* and left the charred husk in a waste paper basket. While on cafeteria duty, Will discovered the ashes but couldn't find it in his heart to blame the arsonist.

Finally, the bell. Before tidying his floating desk for the road trip across the hall, he turned off the airplane mode on his cell.

Two missed calls from his mother.

Your father is missing. He's been missing for two hours. Call me.

I called Terri. I didn't know who else to call.

The 9-1-1 operator had been patient, courteous and possibly mentally challenged. She asked Barb Larkin three times if her husband was out for a walk and simply forgot the time. Mrs. Larkin said no, he has Alzheimer's, and he doesn't know the way home much less the time.

"You need to find my husband. *Now.*"

"All right, Mrs. Lincoln."

"No, it's Larkin. My husband is William L-A-R-K-I-N."

"Yes, ma'am," the young operator said before dispatching a patrolman to the Larkin/Lincoln residence at St. Mary's and Compromise streets, two blocks from the Annapolis Harbor.

Didn't they have sophisticated 9-1-1 equipment that immediately tracked the address through the phone number? They'll never find the house. How far could he have gone? The man doesn't drive anymore. Last month she stopped covering for him. She didn't have the strength or patience anymore to lie. My husband has Alzheimer's, she practiced saying in the mirror before telling their friends. And now her husband was missing.

"Start from the beginning, Mom."

She was taking her morning shower after locking the front and back doors with the keyed deadbolt, a suggested precaution in case an Alzheimer's patient attempts to leave the home unattended. Her husband was settled in at the kitchen table eating a bowl of Wheat Chex and drinking his cranberry juice. Her showers never ran more than 15 minutes; she had become more mindful of that, too. But when she came out of their bedroom, he was gone. She checked every room, checked the doors again, climbed the stairs and out into the widow's walk. He wasn't there. But on the north railing, the tip of a yellow extension ladder was visible. On the short side of the house, it was 25 feet down to the ground. An older person, if careful, could handle the descent.

"Maybe he needed to stretch his legs and get some air," Will told her on the phone, immediately regretting it.

"Get some air? By climbing down a ladder?" she started. "Will, your father doesn't know his way home, and he probably doesn't remember his name. Do you understand what I'm saying? He's *gone*. He doesn't need to get some *air*. If you think this is some kind of adventure, you are not only wrong, you are being cruel."

"I'll be right over."

She picked up the brochure on the kitchen counter, the brochure about an assisted living facility near Annapolis. She ran through the checklist again:

You are doing everything you can to keep your loved one home.

You feel guilty and frustrated.

You feel like a spy following your spouse around everywhere.

You feel like a stranger to your spouse.

You are mentally and physically exhausted.

In addition to private suites, Somerset Assisted Living staff helped with bathing and grooming, three nutritious meals a day, secured doors and courtyards (gardens, footpaths), and visual cues to help residents remember their way. *Remember, Somerset is not an institution – it's home!* Private telephones were not included, but the rent tax was deductible. That was all fine, but they better carry the Orioles games.

She heard a car pull up, but it wasn't Will's. His car always sounded like it was dragging a loaded dishwasher. In the driveway, she hugged Terri Morrow, who was wearing her hair shorter these days.

"Thanks for coming, dear."

"Please. You know to call me any time, right?"

"Let me look at you," Barb Larkin said, stepping back while holding both of Terri's hands. "Are you getting enough sleep?"

"No, but who is?"

"I like your hair. Very hip."

"I've missed you," Terri said, eager to look for Bill. She had always called him Bill – "Dad" was a stretch. She wasn't the daughter he never had; she was the daughter-in-law he could not have loved more.

A brown-and-white patrol car from the Anne Arundel Sheriff's Office pulled into the gravel drive, the deputy got out of his patrol car and, with a heavy walk, joined the growing search party.

They all heard him coming.

The silver Honda clanked and ground its way onto the driveway. Through his water-spotted windshield, he counted not one, but three people staring at his car. Will studied the features of the sheriff's deputy and determined he had *not* taught him at Lakeview.

Will walked up to his mother. "Go look for your father. Check around the harbor. Check up and down Compromise Street and Dock Street. I'll tell the officer what he needs to know. I have my cell. Answer yours, for a change. Terri, go with Will, please."

They walked past the Marriott Waterfront, Annapolis Yacht Club, West Marine supplies, and the U.S. Naval Academy Gift Shop. At City Dock, they checked at the Alex Haley statue. No Bill Larkin. Maybe he climbed aboard one of the Zodiacs tied up at dock's end. Or he could have boarded *The Woodwind* schooner. They ducked into the Marriott, walked through the air-conditioned lobby, came through the restaurant and out the back door to the dock. They asked the kid at the ticket window if an elderly man boarded the schooner. Two deckhands were enlisted, but no one saw a man traveling alone. Nothing but a bachelorette party – twelve overdressed ladies hopped up on watery Cosmopolitans.

"Maybe he hitchhiked to California," Will said.

"I don't think people hitchhike anymore," Terri said. "And you might want to take this a little more seriously."

"You want serious? Why are you here?"

"Not for you, trust me. I'm here for him."

At Market Square, at the corner of Randall and Dock streets, the Middleton Tavern had claims on being the oldest continuously operated tavern in the country. Civil War muskets hung on the walls, as customers chose between oysters or clams on the half shelf with their pint of Middleton Ale. Bill Larkin was sitting at the bar having a Yuengling and a dozen littleneck clams. He ordered the smoked bluefish, which would be up any minute. His face was unshaven and speckled in gray, his white T-shirt frayed at the collar. He looked like a man, after having come down from a ladder into a mulched bed of rhododendrons, treating himself to beer and seafood.

"Dad?"

The man didn't look up from his Keno card.

"Bill?"

He turned to see where the sound of his name was coming from exactly. Terri stepped closer to the barstool and smiled.

"I was hoping to find you here," she said.

"And you have! Please sit. Have a beer with me, young lady. Do you like clams?" He attempted to tuck in his T-shirt and comb his hair with his hand.

Terri and Will took seats at the bar. A bartender named Tim took orders for two Yuenglings and water for Will. A bowl of oyster crackers appeared. Smoked bluefish soon was delivered.

"What's this?"

"The smoked bluefish, sir."

"I didn't order bluefish."

Will looked at the bartender and tried to send a message to him: My Dad is not well, don't press the bluefish issue.

"I ordered it," Terri, interrupting. "Thanks. It looks great." Without speaking, she messaged the bartender.

"Oh, that's right. You did. My mistake, ma'am."

"No problem, young man," Bill Larkin said. He offered Terri a littleneck clam on a soaked napkin. Nursing his water, Will watched his ex with his father. She cut the tender fish into strips with her fork. They enjoyed the smoked bluefish and finished the littleneck clams and after Will settled up with Tim the bartender – 30 percent tip. Will thought his father might not *want* to go home, so he needed a ruse.

"Can I show you my favorite house? It's right across from the harbor. We can walk there. It has a widow's walk," Will said.

"I have a widow's walk."

"Let's go see this other one. Do you mind if this young lady comes along?"

"As long as it's OK with you," Bill Larkin said, winking.

"It is," said Will, who led his father by the hand out of the Middleton Tavern on to Dock Street.

The street was clogged with high-socked tourists and local men in white Fedora Safari lids and other folks being hauled around by exceptional dogs mostly in the Labrador family. His father glanced at the yacht tenders tied up at Ego Alley. They should rent one of those, one of these days, the two of them. That's a good idea, Will told him. He almost forgot about Terri, who was trailing just a few steps behind, as they both brought his father home.

That evening, Will tried twisting open a Sierra Nevada, but it wasn't a twist-off. He rubbed his injured palm and searched Craigslist for basset hounds and clicked on a rescue group in D.C. The site featured photographs and descriptions of one adoptable dog after another. There was COLA, who was "Too young and active to be stuck in a kennel." And SALLY, a "young tricolored hush puppy with one blue and one gold eye!" And ANGUS, "a real couch potato. Has a beautiful singing voice."

Angus was a singularly strong name for a boy or dog. Will inspected the color photo of Angus: the tricolored hound was sleeping on a couch.

Will's cell buzzed.

"Hello."

He knew her pauses.

"I should have thanked you for not letting Dean suffer."

She knew his pauses.

"I should have thanked you earlier for helping find Dad."

"You're welcome."

"You, too."

Terri's voice caught, and Will pictured her wiping her eyes and cheeks, sitting up straight, and shaking her head a few times, regaining her patented Terri Morrow composure.

"What are you doing now?" she said.

"You won't believe it."

"Watching *Deadliest Catch*?"

"Staring at ads for basset hounds. It's unbelievable how many people give away basset hounds."

"I know. I looked at sites last week." She spent an hour searching rescue sites but could find 16-20 basset hounds, any one of them she would adopt on the spot. Terri knew when the day came for Dean, she would not have been able to take him to the vet by herself. She would have asked Will – and, now, he had done that hard thing by himself.

He asked if she wanted to come over to look at basset hounds. He printed a dozen photographs of dogs in the Annapolis-D.C. area – Sally, Miles, Cola, Angus. Terri really should see Angus.

"I don't know if that's a good idea."

"It's just looking at dog pictures. We can be in separate rooms and tap on the walls using a special code. Plus, I'm injured. I ruptured my hand trying to twist off a beer bottle cap."

"You didn't use a chainsaw, did you?"

"Funny."

"By the way, how are the captions coming?" Terri said.

Terri's *New Yorker*s followed Will to his new apartment. She either forgot to stop the magazine or was her way of leaving him something besides Dean. When he was a boy, Will credited Charles Addams for his first sexual inkling. His grandfather collected Addams' cartoons, including one that featured a collegiate crew race with men rowing in one shell while passing them was this lavish rowing boat with its coxswain pampered by half-naked attendants – a brush stroke of bare hip and nothing more. It was a start.

In honor of Mr. Addams, Will turned to the *New Yorker*'s weekly caption contest where, three weeks ago, he submitted a caption to accompany a cartoon of a Clifford-sized dog sitting behind and nearly on a couple in a family room. "I'll work, you shovel," was the winning caption. Will suspected he lacked the necessary humor gene to write winning captions. Didn't make him a bad person.

"Keep trying," Terri said. "You'll win one of these days."

Caption pity. It had come to this.

"Are you coming over?" Will said.

"Do you have any wine?"

"Beer."

"What kind?"

"The kind that doesn't twist off."

• • •

They missed the window for hugging, so they shook hands. Terri's hair was shorter, darker. She got contacts. Terri looked younger, which didn't seem possible or fair to Will, who looked like he hadn't slept in two weeks and needed a haircut. This was Terri's first time in Will's apartment on West Gate Street near Church Circle. She wondered if he still had her DVD of *The Bicycle Thief* and her J.D. Salinger books. Wondered if he still slept with four pillows.

"Do you want a beer? Dumb question. Let me get you one."

"In a frosted mug."

"I remember," he said.

Terri toured the apartment as if trailing a realtor during an open house. The refrigerator magnets looked familiar: kitschy souvenirs from trips to the Rock and Roll Hall of Fame in Cleveland, Acadia National Park, South of the Border and a pink surfboard magnet from Maui. Terri kept poking around. Will still had a thing for Green Bay Packer memorabilia. She peeked into the bedrooms and the family room to check out the built-in bookcases and mud room where, in the corner, Dean's bed was heaped. Will found her there and handed her a beer in a frosted mug.

"How sick was he?"

"He hadn't eaten for days. Couldn't lift his head or drink water from my hand. His coat was still beautiful. He could wag his tail, a little. The vet told me the sooner the better. He told me it was my call."

"It was."

They put their beers down. She noticed Dean's Christmas-red collar on the peg above and there the tick remover and packages of Heartgard chewables, unopened. Will turned away, his shoulders shaking. Terri wrapped her arms around him from behind and rested her face under his shoulder blades. They stayed that way much longer than any two people who moments ago botched a simple hello hug. He slowly turned to her and finally saw new lines around her eyes. Hooking her jeans' pockets with his thumbs, Will pulled her closer. She pulled away.

He remembered (how could he forget?) how he had to bend kiss his wife, how he would unlock his knees so he could drop a little height; and, if necessary, he was never too proud to stoop. (And Will always went right to kiss her; he went right, she went left, starboard-to-port.) In the mud room next to Dean's bed, Will unlocked his knees and tried again to draw Terri close. Again, she held back.

"What's wrong?" he said. "I mean besides everything other than maybe this moment."

"Why are his heartworms pills unopened, Will?"

"What?"

"Those are either new packages or the same ones I bought I-don't-know-when. Please tell me you remembered to give Dean his Heartgard."

Without moving, Will collapsed, an internal collapse, as he felt himself being slowly hollowed out.

"Tell me his symptoms again."

He listed them in a whisper, as he backed out of the mud room, almost tripping over his own foreign feet.

"Say it. I want to hear you say it," Terri said, sobbing.

"I forgot to give him his pills. You always took care of that."

"That's right, I did. And when we agreed to let Dean stay here, you couldn't remember to do this one simple thing? This one simple thing that would have saved his life."

He ran out of his house, leaving Terri to leave any time after she wanted. Will ran the length of his block before walking three more blocks before dropping to his knees into someone's front yard at 11:45 p.m. and into their mowed, dew-slicked grass. There were applicable prayers, there must be, but he had only pretend-prayed as a boy those few years his parents managed to keep him going to church. No prayers tonight, but Will howled for forgiveness, invoking Dean's name and then the Lord's name out of panicked habit. He lifted his hands and saw their clenched imprint in the wet grass and began pounding the ground with balled fists until a front porch light lit then another and a front door opened, and he had to run again.

Chapter 5

His name was John McGuire but they called him Mack, and they were the only ones allowed to call him Mack. A certified financial planner, he made excessive amounts of money investing for people, a foreign and mysterious talent in the opinion of his friends, Will Larkin and Kyle Dixon, a reporter at the only Annapolis news-talk radio station. Kyle made virtually no money and appeared enormously happy. Mack, who self-identified as an apex predator, boasted of devouring all competitors. He bought a black BMW every other year, owned a beach house on the Eastern Shore and nurtured a childhood grudge the source of which only Will knew.

"I have two close friends in this world, so it's only fitting I share the news with you both," Mack said. Unlike his rangy and fair-skinned best friend, Mack was built low to the ground, his dark features implying a ruggedness he did not disprove. And while Will struggled to occasionally grow the most rudimentary of facial hair, Mack shaved twice a day, including down where he called his "dance floor." As for Kyle, he simply looked like a Kyle, which was the extent of his friends' descriptive powers. Of his habits, Will and Mack would always remember Kyle's anti-litter crusade (begun in grade school), his penchant for watching for deer along the highway during any road trip, and the boy read *novels*. Hemingway and Steinbeck, those dudes. This level of reading mystified and escaped his friends.

The trio from Lakeview High (Class of 2004) still met monthly at Buster's, a wing joint on Green Street. Behind the bar, two ancient Hamilton Beach blenders and a framed dollar bill were dwarfed by skyscrapers of gorgeous booze. Above the cash register hung a decommissioned life ring from the USNS Comfort, a Navy hospital ship out of Baltimore. The bar's mascot, a goldfish in genetic shambles named Maurice, hid in a Jim Beam bottle with its hull cracked open (the tank's gumbo water hadn't been changed in weeks). Buster's was also known for its men's urinal – a 5-foot tall industrial dandy.

Buster's had good food and bad service. Customers begged waitresses behind the bar for a beer; the wait staff was habitually caught off-guard by food and drink orders. They looked like they wanted to press charges. Four months after Dean's death, Will agreed to meet his friends at Buster's on a rare Thursday night. He hadn't seen them or anyone in that time, but they had convinced him to come out of exile.

"So, are you done?" Mack asked him.

"Done what?"

"Rolling around in your sewer of self-pity?" Mack's sympathy was often compact and lacerating.

"I'm feeling only slightly less horrible if that's what you're kindly asking."

"Good," Mack said. "Now on to my news. I am no longer employed."

"This is your emergency?" Kyle said. He guessed cancer; Kyle thought everything in life revolved around cancer. Someone was always *battling* cancer. That was the chosen verb: *battling*. Kyle was convinced one day he would be *battling* cancer after they discovered a tumor the size of a *grapefruit*. Never the size of a mango or one of those Meyer lemons. Always a grapefruit.

"What would you fucking call unemployment other than an emergency? A mild, unassuming setback?" Mack said.

"What happened?" Will said tepidly.

While cradling his beer, Mack explained the circumstances and intricacies of his termination from his unstinting and perhaps unreliable point of view. The explanation was impenetrable. The friends observed a moment of silence. The very notion of Mack not making money was too much to process.

"Well," Kyle finally said. "That is unfortunate news."

"Gee, you think, you reporter fuck."

"Can we do anything?"

"Yes, William you can," Mack said. "I need you to be a stand-by."

"Stand by for what?"

"Stand by me, that's the fuck for."

Sure, yes, of course, Will said. "I might actually have some not-terrible news."

"Besides the tri-fuck-ta of getting arrested, divorced, and killing your dog?" Mack said.

"I met someone a while back." An innocent meeting at his vet's office then a random visit at City Dock, he explained. "I haven't thought about girls since Terri. I never thought I'd think about a girl ever again."

"You just needed time," Kyle said. "Have you called this mystery person?"

"I tried, but I got rattled. I hit star or pound key or both. I think I took a picture."

"You don't deserve a dog, phone or a girl," Mack said.

"You're not helping," Kyle said.

"This will help then. Yesterday I saw a woman driving with her vagina. I was next to her at a light. I was looking right down at her. There was her stomach and there was like this other thing mashed up against her steering wheel. When the light changed, she took off driving with her vagina."

Will looked sadder.

"I thought my little story would cheer you up, William."

"You know," he said, "normally it would."

• • •

Will imagined Parker drove just fine with only her hands. But she probably said "verse" instead of "versus" or preferred Wheat Thins over Triscuits (Rosemary and Olive Oil Triscuits no less!) or flossed in front of significant others. A deal breaker must be lurking in the shadows. She probably didn't date guys who were married 2.92 years, drive a boring silver Honda, liked Triscuits, solitary flossing, and the Green Bay Packers (she did not strike him as a football kind of gal). He vowed to never tell her about the heartworm pills.

Impulsively, he drove to the Annapolis Animal Hospital. He also vowed to never step foot there again after what happened, but he wanted to see her.

"Needs a Good Home" cat and dog posters hung on the lobby's crooked bulletin board, along with the office's permanent exhibit: an in-house photographic montage of a spaying operation. Will looked closely and recognized Parker, masked and in her scrubs, assisting with the delicate piece of office business. Will instinctively reached low for himself, then drew back his hands.

"Well, well," Parker said.

"Thought I'd drop by."

"Oh, really."

"I was thinking about you."

"Were you now. Allow me to recap. You come to the animal hospital with your dog. After an embarrassing false start, I help you. We run into each other at City Dock. It's nice – at least I think it was. Against my better instincts, I call you two times, and you don't return my calls."

Will upgraded his cell phone but the device paralyzed him. Mack graciously programmed his phone numbers and had added, for spice, four phone sex numbers, both gay and straight (accepting assistance from his friend came with known risks). Will had not attempted texting, but maybe one of the kids at school could help him. Every single kid. He began to question whether his self-identification as an *old soul* was just a more poetic way of saying *old*.

"I'm sorry for not calling you back. I seem to struggle with 21st-century communications." He pivoted to their handwriting contest.

"Wasn't that fun?"

"I thought so," Parker said.

"This might be fun, too. I created a test for us to get to know each other. I'm going to ask you a series of questions. Don't think, just answer. There are no wrong answers and trust me, I have never said that in my life."

"Maybe you are *evolving.*"

"Sounds painful."

"You bet," Parker said. "If we're doing this, let's go outside. There's a picnic table out back where we walk the dogs."

They went out back and aimed for the raggedy picnic table. Watch for splinters, Parker said. Oh, and dog shit, watch for a field of dog shit.

"Ready?

"If you insist," Parker said.

"Wheat Thins vs. Triscuits?"

"Wheat Thins."

Will made a buzzer sound to indicate the utter wrongness of her answer.

"Weirdest product name."

"Tyvek."

"What?"

"You see it wrapped around houses under construction – TYVEK in big letters," Parker said. "When I was a kid, I thought it was the name of the family who lived there. I couldn't believe how many families were named Tyvek. My dad broke the news to me that Tyvek was a brand of home insulation."

"That's kind of the best childhood story I've ever heard."

"Your bar must be low."

"Moving on to the world of sports, who won this year's Super Bowl?"

"The Houston Oilers."

"There's no Houston Oilers anymore."

"How tragic."

Will reached into his pocket to find his cheat sheet.

"Best name of a thing that no one knows the name of."

Parker rose to it.

"A crumber – what waiters use to wipe the crumbs off the table."

"Impressive," Will said. "Favorite word?"

"Honeysuckle."

"Favorite saying?"

"We had a neighbor, a real Southerner, whose daughter went out for cheerleading," Parker said. "She didn't make the team and was crushed. Her mom told her, 'Honey, cheerleading won't get you across the street.' *Won't get you across the street.* I love that."

"What's your dream job?"

"Besides novelist or Tyvek Saleswoman of the Year? Drummer in a rock band." Parker's only brush with music came in seventh-grade band when her rental trumpet attempted to swallow her whole.

"What's your go-to music?"

"Tedeschi Trucks, Neko Case, LCD Soundsystem, Richard Thompson, Beck and of course, Lucinda Williams."

Will owned none of their music and decided not to mention he was in possession of his grandfather's Kingston Trio albums – no need to frighten the girl. He did know one song that might be classified as new (he wasn't positive).

"Ever heard 'Rock & Roll is Cold'?"

"To death," Parker said. "Have you heard Bambi Lee Savage's 'Darlin'?"

"Bambi?"

"Find it, listen to it, commit it to your heart."

"Yes, Bambi. If I may call you that."

"No thanks."

Will was out of music questions.

"OK, math man. I have a few questions for *you*. Do you like Howard Stern?"

"Uh…yes."

"That question made you nervous, didn't it? You are wondering, does *she* like Howard Stern."

Will often struggled to find a foothold with multi-part questions.

"Greatest Wack Packer?"

Parker: "Easy. Eric the Actor."

"Agreed. And now Ms. Cool, tell me something shocking about yourself."

She thought about her desire to return her childhood seashell collection to a Delaware beach where she took the shells in the first place. Instead:

"I have a daughter."

She looked at Will and imagined a cartoonist's bubble sprouting over his head. The caption saying "How do I ditch this chick?" But Parker never had a feel or trust for her captions. Rather than shock, Will was curious.

"What's her name?"

"Dailey."

"I've never taught a Dailey, and I've taught every name in the baby book. Parker and Dailey. Two great names."

Was he flirting? An algebra teacher had never flirted with her before. Dog owners of nearly every occupation and age and marital status, but never a math man.

"I have another question for you."

"Ask away, Parker Cool, mother of Dailey."

"What scares you?"

"Boats."

"And you live in Annapolis?"

"I had a bad experience when I was young."

Will looked like he swallowed a sword.

"Carry-on emotional baggage or the kind you have to check?"

"What?"

"Nothing, sorry," Parker said, trying to tug him back.

"So, what makes Will Larkin happy?"

"When life adds up."

"How's that been working out for you?"

"Not tops."

"Me, either."

"So, how do you think this went?"

"I think it went pretty well, math man. *Pretty, pretty* well. Next time you call me."

"Next time?"

"That's what I said, buckaroo."

That night, Will stepped down into his unfinished basement. He bought a 70-pound Everlast heavy bag along with a speed bag and stand at Dick's Sporting Goods. He picked up 16-ounce gloves and wrist wraps and taught himself to outfit his hands since he had never boxed before in his life. Mack had recommended the activity to relieve stress and as a private, safer alternative to actually punching someone. Will pilfered a kitchen timer from his mom's house to double as his ringside boxing timer. He had no idea what he was doing and enjoyed the not-knowing very much.

The initial bouts were two, three rounds with Will stung and shocked by the hardness of the heavy bag and the softness of his teacher's hands. Clearly, he would have to build up stamina and tolerance to stick with this hobby or whatever it was. In the ensuing weeks, he managed to hyper-extend his elbow, jam his right thumb, and strain his Achilles all while punching a defenseless hanging sack of compressed newspaper shreds. The injuries were embarrassing, but Will finally had grown shoulders. If only he had discovered this devil exercise in middle school.

He set the white kitchen timer set for the first 3-minute round of tonight's main event in his basement. The big bag, once unyielding, had developed a paunch from where he pummeled it for six rounds, three times a week. A righty, Will was determined to strengthen his weaker left arm. He desired a left jab – like a sixth-rate Ali (his grandfather's favorite fighter). Once he felt good about his left jab, he developed combinations and worked the body of the bag with hooks and uppercuts, mindful to keep his thumbs tucked aided by wrist wraps. Instead of his usual six rounds, Will stayed on his toes tonight and pushed himself to go seven, then eight rounds. When he told Kyle about his boxing, his friend assumed a Zen stance by stating the marksman fundamentally aims at himself.

"You think I'm doing this to beat myself up?" he asked Kyle.

"It doesn't matter what I think. What do *you* think?"

"I don't want to think. I want to hit something."

When the kitchen timer quit, so did Will. His body was soaked, his arms sand-bagged, his left arm particularly limp and punished. His left wrist was sore from an uppercut that caught the bag low where it hadn't been punched soft. There were no mirrors in his basement. Maybe he looked stronger. He always felt stronger and more relaxed after boxing, the day's toxins excised.

He wanted Parker to see him box. He wanted to see her again. He needed to discover what exactly was a *buckaroo*.

Chapter 6

He picked up this time.

"Happy birthday, dear."

"Hey, Mom. Thanks for remembering."

"How could I forget my son's 30th birthday? You're coming over, right? Your dad is cooking ribs, and I made the coleslaw you like," his mother said. Will did not like her mother's coleslaw. Too much mayo.

"You didn't forget, did you?"

The birthday lunch reminder might have been on that batch of Post-its Will accidentally washed and spun dry along with his jeans, shirts, and dachshund boxers. He remembered picking out shards of yellow paper plastered against the drum of his Maytag dryer.

"I'll be there."

"Good. Did you give any thought to what we talked about?"

On Sundays, St. Gregory's Catholic Church in Annapolis had a vespers service. His mother wanted to know if her son would come with her. She conceded Will wouldn't be going to Mass with her anymore. Those days were over, but vespers sounded spiritually neutral.

"About the vespers thing? Sounds like Scooters for the Lord," Will said. She had read to him from the vespers literature:

"You will enter a world of ancient chant. You will be bathed in illuminating candlelight as gently rising incense and ancient music provide the context for quiet meditation. What you won't find is a sermon, a confusing service bulletin, or proselytizing. We invite you to experience for yourself the sacred mystery of divine encounter."

"Think I'll pass."

"But you're coming over, right?"

"I said I would."

Downtown Annapolis, its history hermetically sealed, has crowned streets – King George, Duke of Gloucester, Farragut – and two radiating, signature hubs – Church and State circles. But Compromise Street, a mite of a road, has the best waterfront view of the lot. Compromise runs north to downtown Annapolis and Ego Alley, then south past the Summer Garden Theatre, yacht club, and Marriott Waterfront before the drawbridge at Spa Creek.

Will's parents lived in a 19th century Colonial home at Compromise and St. Mary's streets. Like a few other homes in the area, the Larkins' house featured a widow's walk, so named for the ancient wives of ancient mariners who watched their husbands return from sea. They often did not, leaving the women to pace the rooftop awaiting their return. Barb Larkin's husband was not a mariner, although he owned a 17-foot Carolina Skiff for 29 days. On the 28th day, while zipping around Spa Creek, a Sea Ray about capsized him or that's what he told his wife. There had been no Sea Ray, just a first-time boater making a common and near-tragic mistake on the water. Their 6-year-old son had been with him. Their son almost died. He sold the skiff a month later but bought an inflatable boat called a Zodiac that he hoped Will would want one day.

Bill Larkin never boated again or talked about what happened. He dedicated his spare time (and resources) to finding a home with a widow's walk and a view of Annapolis Harbor.

"And now you have one," Barb Larkin said 12 years ago when they bought the house. "But I don't know what you expect me to do. Go up there and watch for your return from the law office every day?"

He didn't expect that *every* day.

"Bill, you need a dog. He can stand look-out for your homecomings," she told her husband of 41 years. In 2008, they adopted a corgi named Otto. Despite the dog's molting and relentless pursuit of used Kleenex, the Larkins became dog people. Otto adopted the widow's walk, and his owners didn't mind once they broke him of a certain habit associated with dog walks in general.

On nights she couldn't sleep, Barb Larkin played the memory game. She replayed the second, third and fourth dates with her husband. The first date wasn't remarkable (coffee, somewhere). On their second date, Bill Larkin attempted lasagna, and there was almost nothing cuter than a nice man botching a meal the first time out. Barb replayed the birth of their only child: 12:45 p.m., Friday. Drizzling. Got to the hospital the night before. Water broke in the middle of *Cheers*.

Should we leave now? Bill kept saying.

Yes, dear.

He drove to the hospital and used two hands on the wheel, a first. Mr. Turn Signal, all of a sudden, too. When they dated, Barb kidded him about keeping two hands on the wheel. She didn't mind his one free hand. Now, she couldn't remember the last time they drove together or held hands.

It wasn't only that Bill forgot his son's birthday or where he put his keys (right where he always left them – in the Route 66 ashtray on the kitchen counter) or to pick up a half gallon of skim. He got lost on a short walk in their neighborhood and, worse, had climbed down the ladder and wandered off downtown. The man forgot their house number when addressing an envelope to State Farm and joked about wishing he could forget to pay every bill. Last week, turning on the oven to medium stymied him.

She finally told a close friend about her husband's behavior – she didn't use the word *symptoms*. Pat Rogers lent her a book, David Shenk's *The Forgetting*, a portrait of the Alzheimer's epidemic. Barb made it to page 13 when she learned what she already knew. Her husband was losing himself, gradually, definitely.

On Will's birthday, Bill Larkin watched from his widow's walk as the Honda pulled up. Will's back rear tire could use some air, he surmised from his vantage point before descending. Will hugged his mother in the driveway, his chin perched momentarily atop her silvery styled hair.

"You're never too old for a hug," she said into his chest.

"Don't suffocate him," her husband said, shaking his son's hand.

Will didn't grow up on St. Mary's Street, so the house never felt like home. He never felt he could plop down on the sofa or stretch out on the floor, which was his preferred position in childhood. He missed their old home on St. John's Street across from the college of the same name. He missed where he set up his Hot Wheels tracks in the unfinished basement next to the drier that always sounded like it was running over road kill. He papered his bedroom walls with *Sports Illustrated* covers – must have had six Michael Jordan covers. In middle school, his friend Mack brought over copies of his father's *Playboys* to grace his friend's bedroom walls, but Will never had the nerve, so they surveyed the centerfolds behind locked door.

Will never understood why his parents moved. Why move? Why change?

The birthday boy sat in a nondescript second-string chair in his parents' family room. The leather recliner clearly belonged to his father; the indentation in the cushion mirroring his father's proportions. The recessive gene carrying butt-less-ness – Will was a carrier – must have come from his mother's side.

"I saw you drive up," Bill Larkin said. "You've got a tire that looks a little low in the back. I've got a compressor in the garage."

Will wished he knew the age when tire pressure became a dominant issue in a man's life. The well-being of his tire pressure extended beyond Bill Larkin's nuclear family and into the neighborhood. His mother reported last month that Bill alerted a neighbor to *his* car's tire pressure – judged again from on high in the widow's walk.

"I'll take a look before I leave," Will said.

"You don't want to be driving on underinflated tires."

Will imagined a NASCAR-level blowout on the way home. He wasn't sure how to change a tire, wishing he had paid attention to the man who preached the need for a 4-way lug wrench in every car trunk.

Barb Larkin returned to the family room with a pitcher of unsweetened iced tea and a tray of Berger Cookies. The Berger Cookie, a Baltimore institution, was roughly four parts chocolate to one-part plain cookie, whose only role is to hang on to all that chocolate. Otto eyed the cookie tray.

"I'm so sorry about Dean. He was such a sweetie."

"Thanks, Mom."

"In happier news," she said, "someone has a birthday. Thirty years ago today was a special day for us. Our baby boy was born. Nine pounds 11 ounces! Twenty-three inches long!"

The big 3-0. Will wondered if it was too late to learn the alto sax or develop a sitcom. He found himself loitering inside Stevens hardware store on Dock Street. Last Wednesday, he bought a pack of overhead ceiling hooks because he liked the way they looked (he had nothing to hang). He bought Krazy Glue even though he had six desiccated tubes at home. He saw a magnificent crowbar for sale and bought it. Was grout next? On school nights, Will performed his dad's sock trick. After coming home from work, Bill Larkin would hunker down in his leather recliner, take off his shoes, and slip his socks half off his feet; his toes looked they were wearing floppy nightcaps. *My God, I'm becoming more like my father than his son.*

Physical fitness reared its head. As a birthday gift to himself, Will bought a treadmill, but the machine required programming for speed, calories, distance, elapsed time, pace, and elevation. The treadmill's display panel resembled the cockpit of the space shuttle. He could not immediately locate the start command, so, unstarted, he gave up. Will Larkin at 30.

"That boy was a whopper!" his father said.

"Bill, you were scared to hold him. You were scared you'd dislocate his shoulder when you had to change his little T-shirts." His wife sipped her tea and nibbled a bit of chocolate lava off a Berger Cookie.

"I was never scared of changing him."

"I don't recall you changing many diapers."

"I changed plenty."

"Never the bad ones."

"What exactly were the good diapers?" he said.

"You know what I mean."

Before his head exploded, Will asked for a beer, asked because he still wasn't comfortable going into the kitchen and getting one himself.

"Have you heard from Terri since, well, our little episode here?"

Barb Larkin: Dominatrix of Segues.

"In a way."

"You mean you don't want to talk about it," she said.

"What do you say us men folk take a walk. Got beer stashed on the roof," his father said. The Larkin men excused themselves to the widow's walk.

There are man caves – garages outfitted with 78-inch HDTV plasma screens, stocked refrigerators, pool tables, dart boards, plush seating for six or even twelve – and there was Bill Larkin's economy-class man cave. The widow's walk had room for two, weather-tortured Adirondacks and an Igloo cooler. From the widow's walk, the altitude and view created an artificial sense of boating; hard not to feel like a captain here, hard not to want someone waiting for you to return home.

Among other roof-top amenities, Will's father maintained an extensive library of *Reader's Digest*s.

"They've dumbed down Word Power. They used to give you four choices, now it's three and two are obviously wrong. Anyone who passed eighth grade should know these words," he said.

They had other potential subjects to discuss, but Will couldn't think of any. Sometimes, it's easier to talk about the *Reader's Digest*.

"Button up your overcoat and put on your thinking cap," Word Power advised. The Larkin men obliged.

They blazed through *arctic, hibernate, tundra, gelato, toboggan,* and *permafrost* before they put an end to the cushy quiz. An insulted Bill Larkin said he would write the magazine to complain. "And I'll use really big words."

Next up, "Laughter, the Best Medicine." The *Digest's* joke page was another anchor in Bill's rooftop entertainment complex. For Will, one of the more frightening aspects of aging was that the old jokes got better.

"Read me one, Dad."

"Who's the patron saint of e-mail? Answer: St. Francis of a CC."

"Not bad, not bad."

"I got you something," his father said. He handed his son a floppy bag. Fearing another fleece jacket, Will reached into the mystery sack. Nothing but mesh – lightweight, floatable, insured against loss, guaranteed for life, "handcrafted with Canadian persnicketiness", mesh. And the correct size: 7 7/8.

"I heard you wanted a Tilley."

He didn't. A Tilley was for an old guy. My God, did even his own parents think he was old? Plus, a Tilley was for a boater. Will was not a boater.

"Try it on."

Will lowered the Tilley onto his head; the hat's drawstring tickled his neck. Drying instructions came with the hat and a campy testimonial: *Most Tilley Hat wearers and the person beside you is a prime example, are interesting people of sterling character...*

"Dad, can we talk about something?"

Bill Larkin flicked a dot of morning bagel off his shirt.

"I want to talk about the boat ride. When I nearly drowned. You remember. Do you? Do you remember?"

"I don't remember any such thing." He tried to stand but lost his balance and fell back into his chair. "I don't know what the hell you are talking about!"

Barb Larkin heard her husband's raised voice from the kitchen. She hadn't heard him sounding so upset in years.

"What's all the commotion?"

"Nothing," Will said. He looked at his father. "I heard you made ribs."

"I never said that. Why are people always telling me things I said!"

"I told Will you made ribs, dear. Come on now, let's all go eat."

They came down the stairs from the roof. On the kitchen table, a birthday cake from Graul's – chocolate with white frosting. His mother opened two top drawers looking for candles and matches.

"I noticed when you drove up your back rear tire could use some air."

"You told me already," Will told his father.

"God dammit, I haven't said one word about tires," Bill Larkin said.

After they ate his ribs in stone silence, Barb Larkin lit three candles on Will's birthday cake – one for each decade. She cut three small pieces and left a plump yellow rose for her son. Barb Larkin, alone, sang "Happy

Birthday." Will unwrapped her gifts – two dress shirts from Orvis, a splurge. At the front door, he kissed her on the right cheek.

"What's happening?"

"He's worse."

"What can I do?"

She took her son's hand.

"Be nice to him."

"I am nice to him."

"Be nicer."

Chapter 7

He called the next time.

Will wanted her to see his place – a big step in what he hoped was the stirring of a relationship. A cold wasn't going to stop him, although he never understood the roots of the common cold, which was not caused by a draft as he maintained. Whatever the alleged cause, Will knew he had a cold and he chugged Nyquil, whose active ingredient, the antihistamine Doxylamine succinate, commonly induced drowsiness in users. Additionally, combining Nyquil with alcohol led to increased drowsiness and was not recommended. Feeling a surge of medicinal courage, Will flipped open his cell. Thanks to Mack's help, Will had Parker on speed dial.

Two rings.

"Parker?"

"Well, hi."

Will dove right in for a change.

"Do you want to come over tonight? I have Netflix." (How could any girl say no to such a seductive offer?)

Parker said yes.

Will issued three directions to his home and was working up a fourth route when she politely asked him to stop for the love of God. Parker and verbal directions had a strained relationship. She Googled it.

"If I'm not there in an hour, Google misled me."

"If you're not here in an hour, I'll come find you."

Parker asked if he would be providing soda and popcorn for movie night. Bring the popcorn, he told her. Will showered, shaved, Scoped-up, and dabbed his neck with Kenneth Cole cologne; the gauge on the bottle hadn't moved in a year. He killed time watching blooper reels from *It's*

Always Sunny in Philadelphia. Will wanted a job where the highlight of the work day was cracking up. There were no blooper reels in teaching.

Fifty minutes later, Parker knocked twice on his door. She wore black Levi's and brought microwave popcorn. Have a seat, he said. She plopped down on the khaki sofa in front of the TV. Will took the popcorn to the kitchen, unfolded it, and centered it in the microwave. Straining to muffle his sniffling, he drank another plastic cup of Nyquil before filling two glasses with ice. He rushed the pouring job, and Coke foam erupted over the sides.

Will sat on the sofa two cushions away, as if they were separated by a coil of concertina wire. He wanted to talk to her and look at her all night long but was overcome with an insatiable desire to nap.

"Is it show time?" Parker said.

The Netflix menu proved unappetizing. Will suggested something from his home collection:*Anchorman, Tommy Boy, The Big Lebowski, Apollo 13, It's a Wonderful Life, Old School, Wedding Crashers, Silver Lining Playbook, The Royal Tenenbaums.*

"I've seen *Tenenbaums* probably 10 times. Might be my favorite movie," Parker said.

"It's a Wonderful Life?"

"How old are you?"

"30. You?"

"A mere 28."

"Wedding Crashers?"

"'MA! THE MEATLOAF!!!'"

"Agreed," Will said.

Parker curled up her legs on the sofa, a sliver of tummy exposed. In the kitchen, Will dumped the popcorn into a Tupperware bowl and plunked the treat down between them. He started the movie and fast-forwarded through the previews. As Will attempted to stay conscious, he noticed Parker was not a dainty popcorn eater.

"How's work?" Will said.

"Oh, the usual. I fell in love with about a dozen dogs that came into the office. I talked to my folks. I went to my brother's fish picture party."

"What?"

"A fish picture party. Have you not experienced a fish picture party?"

Although not a fisherman, Steve Cool did enjoy a good fish picture. His annual Fish Picture Party required that guests arrive bearing a picture of them holding a fish they caught. The photographs were clothes-pinned around the house so all could admire. Sons and daughters brought pictures taken by their parents – crinkled snap shots of rockfish, flounder, catfish, bluegills, perch, barracudas, mangrove snappers, gar from the Everglades. Parker brought a 1996 picture of her holding a small, silver jack with black bulging eyes from when their parents took the family to Islamorada.

"Do you have any fish pictures?"

"One," Will said. "Not much of a story behind it."

They started *Wedding Crashers*, which featured a cameo of *The Woodwind*, a popular tourist schooner in Annapolis. They ate popcorn and drank soda before Will switched to Ravenswood Zinfandel, the only brand he knew. He heard that a safer opening drink gambit was wine rather than beer. He really didn't know, but the wine did loosen their gears.

"Are we going to talk at some point about the wedding ring on your finger?" Parker launched.

"I'm divorced."

"But you still wear your ring."

"Habit. And I'm not sure I can get it off. I appear to have gained a few pounds over the years. But I'm working on it."

"Working on what?"

"Losing weight. Changing habits."

"I grind my teeth at night," Parker said. "And crack my knuckles."

"Well," Will said, "*that* won't get you across the street."

Parker's laugh was of Old Faithful quality – a superheated geyser worth sticking around for each time.

"Me and 40 million others are proud sufferers of Bruxism. I have to wear a plastic night guard. It's sexually irresistible."

Will pictured an angry, protruding orthodontist's headgear, keeping the men (man?) in Parker's life at bay, jabbing them back to their side of the bed.

He also imagined himself sleeping for three days thanks to this moonshine cold medicine.

"Not to brag, but I have Restless Leg Syndrome. At night, my feet rub together like horny crickets," he said.

"Big deal."

"I'll have you know RLS is a recognized neurological disorder and affects 10 percent of the population. There's no known cure."

Will was feeling proud, defensive and drugged.

"Maybe it's not Restless Leg Syndrome."

Will was positive about his Restless Leg Syndrome. Once you read something on the Internet, you can't go back on that. The man had a syndrome!

Parker noticed Will had assumed a position of rest on the sofa. Guess this was nap time.

"Will?"

He was nonresponsive. She expected his feet to start cricketing.

"Maybe I should go," Parker said.

Came a slurred mumble: "Don't go…. let's…"

She waited.

"… let's drive over to the little beach at Horn Point…and drink beer on the hood of my car and look at the lights on the bay bridge and take our shoes off …and…and…there's an osprey nest and we can stay there until…"

Which sounded like a lovely Jimmy Stewart-ish plan until she heard Will's snoring, a benign death rattling. As Parker stood, popcorn high-dived off her shirt. She found something resembling a clean blanket and covered the man for the night.

He never heard her leave.

In the morning, Will still had his cold plus a strange hangover that left him not so much hurting but concerned he would never again be able to operate a motor vehicle much less instruct youths on algebraic equations. While convalescing, he thought about Parker's scar-crossed hands, how she walked with a slight hitch and how she told him when they first met that she never wanted to be tied down to a coffee card. He wanted to know everything about her.

He called her at 8:02 a.m.

"I'm a little rusty in the dating department," he said.

"A *little?* You passed out. Were you drinking before I got there?"

"I mixed cold medicine with wine. Both, I can report, don't play well with each other. It was a stupid thing to do."

"We're not clicking, are we?" Parker said.

Will felt sick to his stomach.

"I don't know what's wrong. Life used to be predictable. I used to be likable, I swear."

She almost smiled.

"Can we try again? I promise not to mix alcohol with cold medicine again."

"A girl can dream."

That night, he tried leaning into sleep but it would have none of him. Will, who still owned a CD player, slipped in both discs from James Taylor's live recording in 1993, a gift from his father six birthdays ago. After listening to the first 6 songs, Will noticed his alarm clock's double-jointed numbers read 2:45 with the red dot to signify AM. He hated that dot.

• • •

"Are you still mad at him?"

"What?" Parker said, flicking on the Lady Bug night-light in her brother's spare bedroom. Nightlights were a novel addition to Steve's home as had been the addition of a 6-year-old girl. He retrofitted his house with kid-proof cabinet latches and plastic covers for the electrical outlets; Steve even canceled his premium movie channels for fear Dailey would accidentally stumble on adult fare.

"Are you still mad at him?" said Dailey, who was busy not sleeping.

"Daddy?"

"Uh-huh."

Parker steadied herself.

"I know we haven't talked about this enough. And I know I didn't do a good job telling you why we left. I'm sorry, sweetie. The best I can do is tell you I wasn't happy there. I always feel happy with *you* but not with your father. I love you more than anything and that goes for Lambie, too. Although she's long overdue for a bath."

"Lambie told me she doesn't like baths," Dailey said.

"Oh really? Well, that's funny because that sounds like a certain girl I know. A certain girl who needs to get some sleep. Lambie, too."

Along with a night light, Dailey insisted on sleeping with Lambie, a stuffed animal that had undergone so much reconstructive stitch work the body and head were grossly disproportional. A pattern of failed laundering left a gray paste to Lambie's countenance. On her best days, the beloved doll smelled like regurgitated milk. Dailey had also fallen under the spell of "Charlotte's Web," her mother's favorite book and together their favorite bedtime reading. But no chapter tonight.

Parker tucked in Dailey's sheets, which she promptly untucked with a shove of both feet. Parker smiled – she was an un-tucker, too. Lambie's head rested on the pillow next to Dailey's. The doll's arms were folded peacefully like a limp, smelly Buddha. Dailey folded her arms on her chest and didn't budge. Neither did Lambie.

"When can we see Daddy?"

Parker swallowed a mouthful of resentment and anger toward her ex-boyfriend.

"Soon."

"Promise?"

"Yes, I promise. Now sleep! It's a school day tomorrow. You, too, Lambie."

Parker kissed Lambie's misshapen forehead and closed the bedroom door behind her, caught herself, then cracked the door half-way. Downstairs she plopped down on her brother's sectional. She turned on Turner Classic Movies hoping to find a Barbara Stanwyck movie but no luck. She peered at her phone and saw five missed messages.

All from Alex.

Chapter 8

In the home with the widow's walk, Bill Larkin looked for *something* to repair, but there was nothing to take apart, tighten or spray with WD-40. He wasn't sure of the day or time; he couldn't remember if he had replaced his watch battery or not. He walked up to the widow's walk and sat in his faded Adirondack chair. He couldn't remember why he had taken off his shoes or where he put them. His feet looked strange as if they belonged to another man, or maybe all old men's feet looked spotted, cracked, slow. Bill Larkin covered his feet with a beach towel and hung the green field binoculars around his neck. He looked out toward Annapolis Harbor and watched yachts thread the channel, saw where the tenders tied off at the end of City Dock. He had a bleached memory of owning a boat.

"Did I give Will that Zodiac?"

"Yes, dear."

"Does he take it out?"

"Bill, you know he doesn't go out on boats."

"Do I still own the skiff?"

"Not for a long time."

He had been so excited when he bought the Carolina Skiff. Against her wishes, he took it out the first day on Spa Creek with Will, who had just turned 6. The Larkins were not boat people, and she was not bossy by nature but repeatedly told Bill to not go far, go slow, and wear life jackets. We haven't even taught Will to swim yet. And please let me know when you'll be back, Bill. No longer than an hour. Please. He promised all of the above.

The skiff was more unwieldy than he imagined as he chugged up the squiggly creek. A boat is not like a car; chiefly, a boat has no brakes. A boat *appears* simpler and safer. He thought it would be fun for Will to ride in the bow and dangle his feet over the front of the boat as they cruised through calm, cloudy Spa Creek. He hadn't taken any boating safety class or checked a chart book which, along with providing water depths and navigational aids, educated boaters on 14 types of underwater obstructions from wrecks to rocks to pilings and shoals. Too stubborn to wear a life jacket, he used his as a seat cushion. His son wasn't wearing one, either.

Feeling liberated from his clinging law practice, Bill Larkin imagined himself a free man on his skiff. This was no ocean, not even a river, but he had disconnected from land and everything and everyone on it. By God, the man finally had a hobby (he had tried his hand at golf and while not a bad golfer, he was a terrible scorer). Unlike at work, he was the boss on the water, the captain. He didn't need to learn the nautical rules of the road. He had earned the right of way.

"After we get the hang of this little creek, one day we'll head out to the bay," he told his son, who *was* dangling his feet over the bow and smiling, the wind whipping up his blond hair.

"Can we find our own island?" Will said.

"One day."

"Promise?"

"I promise."

The skiff was still hugging the shore when it slammed into a submerged tree stump. The jolt launched the 6-year-old over the bow and face first into the murky water, his face scrapping the shelled bottom. The boat's momentum carried it past where the boy plunged overboard, and his father didn't know how to slow and reverse the skiff. Eventually, he jammed the throttle into reverse and the Merc 25 churned backward toward his submerged boy, ripping him out of the water by his arm. It had all happened in the longest of seconds, and the boy was breathing, yes, but he was hacking out creek water, and his father saw terror in the boy's eyes or the reflection of terror in his own eyes. He took off his shirt to warm Will and held him tightly as the skiff, unaware, harmlessly beached itself on the muddy shore.

Bill Larkin decided they couldn't go home with Will soaked, shaking, his face scratched, his arm bruised. He took the skiff to his friend's house up

Spa Creek. As they rode to Leeds Walker's home, Will sat next to his father on the bench seat. I'm sorry, I'm so sorry, his father said. Don't tell your mother. I'll tell her. But he told his wife two hours later that Will promised never to stand up when the boat was moving but he didn't listen and fell face-down in the skiff – but not before they both had been warmed, fed and sheltered by Leeds Walker. Not before Leeds Walker, a boater, lectured his friend on the danger of bow riding, citing numerous cases of children hurled overboard and killed instantly by boat propellers. They were lucky, said Leeds Walker, who agreed no one else needed to ever know. Nobody was seriously hurt, after all. Your boy probably won't even remember what happened.

• • •

"Lunch is ready," Barb Larkin said, stepping onto the widow's walk. She brought her husband a beer and shrimp salad sandwich and four chubby strawberries. He strained to look out toward the water, the binoculars dangling like hiker bling.

"Why don't you use the binoculars?"

"Where are they are?"

He followed her eyes down to his chest. When he saw the binoculars, she looked away so not to embarrass him.

"Good, you found your binoculars," she said. She had placed his lunch, a cloth napkin, and the pepper on a wooden dinner tray.

"Is it lunchtime?"

"You're having lunch, so it must be."

His wife, more tired these days, took the binoculars from around his neck. She balanced the dinner tray on his lap. Her husband's clothes were again mismatched, but she could live with his loss of color and design sense. Preventing her husband from driving and installing locks on the *outside* of their doors were enough to adjust to this month. Who cared if the man wore gray with black or gray with gray and forgot to wear shoes sometimes?

She was the keeper of his memories and history. One memory: the time she convinced him to drive to Baltimore to see a movie at the Senator

Theatre. It was July, and the Senator's air conditioning was on the fritz. Anyone in the vicinity was invited to come on in and watch *Liberty Heights* for free. The popcorn was free, too. Even Bill admitted it was a wonderful old theater – despite no AC and springy, worn seats.

Another memory: They never owned a dishwasher because they both liked washing and drying the dishes together, and together, they put away the dishes every night. In the process, they had a glass or two of red wine. They talked about their day or didn't talk at all. Their friends never understood why the Larkins didn't pony up and get a dishwasher, but their friends didn't know Barb and Bill had a date every evening to do the dishes together.

She touched her husband's shoulder to nudge him back to the idea of lunch. Bill Larkin took two small bites of his sandwich and bit into the belly of a strawberry.

"Is he coming?"

"Who, dear?"

"Our son."

"I called him. He said he would be here."

But he hadn't said a word to Will about coming over. She knew that. She knew he wasn't using the phone anymore. It was too confusing. They hadn't talked about Will's arrest either, of course. Maybe Bill would never have to know.

Last Wednesday, her husband had rooted around in an upstairs closet and found a box of gifts he got on Father's Day: a Smiley Face necktie; the wrong car polish; a magician's "Rising Card" deck; two sweaters; and four dime store wallets, all stiff as a saddle and fitted with family photos in the plastic sleeves. Typically, the four family members (father, mother, brother, sister – in descending height order) in the black and white photographs were smiling and looked dressed for a funeral. Bill took one of the wallets and kept the 1960s family picture in the sleeve. Surely, he was asking about *their* son and not the grinning boy in the crew cut towering over his sister in the wallet picture.

"He's coming over to watch the game. O's and Yankees."

"That sounds like a wonderful idea, honey."

"Why wouldn't it be?" He took another bite of his shrimp salad and left some on his chin.

She went back to the kitchen to check *The Capital's* sports section. The Orioles and Yankees were playing three games in Baltimore. Thank God.

She walked back up to the widow's walk. Her husband's lunch tray had toppled off his lap. Otto, the family Corgi, pirated the fallen sandwich but left the strawberries untouched. The beer bottle managed not to break.

"Is Will here?"

"He's coming soon," she said, touching his shoulder.

Will arrived at his parents' home ten minutes before the national anthem and the start of another 3-game series with the Yankees. The six-pack of Yuengling was lukewarm, so Barb Larkin put the beer in the freezer. She was raccoon-eyed and too thin, Will thought. They hugged at the door and spoke in code about the arrest. Thank you, Will said. I have a long hard road ahead of me, I know. I don't know where all this anger is coming from. You need to find out, dear. You know I am here and will help you any way I can. But I can't fix your problems, and I can't change your life for you. I know, I know…

"How have *you* been?"

"Your father has become a lot of…work," she said. "Lately he's been obsessing about women's breasts."

"What?"

"You know, Will, *breasts.*"

"I know what breasts are." Will vaguely remembered breasts being fun things, the both of them in fun conjunction.

"So, Dad talks about breasts. In what context?"

"He has Alzheimer's. That's the context." She didn't mean to be testy, but she was testy with everyone these days.

"Somehow he got his hands on a *Playboy*. He never brought *that* into our house. But now it's 'tits' this, 'tits' that. He never used that word before either – at least never around me. Did you buy him that magazine?"

"No, I didn't." (Leeds Walker was the culprit, thought his old friend needed cheering up.)

Will never thought of his father a breast man but why would he? He had trouble enough seeing his father in swim trunks years ago (did all fathers just one day give up trying to get sun on their legs?)

"Hey, I'm in time."

"For what?"

"The game. I'm in time for the game, Dad."

Will had grabbed a six-pack of Yuengling out of the freezer. The windows were open in the family room, allowing a slight breeze in off the bay. O's announcers Gary Thorne and Jim Palmer were calling the game. Bill Larkin put down his *Playboy,* as the national anthem ended. The Orioles bounded out from the dug-out and took the field at Camden Yards.

Bill Larkin picked up the magazine again and unfolded a traditionally popular section. It wasn't the father-son moment Will imagined, although their moments had always been rather low key. Maybe they should have golfed together. Opened a hardware store together. Hunted wild game. Run rum to Cuba. Played chess. Chess would have been a good game for the Larkin men.

"Do you see these tits?"

Will looked at the tits and nodded in loyal confirmation. His father placed the magazine face down on his lap, right on his Corduroys. Will was determined to stay for the entire game even if that meant competing against Miss July, who was planted squarely on his father's crotch. He began to realize his father was *declining* and would need another person around the house to help him until he would have to be moved to one of those *facilities.* But for today, Will focused on the slumping O's and Miss July, who was not experiencing the slightest of slumps.

Chris Davis slapped a double in the third inning. Bill Larkin stunned his son by scoring the game; the man who announced this morning he had never seen a spoon was noting on his scorecard, among 1.4 million other possible notations in baseball scoring, a "Ks" for a swinging strike-out, a slash mark for a single, and the revered 6-4-3: the shortstop (#6) throwing to second (#4) for one out, then on to first (#3) for the double play. His father noted the start of the game (1:35 p.m.), the weather ("hot"), and below, on another microscopic line on his scorecard he scribbled: "Watched game with son."

"Looks like Davis is getting untracked," Will said. He went to maybe two out of 81 games at Camden Yards every year and couldn't explain satisfactorily to himself why he didn't get out to the park more often. It felt like a personal failing.

Will turned the sound down. His father marked something on his scorecard – probably noting when his son turned the sound down.

"How are you doing, Dad?"

"I'm fine. Why are you looking at me like that?"

Davis launched a 3-2 fastball over the centerfield wall to break a scoreless tie. The Orioles were beating the New York Yankees and over the skies of Annapolis, pigs were somersaulting among the clouds.

Will opened a beer for his father.

"I want to know you're OK."

"Of course, I am. What's wrong with you?"

Oh, lots.

They didn't talk for two innings. The O's won 6-1. Will's father turned off the TV. He collected his scorecard and tossed it toward the ottoman. He missed by a foot.

"Did you have fun?"

"What?" Will said, blinking away tears.

"Did you have fun watching the game?"

Bill Larkin reached into his back pocket and brought out a black, stiff wallet.

"Do you want a see a picture of my family?"

• • •

Will got home after 11 and poured himself a heaping glass of pulp-free OJ and revved up his laptop. Killing time, he began hacking through his work emails, most of which were disingenuous, cunning reminders from the front office. One email, subject head: Best Email of School Year," was interesting, however. "Anyone have a metal detector?" the drama teacher wrote, before explaining school-wide how she planted her gardening tools along with her new plants and would like very much not to dig up the whole garden bed again. Will noticed the bulky email chain included Teresa Morrow's name, so he deleted the best email of the school year. From his Netflix queue, he bumped up the third season of *Peaky Blinders*. Then he Googled "Alzheimer's" and crash-landed on a series from the *New York Times*.

"The disease slowly attacks nerve cells in all parts of the cortex, thereby impairing a person's abilities to govern emotions, recognize errors and patterns, coordinate movement, and remember. Ultimately, a person with AD loses all memory and mental functioning. Most drugs used to treat Alzheimer's are aimed at slowing progression. There are no cures to date."

Will printed out the health guide. After midnight, he called Mack.

"What the fuck time is it?"

"I don't know," Will said.

Mack waited him out.

"It's dad," Will said. "He carries a picture in his wallet of someone else's family. He thinks it's *his* family."

"That's Grade A fucked-up."

Mack's delicate communication skills hadn't changed since sixth grade, and Will was grateful.

"What are you doing? And don't say revving your Johnson."

"I revved my Johnson earlier, a splendid solo journey featuring a cameo by Angelina Jolie and a cock ring."

"Yours, I hope."

"I'm very, very ashamed. But since you woke me, I have turned my energies to Turner Classic Movies and an Elvis movie called *Girls! Girls! Girls!* If I'm tracking it, Elvis is a poor fisherman and babe magnet."

"Channel?"

"230."

They watched separately. Elvis turned out, didn't know how to fish and didn't appear entirely comfortable on a tuna boat.

"I got to sleep," Mack said.

They both hung on.

"My dad won't talk about the accident or doesn't remember it."

"It was, what, 25 years ago? What do you expect?"

"I don't know. He can't even remember if he's wearing shoes or not."

"Does this have anything to do with this new girl?" Mack said.

"Maybe. I just need a fresh start, you know?"

"I know, buddy."

Chapter 9

Parker agreed to meet Alex Cavanaugh at a driving range with Dailey. Golfing would be a first for the girl, but the activity couldn't be worse than summer camp. Parker tried three-day camps for Dailey, who lasted a single day at each location. The girl lasted one hour alone at the Riderwood Pool Club before she informed staff members she would not be entering any part of the pool. Beyond the unreasonable swimming demands, one of the camp kids brought a tape measure the first day and snuck around measuring everyone's butts. The snotty culprit was sent home but not before taking aim at Dailey with his tape measure.

After Parker picked her up, they decided that camp was overrated and that two scoops of chocolate mint ice cream on a waffle cone was a more suitable summer activity for a 6-year-old girl not entirely comfortable in the water – despite a stunning appearance by her Dora the Explorer pink swimsuit. With ice cream seeping from her cone, Dailey confessed that one of the camp counselors, a blond-haired guy named Ben, was nice and wasn't pushing the pool on her. Ben even gave her a nickname – Little Champion. Her mother ran with it.

"So, Little Champion, maybe you will give the place another try?"

"Maybe," Dailey said, licking ice cream off her thumb. "Do you think I have a big butt?"

"You hardly have one at all," Parker said. She tried pinching said butt and came up with practically nothing.

A week later, camp was still out, and golfing was in.

"He's late," Dailey said. The girl was *ready*: a sun block-greased nose, pretty sleeveless pink top from Gap Kids, Parker's old Ray-Bans, and funky anti-golf shoes – Converse All-Stars, glow orange. Not yet, her mother said.

The Pines Driving Range outside Annapolis was outfitted with a new shelter and three security cameras, but the range retained its mission and function: give a person a bucket of balls to experience the thrill of skulling golf balls down a wide corridor of green space. Just mind the deer nibbling around the 150-yard sign.

Alex lugged his mothy golf bag from the gravel parking lot to the range's hunter green clubhouse. He punched four numbers into the ball machine and out plopped 34 range balls into a yellow bucket. A diving pad became available under the sign: "Please Check Your Swing Clearance." Parker and Dailey spotted him there. He scooped his daughter up in his arms and held her aloft, lifting and lowering her over his head like she was a human barbell. Dailey kicked her feet as if running in mid-air.

"We're all here!"

"At a driving range," Parker said.

"A little more enthusiasm in front of the youngster, please?"

He finally put Dailey down. She studied the line-up of golfers and began watching a Korean man hit ball after ball. His driver made the same clicking sound each time, and each ball started straight and low before throttling up toward the speckled deer loitering near the 250-yard marker. Alex and Parker even stopped to watch the take-offs and landings as the deer fled and the other golfers in their driving pads became self-conscious and pulled out their lob wedges. Alex told Dailey that when Koreans were done with their clubs, they traditional gave them to beginning golfers. Having spotted several Big Berthas in the gloved hands of nearby Koreans, Alex hoped to get lucky.

"Dailey, I've let you down, I know I have. But ever since you and your Mom moved out, I didn't know what to do. I still don't know what to do," Alex said. "I don't even know why you both left."

"Not now, Alex," Parker said. He noticed she had made an effort to look golf-like. Her ponytail was tucked through the back of a Ravens visor. She wore shorts and smelled of Banana Boat sunblock. Wisely predicting blisters from swinging a golf club for the first time, a Band-Aid was slipping off her ring-less finger.

"Fair enough, Park." (She hated his nickname for her.) "Now, it's time our girl sees what she's been missing," Alex told Dailey, reaching into his golf bag.

A 5-iron had always felt good in his hands, but today Alex hit the first 10 range balls with his 9, another club he once had a crush on. When he pulled out the 5 and hit the first ball, the club electrocuted his hand. The deer never looked up. He put the club down and motioned Dailey over to the driving pad. He put a 9-iron in her hand and realized the club was far too big for her – he hadn't thought that part through. She whacked at a few balls. Some skidded into the grass; others were missed entirely and stayed put on the rubber tee. Alex took another turn, then Dailey. Combined, 11 of the remaining 25 balls achieved flight. When the bucket was spent, they sat with Parker on black wrought-iron furniture well behind the golfers.

He stood up his golf bag by the table and turned it so the handle faced him. The tag said, "Women's Collection," and Alex realized he had been carrying a women's golf bag his adult life. He wondered if Parker would find that funny.

"Are we done?" she said.

"Oh, not so fast. I have another surprise," said Alex, turning his golf bag around. "I bought Dailey a golf lesson."

They walked over to the clubhouse and found a man named Rick. The club pro had a set of children's clubs, and Rick and Dailey walked to the end of the range for their lesson. This left Parker and Alex alone for the first time since she left him.

She snuck a peek down the row of driving pads. He saw club pro Rick, straightening Dailey's left arm before she attempted her first backswing. To be on the safe side, Parker had told Dailey land monsters have never been spotted on the driving ranges of North America. The girl appeared to appreciate the information.

"You said on the phone you wanted to talk. So, what do you want to talk about?"

"I want to talk about us."

"Us as in you and me?"

"Yes, Park, you and me."

They watched Dailey with the club pro. Much instruction was spent on where she lined up her feet and hips in relation to the ball. Getting Dailey to face *away* from the clubhouse when swinging was a watershed moment.

"You mean you, me and *her*, right?"

"Not that again. I apologized a million times, Park. I ended it. It's history."

Five of the 25 range balls achieved lift-off on pad #64 before the club pro and his new pupil walked to the clubhouse to get two Sprites from the vending machine. It was getting dark at the Pines Driving Range. The deer and Koreans were getting ready to leave, too.

"We should get married," Alex said. "I can't be a gym rat for the rest of my life. I need to settle down."

Parker's veggie burger lunch about lurched into her throat.

"We can raise Dailey together for real and have family vacations together and dinners together?" Parker started, "and we even can do laundry together again!"

Alex's pinched expression reminded Parker of a dog's expression when he's about to get his shots. Parker gave Alex his shots.

"And when I find another slut-red thong in our laundry that doesn't belong to, say, me, then Dailey and I can leave again and it will be another wonderful family experience, won't it? So, yes, absolutely Alex, let's get married ASAP!" (She trusted he knew the acronym but could never be sure.)

Club pro Rick and Dailey walked up to where the grown-ups were sitting. The girl was still holding her Sprite with a bendy-straw.

"She's a natural," club pro Rick said, lying.

But Dailey's parents seemed lost in conversation. Without saying good-bye, Parker drove off again with her daughter and with Alex again shuffling beside the car. As she sped away (disrespectfully exceeding the facility's 15 mph speed limit), Parker wondered if Will liked golf. Christ, she hoped not.

Chapter 10

All he said on the phone was it was an outing. He was inviting them *both* on an outing. But moms don't just go on *outings* without knowing where and how to pack especially for a 6-year-old girl, Parker told him. So, Will spilled his plan for a boat trip, sensing the element of surprise would backfire. No need to announce this was his maiden voyage on the water as an adult.

Bought for him by his father, the unused gray Zodiac Yachtline with a Merc 50 was still tendered to *Seas the Day*, Leeds Walker's 37-ft. Sea Ray Sundancer. The Zodiac bobbed in the Annapolis Harbor, clinging to the mother ship's nylon umbilical cord. Leeds Walker pulled the 15-foot inflatable closer to the dock and held it steady for his guests. As a favor, he kept the Zodiac although no Larkin had ever checked on it. Last week, Will called to say he wanted to take the boat out. Knowing full well Will hadn't been on the water since that one time, Leeds Walker tried to talk him out of it. He had no boating experience – no good experience, he meant.

"I want to do this," Will told his father's friend. "I need to do this."

Parker and Dailey weren't sure where and how to step into the Zodiac. The thing didn't look steady. Will helped Dailey first, insisting she sit next to him behind the console. Parker sat in the bow gripping the tubular sides. Keep your feet inside the boat at all times, Will told them both. He fitted them all with personal flotation devices. He didn't tell Parker he hadn't stepped foot on a boat in 26 years.

Will assessed the riddle that was the outboard. Maybe there was a handle to pull like on his lawnmower.

"It has a key like a car. It's on the console if you turn around," Leeds Walker said, his worries compounding. "Before you go *anywhere,* did you file a float plan?"

"A what?"

"A float plan. Let's people know where and what time you are heading out and expected back, names and number of people on board, emergency numbers, boat's registration number. A float plan."

Parker looked at Will. Dailey looked at Lambie, her stuffed animal. It was her first boat outing, too.

"Can't I just tell you my plan?" Will said.

Leeds Walker knew he shouldn't let Bill's kid out of the harbor, but he was a grown man. Weather was good, little to no chop in the bay. What harm would a little spin around the creek do? He knew what harm but chased off the memory.

"Stick close to shore and stay in the creek. Don't let anyone ride on the bow. Ever. Let's see. It's about 2 o'clock now. Let's say you will be back in an hour – one hour tops."

"Aye, aye, captain."

"Don't be a wise-ass. I'm serious."

"Yes, sir."

Will turned the key and the outboard almost breathlessly started up. He gripped the steering wheel, as Leeds Walker shoved the rubber boat away from his cruiser and out toward the open water. The Zodiac coasted with the Merc in friendly neutral. Will jiggled the throttle forward and felt a slight jolt.

"Stay in the creek and no bow riding," were Leeds Walker's last repeated commands.

Baby waves slapped up again the sides of the Zodiac, as Dailey bravely ducked a finger into the water to feel the tiny swells. Let's keep our hands in the boat, Will told her, as he steered clear of the *Stanley Norman,* a retired skipjack. Inflatable boats look like they could spring a leak and sink like a cheap beach raft, but multiple air chambers keep them afloat. Like any boat, they can break down, get swamped or float away if not anchored down, but Zodiacs are sturdy, reliable watercraft.

"Crew, this is your captain speaking. Are you ready for high adventure on the low seas?"

He heard faint acknowledgments from his two passengers.

"Louder, please! Also, I'm going to have to insist on being called Captain."

"Oh captain our captain, where are we going?" Parker said over the din of the outboard.

"Just you wait."

Dailey squirmed on her bench seat and whispered into her mother's ear. Will noticed even Lambie's nose was coated in sunblock.

"Speak up, Miss Dailey!" Will said.

"She wants to know if you are taking us golfing," Parker said.

Golfing from a boat?

"My dad took us golfing," Dailey said, her voice barely carrying.

"No golfing today," Will said. For damn sure.

Leaving Spa Creek, the Zodiac cleared the moored sailboats and live-aboards in the harbor and past the buoys with NO WAKE signs. The boat veered northerly toward the looming spans of the Chesapeake Bay Bridge. A warm splash of wind kicked up. Will had studied the bay chart and at least by chart, generally knew the way. They passed under a minor span of the bridge, clear of the deep water channels for the big cruisers and cargo ships. They passed real boats with names and with cabins and flags flying and Labradors' ears flapping from bow perches. He didn't let Dailey near the bow. Will pushed down the memory of going overboard, face down in the jagged mush of Spa Creek, hearing the muffled sound of the outboard overhead, feeling his left arm then right arm yanked so hard he thought his body was tearing apart. His mother never knowing both the secret and lie.

Will lifted the portable gas tank. Still about full. As he put the tank down, wake from a cabin cruiser passing too close broadsided them. Pearl gray water rolled over the boat's cones and pooled at their feet. Then another wave smacked the boat sending more of the bay into it. Quickly, he opened the storage locker in the stern. Inside, sunblock, gallon of drinking water, a six-pack of Yuengling, dock lines, First Aid kit, the spiral Chesapeake Bay chart book, and a Clorox plastic bottle sheared off at the bottom with the cap still on. He was prepared.

Will bailed until it was safe enough to give Dailey a turn at the Clorox bottle.

"We're OK. Just a little water from that big boat. I got it all except a little smidge of water. Can you take this bottle and scoop it up and throw it overboard for me?"

Dailey studied the inch of water at her feet.

"A little smidge," she parroted, scooping out the water and flinging it overboard. Flinging anything is fun.

"Stellar job. You're a real captain's mate."

Fearing a swamping, Will punched the throttle forward and zipped further away from the channel. The Zodiac was hugging the shore now; if they had to, they could step out, walk to the shore and right onto someone's private dock or back yard. The boat drew about as much water as a ski.

Skirting North Point State Park, baitfish snapped the water around them. A blue heron caught Parker's eye at the water's edge – a thrilling, stilted creature, all four feet of it, and all in gray, white, brown and chestnut. She wanted to reach out and stroke its long neck, touch its crest, name it. Bert. Pete. Dexter. No, Pete Dexter is a writer. Bert. Yes, Bert the blue heron.

"I like the cut of your jib, Bert the blue heron," Parker called out as they passed the wading bird. Will smiled as he kept north, northeast toward Horseshoe Island.

An hour later – their return time – they were still a half hour away. Parker said she was getting hungry. Dailey needed to pee.

"How much longer?"

"Not much," Will said, as fatigue swatted at him.

• • •

"How long have they been out?" Mrs. Walker asked her husband.

"Too damn long. I told him not to leave the creek."

Adele Walker considered her husband of 51 years. So this is what he has been missing. Someone to worry about. A project.

"I need to tell Tom. We can use his Whaler." Tom Henley owned the marina where Leeds Walker kept *Seas the Day*. Henley had a 17-foot Boston Whaler he kept for running about and the rare emergency.

"Where do you think *you're* going? To rescue them?"

Leeds Walker cocked his head and looked at his wife

"That's exactly what I'm going to do."

"At least take Bill with you."

Like his son, Bill Larkin hadn't been on the water in 24 years.

• • •

Will lifted the gas tank. Half full. In theory, he could turn around and make it back to the marina. He secreted the option. Past the Magothy and Severn rivers and now in the Patapsco, Will finally saw a gangly strip of island. So-called picnic boats, cocktail cruisers, and other day boats were anchored offshore; people high-stepping in the shallow water, passing drinks to one another, stopping to retrieve cheap sunglasses that had slipped off into the tea-colored water. Looked like a floating party this Horseshoe Island. Ten minutes later, Will needled the Zodiac through aisles of open bow boats and beached his boat. The crossing hardly rivaled the smoothest day of fishing on *Deadliest Catch,* but the journey felt epic.

Parker hoisted Dailey out onto the sand before she and Will disembarked. Seaweed and discarded water bottles netted the shore, the shelled sand felt rough on Dailey's toes. Will pulled the Zodiac up onto the beach. The tide was out.

Parker kept her sweatshirt on, as clouds shut out the sun. She grabbed the water jug, sat on a piece of bleached driftwood, and first gave her daughter a long sip then took her turn. Will cracked open a cold beer. Parker had one, too. Horseshoe Island had all the charm of a de-commissioned landfill. She loved it.

"I need to pee, Mom," Dailey said.

It's not any girl's first choice to pee outdoors on a public beach, but the Zodiac was not equipped to handle basic needs. As Will stayed back, Parker discovered a deserted coast guard station behind a line of scrub pines. The restroom facilities were sealed, so she foraged for privacy, eventually finding relief for Dailey. They back-tracked to the beach and her driftwood headrest. For the next two hours, she watched and joined the beachcombers. The bottom of the shallow bay was silty and felt like mayonnaise on the toes. He downed a second Yuengling. *When did they golf together? Was it Parker's idea?*

They had their picnic lunch (chicken salad from Graul's, Utz barbecue chips, bottled water for Parker and Dailey, four apples, one pack of Raisinets) atop four co-joined beach towels. Will applied more sunblock to Dailey's pinkish nose – Lambie's, too. It wasn't quite warm enough to be hot.

"Are you having fun?" Will said in the direction of them both.

"We are," Parker said.

"Are *you?*" he said just to her.

"I am."

The trip had made him more anxious and nervous than he realized; driving a boat this far and for the first time had throttled his nerves. Spa Creek would have been a smarter starter trip. With dulled senses, Will closed his eyes and imagined floating on a beach raft the size of a King mattress before he fell into a thick nap born of wave riding and worry. Beside him, Parker and Dailey were curled together on the beach towels, both asleep too. Parker, a snore-denier, slightly snoring. Dailey moved about as much as Lambie when asleep.

Two hours later – more? – Parker woke first, rose and stretched.

"Hi."

"Oh, hi. I thought you were still asleep."

"I'm a light island sleeper," Will said, lifting his head off the driftwood, his neck stiff from the makeshift pillow.

She plopped down in the rough sand next to him. They had the place to themselves minus the dozen off-shore party boats, countless midges, and one sleeping 6-year-old.

"Can I ask you something?"

"Anything," Parker said.

"Do you know anything about heartworm? Of course, you do. What I mean is do you know how long a dog will live without heartworm pills? I think I killed Dean. Terri thinks I did."

Parker imagined a more recreational line of questioning, and she had not lied: she would have answered any question from Will Larkin this afternoon on Horseshoe Island. Heartworm in dogs, while serious, wasn't exactly island pillow talk.

"Do you remember how many months you missed?"

"I don't know. Maybe four, maybe more."

"I don't know what to tell you, Will. Dean was very sick, and we saved him from suffering. *You* saved him from suffering."

A bitter consolation, but one for which he thanked Parker for offering. We probably should start thinking about getting back, he told her. She nodded before nudging Dailey awake. Will looked up and toward his beached Zodiac.

It was gone.

• • •

The search party numbered three: Bill Larkin, Leeds Walker, Tom Henley. They met by the slip housing *Seas the Day*. It was almost 5 p.m. — some three hours after Will Larkin departed Annapolis Harbor.

"Did he file a float plan with you?" Tom Henley asked Leeds Walker.

"No."

They looked at Bill Larkin.

"I talked to him about it when he left, Bill, but I let him talk me out of it. I'm sorry."

Silence between old friends is a loud passage.

"I told him to stay close by, suggested they might go up Spa Creek. He told me he would. He told me he'd be back after two hours, tops."

"Who would be back?" Bill Larkin said.

"Will."

"What does he have to do with this?"

"Bill," the marina owner said, "we're looking for Will, your son. Do you have an idea where he went?"

"How would I know?" he said, puzzled before a memory *surfaced*. "Maybe he went…to an island."

"What island?"

"Our island."

The answer came simultaneously to Leeds Walker and Tom Henley.

"We better go," the marina owner said. "It's a haul to Horseshoe."

Marcus Greene was Leeds Walker's neighbor over in slip 32 where his Sea Ray, *Salary Cap*, lived year-round. Greene was a former defensive end for the Baltimore Ravens. One season he led the Ravens in sacks but two years later, he shredded his ACL against the Tennessee Titans. Since moving to the marina two years ago, he had become a hyper-local celebrity. The men – retired accountants, CEO's, former U.S. under-secretaries – interrogated him about the Ravens' chances each year. He didn't mind talking football, but he never discussed his injury. It wasn't like when the Giants' Lawrence Taylor snapped Joe Theismann in two on national television. Greene went down, rather quietly, and never got back up into the NFL. Hardly anyone seemed to notice.

As for his boating life, Marcus Greene favored Horseshoe Island. He was a single man, and the playful environs enriched his social life. And being it was Saturday, he was due up north to Horseshoe, a crunchy Cheeto of an island. He liked to arrive later in the day, catch a sunset, read, enjoy a chilled adult beverage with a new companion. Around 5 p.m., he anchored *Salary Cap* some 50 feet offshore. The tide was in, but it was still shallow enough for Saturday's island crowd to walk boat-to-boat, sharing adult beverages, rump-shaking to onboard tunes. Because not many 6'3, 255-pound former Baltimore Ravens frequented these waters, Marcus Greene's arrival never went undetected.

He was engrossed in *The Dharma Bums* when he heard yelling through the thumping music bouncing from the nearby boats. Marcus Greene spotted the source, a dude onshore surrounded by a kid stuck like a barnacle to a woman. He stepped out of his boat and forded the shallows to shore.

"Everyone good?"

"We're fine," Will told the stranger.

"We're not *fine*," Parker said.

Sucking up his pride, Will told the man about losing the boat, about not checking the tide chart, about forgetting to bring his cell (Parker hadn't thought to bring hers, either.) At high tide, the unanchored boat had simply floated away as they slept. Mortified by his blunder, he tried to calmly assure his passengers they were safe. A flotilla of boats surrounded the island and surely one of them could tow them back. Mainly, he was worried about Dailey. The last thing he wanted to ever do was scare her. He dug out of the cooler a third ice cream sandwich for her; he had no idea what snacks 6-year-old girls liked so went old-school and stocked up on Klondike ice cream sandwiches for the trip.

"I don't believe this. You lost the boat," Parker said, as Marcus Greene stood neutral on the beach. "You stranded us, Will. At least –" she started then stopped.

"No, say it."

"At least you can't get stranded on a driving range."

It's impossible for a popular beach and boating area on a crowded week-end to become silent, but witnesses – namely Marcus Greene – could verify the impossible happened. Will looked at the former NFL player patiently waiting to help.

"We could use a lift back to Annapolis Harbor if you're going that way."

"I am," Marcus Greene said, as a blue crab nipped at his right ankle. "What kind of boat do you have?"

"A Zodiac."

"Probably just drifted down the Patapsco. No harm done. I've seen far dumber things happen out here, *far* dumber things. Get your stuff and climb aboard. I'll get you all home. Maybe even run into that boat of yours along the way."

After hoisting her backpack aboard, Parker lifted Dailey into the man's boat before joining her daughter in the cushioned bow seats. She asked Marcus if he had ever rescued anyone, and he said this was hardly a rescue but no, he had never rescued anyone. She thanked him.

"This is the peak of my day," Parker said.

"Naw," Marcus said, "We peak twice in life – at our first breath and our last. Everything in between is hard candy."

Forty feet from shore, Tom Henley cut the Yamaha outboard. His Whaler coasted toward *Salary Cap*. Leeds Walks and Marcus Greene exchanged hellos. Bill Larkin about jumped over board to reach Will. There was a woman and a girl he'd never seen before. What was the girl holding? A dead rabbit? Out of habit, Will shook his father's hand.

"What the hell were you doing out here? You don't know anything about boats. Someone could have got hurt."

"I could have said the same thing to you."

"What?"

"You heard me. What were you doing taking me out on a boat? You didn't know anything about boats, either. And someone *did* get hurt."

Leeds Walker moved to the center of the conversation.

"We need to get this young lady and her daughter home. I think we all need to go home."

Will rode back with his father in Tom Henley's Whaler, looking behind every so often at the fading island and Marcus Greene's *Salary Cap* trailing from a paternal distance with Parker and Dailey onboard. Will wondered when or if he'd see them again.

The ride back was imaginably three times longer, choppier and colder. There was no sign of the Zodiac.

Chapter 11

Last month, a discovery.

At a thrift store in Glen Burnie, Parker's brother found a Spandex wrestling unitard. The red suit, with its faded gray striping, clung to a headless mannequin stationed in the storefront window. Steve Cool paid $25 for it. No telling if the suit had ever been washed; it smelled like an all-you-can-eat sausage restaurant. The fabric might spontaneously combust. At home, he dared to wash it twice in cold water. After hand-drying the garment – the drier would have shredded it for sure – Steve stretched it back over the mannequin that cost him another $10. Steve plotted a strategy for his first performance art project, but first, he needed a volunteer. His sister wasn't doing anything except moping around. Parker hadn't heard from Alex, which was more than fine with her but at the very least he should contact his own daughter.

"Do it for me?" Steve said.

"I'm not putting on that stinky suit and don't you dare enlist Dailey into your hipster schemes."

"First of all, it's a wrestling unitard, and it's not stinky. I washed it twice. And I've told you a hundred times, I'm not a hipster."

"Do you drink Pabst Blue Ribbon and wear skinny black jeans even in the summer and quote from 'Howl'?"

"Maybe."

"Case closed. I win. Again," said his younger sister. "Now tell me, do you know how many crotches have been in that suit?"

"Art isn't easy."

"And what again is your *vision?* By putting on this foul thing people will be transformed into superheroes of their own customized creations?"

"I don't know what people will feel or do – which is the point. Since you have always responded to bribes, I will teach you a few cowboy chords on the guitar if you try the suit on."

Parker, having abandoned her dream of becoming a drummer, could succumb to latent guitar desires.

"Teach me a whole song."

"Agreed."

"Bring on the stink."

In Steve's guest bedroom, Parker stared at the shriveled clothing. The suit looked like something her grandfather wore to the beach in the 1940s recalled on old newsreels. Parker shyly slipped out of her clothes. She slid feet first into the chilly garment. One size must fit all because it fit – mashed her chest, though. Parker looked in the full-length on the back of the bedroom door. The suit miraculously erased the glitches Parker always pinpointed in her figure. Inhibitions fell away. She imagined the wrestling dudes before her who wore this. They must have felt empowered, too. At the mirror, Parker struck a pose like one of those bald, circus strongmen lifting round barbells over their heads. She wished she had a barbell prop or a globe to hoist. She felt strong enough to carry the world in one hand. She might wear the red suit to bed, have breakfast in it, run errands, assume command of the *USS Enterprise.*

"How's it going in there?" Steve asked from outside the door.

"Call me Super Hipster Chick or more accurately, you may address me as Scarlett Johansson."

She wiggled out of the suit. Her figure returned to mortal dimensions, the un-tucking of that she wished tucked. Parker put back on her jeans and Virgin Fest T-shirt. Her superpowers lay in a balled heap of Spandex at her feet. Her brother had indeed made a curious finding. And now to formally introduce the suit, he needed a launch party. The Red Suit Bash could become an annual event to replace his fish picture parties. After six years, friends had run out of fish pictures anyway. Plus, Steve began to suspect certain photographs had been Photoshopped.

The party would be three weeks from Saturday, and Steve hoped someone would be brave enough to don the naughty garment and if comfortable enough in their new skin, have their picture taken for his under-construction Red Suit website. Perhaps fellow disciples could check the red suit out for a week. Take it home with them. Care for it. Steve would promise to wash the suit after each use.

"Are you going to invite math dude?"

"No. We tried, but it's not working. Something keeps tripping us up. You know, drugged movie watching, getting stranded at sea, the usual dating hiccups."

"Not much of a stranding, sis." "What do – or did – you see in him?" Parker hunkered down.

"He's like this old child who hasn't grown up. He's quirky but doesn't know it. Cute, for sure. Tall. He definitely needs more fun in his life. But he was married, and I'm not sure he's over her. And he's trying to prove something. I don't know what he's trying to prove. I don't think he knows. Did I mention I saw one of those old man sailing hats at his house? What are they called? Tilley? That's it. He has a Tilley! And he has this weird obsession with Triscuits."

"Wow. He seems dreamy."

"Plus, he stranded us. Did I mention that?"

"Only six times since your *rescue.*"

Steve Cool was accustomed to his sister's habit of projecting doom and anxiety and blamed her self-defenses on the death of Brownie. No one in their family had died – they were lucky on that morbid front.

"And," she continued, "he has a jittery soul."

Steve smiled, having fallen again into one of his sister's psyche traps.

"OK, what's a jittery soul?"

"Glad you asked, unenlightened one. A jittery soul is a soul out of balance that has not come home to rest."

"I thought a jittery soul was a soul whose bones you want to jump."

Feigning disgust, Parker stood, pivoted and walked outside in what she hoped was a spectacular exit. Steve Cool, armed with intel, called the math man and left a message:

Hey, this is Steve Cool, Parker's remarkable brother. You are cordially invited to a very special party at my house three weeks from Saturday. 9 p.m. till the cops shut us down. No boating required. In the meantime, ask yourself: When was the last time you really had fun?

Will listened to the message four times and still didn't have an answer.

• • •

Fifty Chinese lanterns were staple-gunned throughout the Florida Room of Steve's home in Annapolis. The multicolored string of lights cast a breezy, tropically-muted atmosphere. In the corner, a rented karaoke machine hogged a wobbly card table. The $59-a-day package included an auto-changer player, two microphones, 450-watt sound system, monitor stand, and a selection of 2,000 songs. Game provisions included Twister, Cards Against Humanity and Taboo. But the centerpiece of the room stood center stage on a barstool draped in a black bed sheet. The headless, thrift store mannequin was host to the suit, freshly laundered and lit by a white flood light usually positioned outside to light Steve's king-sized Christmas wreath.

Steve felt a stitch of longing for the fish pictures, but creative change was good and necessary. Guests would arrive soon – Will among them, he informed Parker.

"You had no right to do that. No right."

"I think you should give you two another chance," Steve said.

"That's not your decision. Stop being my older brother and just be my brother, OK?"

"I'm sorry. You're right. I had no right to invite him. Can we just forget about it for tonight? You need fun. I need fun. He needs fun. All God's children need fun. And the Red Suit Bash is going to be nothing short of *life changing*. It will be my crowning moment."

Sensing an unspoken truce, Steve didn't mention that in a round-robin of group emails, he accidentally messaged Alex Cavanaugh, who was also coming. Steve didn't have the nerve to tell his sister her ex-boyfriend was coming; he didn't have to nerve to tell Alex not to come. He was frightened of them both. Her, mainly.

Steve mixed large quantities of mojitos from the kitchen. He had bought a pestle to crush the crucial mint. For his art project to succeed, mojitos would be required. If those ran out, Steve was ready with the tequila for margaritas. He couldn't imagine a sober person voluntarily wearing a used wrestling unitard much less posing on his prospective website.

Parker muscled past Will's unsolicited invite and began to worry her vet office friends weren't cool enough for her brother's crowd.

"Pour me a mojito, prontito," she told Steve.

Soon she was under the ether of mint. In honor of the Red Suit Bash, Parker wore a raspberry halter, jeans, and flip-flops. Her brother noted a rare cameo of Victory Red lipstick on his sister, as she set out the chips and pretzels. She eyed the karaoke machine, as the first guests arrived. "We Are Family," was among the songs available for lip-synching. Good to know.

Steve invited 47 friends, including someone he hoped might be a potential boyfriend. They mostly congregated in the Florida Room, while others snooped around until the hallway, kitchen, and yard. Alex Cavanaugh, looking more roided-up than usual, skulked alone in the back of the family room, undetected by Parker. Will Larkin, who had slithered into the house also undetected, wished he had gotten a haircut; his hair looked like some wooly bad guy from the old Johnny Quest cartoon. The gift wrapping on Elizabeth Bishop's collected poems was coming undone at the book ends. He pressed his thumb on the tape to seal it back.

Tonight would be another chance for them, a chance for him to erase the missteps in his courtship of Parker Cool. Will stood hair-wooly and stork-like in the kitchen, waiting his turn for a mojito. He hadn't drunk mojitos since the gazebo encounter. To medicate his nerves, he drank two glasses of Zinfandel to push himself out the door. Party Anxiety was a particularly searing affliction in his catalog of nervousness; parties and trying to impress a girl who probably wanted nothing to do with him anymore.

"You must be Will," Steve said, filling a shot glass of rum.

"How'd you know?"

"My sister warned me you'd be tall, cute and with a hint of clumsy disorientation."

Cute? Clumsy what? He privately auditioned responses when Steve handed him a robust specimen of mojito.

"Now fly away, Will Larkin. Go forth into the party and have fun. I double dare you."

Steve couldn't make the mojitos fast enough, so the bar operation became self-serve; some of his guests brought their own instruments of enjoyment. The host managed to eke out one more drink for himself before gathering everyone for an important announcement.

"Welcome to the first annual Red Suit Bash. I see a few of you still brought fish pictures out of kind habit. Feel free to put them up but please not in the Florida Room, which as you can see, is occupied."

Parker's mojito was down to its ice-crushed bottom. She thought she saw the mannequin wink at her. Her eyes found Will from across the room. Dailey was in tow, all six years, 42 inches and 41 pounds of her. Her hair was brown and short cropped; her eyes were saucer-round and deep-end-of-the-pool blue. For her uncle's party, she wore a purple Ravens jersey numbered "00" with "Dailey" stitched on the back. Her mother promised her she could stay up 30 minutes past her bedtime tonight.

"Allow me to introduce the real lady of the house, with all due respect to my aging sister and my perfect niece" – Steve pointed to the mannequin – "this red suit is more than what it appears. When worn by truth seekers, the suit will unleash your inner, powerful self." Steve wondered if he had overdone the pitch – and the rum.

"Soon, I will stop talking" (several cheered without malice) "and the musical portion of the evening will commence. But it is my dream that one of you will challenge your inhibitions and routine and honor me by wearing the red suit here tonight. My sister can attest to its powers of transformation!"

Heads swiveled toward Parker, who shook her head and made the universal hand signal for I'm-going-to-get-another-drink. In the kitchen, she cursed her brother for invoking her name in the name of the red suit and, principally, for running out of rum. She broke a personal rule and found the tequila and a Natty Boh shot glass. But she held off on the hardcore booze until later when Dailey would be asleep.

In the Florida Room, the karaoke machine was activated. Eight women glided and hip-shaked to an extended mix of "Get Lucky." Parker and Dailey kicked off their matching flip-flops bought last summer on their mini-vacation at Ocean City.

"Hi, Parker."

"Well, well. If it's not Will Larkin."

She wished she could pull off sounding bad-ass, but in sneaky truth, she was not unhappy to see him. He was still a little tan from Horseshoe Island. So was she. Dammit.

"This is amazing."

"What's amazing?"

"This place. These lanterns. You," he said. "I'm sorry about the whole boat stranding."

"Not much of a stranding," Parker said.

He leaned down and kissed her cheek with a spontaneous intimacy that stunned them both.

"Do you want to dance?" Will said, before seeing Dailey in her Ravens jersey watching him very closely. He smiled at his former first mate and water bailer. "Do you *both* want to dance?"

The karaoke machine's auto-changer flipped to "YMCA," a crowd favorite. But at Orioles games and wedding receptions, Parker could never master the song's choreography. Forming the four letters with her arms and body was beyond her coordination. She thought she might have a learning disability.

"I, we, absolutely want to dance," Parker said. "First, let me slip into something a little more uncomfortable."

Under the Chinese lanterns, they danced around the mannequin. Will never danced so much and so freely. He felt like he had known Parker and Dailey all his life – a sensation so acute and unguarded he trusted it. He guided Parker through the choreography of "YMCA" until she got the hang of it. She looked ridiculously sexy in the tight red suit. He thought he could see the pressed outline of her nipples. He drained his mojito and remembered he was holding another full one in his other hand. One song later, Parker assumed command of the Shure microphone as the lyrics scrolled to Sister Sledge's "We Are Family." She pulled Will and Dailey into her frisky dance circle and at times appeared in a trance; other times, like a cruise director on meth. Her standing order to play "We Are Family" three consecutive times was not countermanded. Will, danced out, peeled off and watched from the living room. Dailey joined him.

The night was moonless, so the only light inside came from the multi-colored paper lanterns and the white floodlight casting a long shadow on the squared shoulders of the suited mannequin. At the conclusion of his sister's performance, Steve wrested the microphone from her, sending Parker to the bedroom to shed her costume and then return it to the mannequin.

"May I have everyone's attention?" the host said.

"Not again!" someone shouted.

"My final interruption, I promise," he said. "I think it's safe to say we have all witnessed the birth of a new diva. Now, who will be the next brave pioneer?"

No one moved. Steve walked over to the mannequin and put his arm around the plastic torso. If it wasn't genuine sadness, then it was a fair piece of acting.

"Can no one else shed their skin and inhibitions? What happened to chivalry? Courage?"

He winked at his sister, who began to think it was Steve's plan all along to goad Will into wearing the red suit. Instead, emerging from the kitchen, Alex Cavanagh strode to the center of the Florida Room.

"Bring it on!"

A state champion wrestler in high school, Alex was familiar with wrestling unitards.

"Anything to impress my girls!"

Parker hadn't seen him until this moment, had no idea Alex possibly could have known her brother was having a party. Surely, Steve hadn't invited him, too. How could he? Alex bounded up to her, kissed her on the mouth, and collected his daughter in his arms, as Will watched like a pedestrian from across the road. Before Parker could say a word, applause rang out as Alex went to the bedroom and slipped feet first into the chilly Spandex still warm from her. He studied himself in the mirror, another familiar ritual. He looked even more buff, as he strutted out to more applause. Someone had pre-programmed "Brick House," and Steve jacked up the volume.

"A toast! A toast to women! They fall in love with you and the second you don't want to get married, they leave you!"

"That's not why I left you, Alex. *You* know why I left," Parker said, before ushering Dailey upstairs and to her bedroom.

"Where did my dance partner go?" Alex said, his words spilling out like Bananagrams, the tequila shots stockpiled in his brain.

Will stepped into the light.

"She's not your dance partner."

"Who the fuck are you?"

"I'm Parker's friend. Who the fuck are you?"

"I'm Parker's boyfriend and Dailey's father. That's the fuck who I am."

A good five inches taller than Alex, Will knew he was giving up a lot of weight and strength as he stood face-to-face with the wrestler at the Red Suit Bash.

"You need to leave," Will said.

"Are you fucking her?"

"Not had the pleasure and everything else is also none of your business."

Parker came down the stairs and saw Alex, shrink-wrapped in that awful suit, dressed like some twisted Underdog in a mankini. She felt slightly ashamed she had dressed up and paraded around everyone, especially her daughter. Her buzz had evaporated, but Alex was beyond drunk. He had been that way twice when they were together and twice she was afraid.

"Stop, Alex."

"Stop what? I'm just having a little fun."

"You're drunk, and you're scaring me."

"Show's over," Steve said, turning off the karaoke machine.

Alex took Parker's arm, high on the elbow, pulling her into the middle of the Florida Room, pulling her close to him, Parker brushing up against the red suit, feeling its cheap, soiled texture. Alex breathing alcohol on Parker's neck, her pulling away, tugging at the red fabric, ripping, freeing herself but not before locking into Alex's eyes and seeing tears and a wild hurt unkenneled.

Will squared up and flicked a left jab at Alex's face. It was like slapping a bear with a flyswatter. Alex, more quizzical than angry, looked at Will almost with sympathy. Will, his guts buzzing, jabbed him again, twice, three times; his left jab crisper. Blood appeared from a cut on Alex's upper lip.

"You're dead, fucker."

Will popped him two more times with the left, then re-setting his balance, hooked him to the belly, and the YouTube boxing videos were right: Alex dropped his hands. Will drove a straight right that rocked him back and folded him out on the floor.

"Don't get up," he told him calmly.

"Fuck you."

As Parker watched, Alex Cavanaugh wobbled up to nearly a standing position. It didn't take much work this time. Will tapped his jaw with a left jab, and Alex collapsed, awkwardly balling up on the ground.

"Stop! Will, stop! You're hurting him," Parker cried.

Will recoiled.

"But he was hurting you."

"I can take care of him, and I can take care of myself. I don't need some knight in shining armor or whatever it is you think you're doing."

Will looked at the fallen man and looked at Parker. He meant to defend her, but now she looked afraid of *him*. Unprotected by boxing gloves, his left hand was throbbing and swollen. His thumb, which he forgot to tuck, vibrated painfully, the ligament possibly torn. The pain sliced through his hand and up his arm. He looked at his fists and saw Alex's blood on his hands.

The doorbell rang like a prizefight bell. Steve opened the door to see an Anne Arundel County Sheriff's deputy possibly born with a congenital neck condition (a party-goer had called the police before slipping out along with most of the guests). He asked to come inside, where he observed a muscular Caucasian man, early 30s, prostrate on the ground wearing some sort of red costume. Fresh blood stains appeared evident on the wall, and the man's lip and chin were lacerated. Deputy Billy Snyder bent to speak.

"Sir, are you able to tell me what happened?"

Alex looked up into the squared landscape of the deputy's face. "He sucker punched me," he said, his speech muddled from two broken teeth. Alex looked down at the bunched red suit sagging around his stomach. He couldn't remember putting it on. He tried to pry himself off the floor but fell back down. His jaw hurt and his shoulder and somehow his teeth.

"Better stay where you are," Deputy Snyder said.

Alex Cavanaugh was able, despite his injuries, to give a reputable account of the fight. How do you know this man? *I have never seen this fucker before in my life.* And he just punched you repeatedly for no reason? *He told me to leave, and I wouldn't leave.* So he punched you for that? *Listen, I don't know why the crazy bastard attacked me. But I need stitches and some serious pain-killers.* Do you need an ambulance? *No, I'll get up and drive myself.* Do you want to press charges? *You're goddamn right I do.*

Then to Will, the deputy asked what happened. *He was grabbing her. I thought he was hurting her.* So, you punched him repeatedly. *Yes, sir.* Did he punch you? *No.* Were you drinking? *Yes.* There were other questions and answers until Deputy Snyder appeared satisfied. They still needed to move Alex from the floor, but he appeared incapable of motion.

"Can he stay here tonight?" the officer asked Steve.

"No, sir."

"Can someone take him home?"

"I will," Parker said.

Will felt sick to his stomach.

"All right then. Now, Mr. Larkin, you're coming with me."

Deputy Snyder led Will outside and told him to sit in the back of his patrol car, which was too warm and smelled of Glade Air Freshener and bleach. Sober but arm-weary, Will stretched out on the hard-plastic back seat and worried whether Deputy Snyder would discover on his dashboard computer that he was still on probation, although he had completed his service hours months ago (he missed the charitable work and even checked online and saw the Shepherd's Table needed a "Casserole Group Coordinator" and a "Dining Room Exit Navigator"). From the back of a patrol car, Will allowed himself thoughts of a second career in the unheralded field of dining room exit navigation.

"I'm charging you with second-degree assault, which is a misdemeanor in the state of Maryland," the officer said from the other side of the car's steel mesh cage. There was a flurry of information, instructions, and rights given.

Remembering "Cops" episodes he watched with Mack, Will turned on his back and kicked at the car window like a sprayed cockroach. There was no end game, no plan to free himself by knocking out the back window and fleeing to freedom. He didn't care. The demoted teacher, dog killer, and divorcee kicked a second time.

"If you don't settle down, I will charge you with resisting arrest, too. Be smart, Mr. Larkin. You are under arrest for assault. You're still on probation for destroying property. Don't make things even worse for yourself."

Will broke down, a small consolation knowing he wasn't the first or last person to cry in the back of a patrol car.

• • •

By some trick of the planet, the night passed in his cinder-blocked cell in the Jennifer Road Detention Center. The metal bed was less forgiving than the patrol car's back seat, and Will's breathing echoed loudly through the jagged hours. He didn't use the steel naked toilet or look out the cell's window, a slender passageway of muted darkness and light. The cell smelled

110

of Lysol and absence. Will had rarely if ever been grounded at home, never suspended in school, never popped for a DUI (and surely could have been), never had any real trouble until this past year and this night spent jailed, the ultimate unexcused absence. His only avenue for levity was that his mug shot was arguably better than Nick Nolte's due primarily to the fact Will tended to keep his hair short.

In the morning, his mother posted his $10,000 bail. Quietly, they waited four hours for the paperwork to clear before getting into her Acura for the ride home.

"Do we need to tell Dad?" Will said.

"I don't think he would understand," Barb Larkin said. "I don't think I understand."

A day after his release, he called the school system's Office of Investigations. A second and final self-reporting was necessary; it was only a matter of days before he would lose his teaching job. He had sealed and self-reported his fate. There may or may not be a conviction, but two arrests certainly would warrant his termination, as they called it in the front office. At 30, the profession he chose out of college, his *chosen* profession, would end by his own hands.

In the days that followed, Will worried about rent, food, work, his parents, money in general; his savings were about shot due to vet bills, a treadmill he didn't use, and four new tires his Honda needed. He replayed the events of the Red Suit Bash and police raid – as much as he could remember. His thumb was still swollen. The thought of drinking made him sick and more ashamed, so he stuck to water and Coke Zero. Mack called him three times. Kyle, six. He didn't want to talk to them. Parker called once and left an expected message: *I'm sorry but I can't see you anymore.*

Will was notified by phone (and then by certified mail) that given the assault charge, the School Superintendent had terminated, with cause, his employment with the Anne Arundel County School System. He was no longer a teacher, floater or otherwise. The letter was signed by Lakeview High assistant principal Thomas Hull, and a long-term substitute freshman algebra teacher had been named. Will was also notified by certified mail his court date had been set for Oct. 5. If convicted, he faced a possible sentence of 10 years in prison and up to $2,500 in fines. He knew enough listening to his father re-hash cases that people convicted of misdemeanors don't do that kind of time; the knowledge was an imperceptible consolation. He knew if he asked his father's friend for help, Leeds Walker would drop everything and find him a lawyer and maybe pay the billable hours himself. But Will was too embarrassed to ask. He knew he had the right to a public defender if he couldn't afford his own lawyer.

Will wished he could feel sick or at least sad. Anything but hopeless.

Chapter 12

Downtown Annapolis inch-wormed with visitors attempting parallel parking jobs along Main Street or any of the slivered side streets, hoping not to get mauled by an SUV or creepy-quiet Prius. The downtown was a portrait in preservation where the political motto appeared to be: "No change is the right change." The threat of carpet-bagging chain restaurants with their *plastic* utensils moving in along Dock Street was met with civic enthusiasm usually reserved for a proposed maximum security prison. Established places of businesses remain established. Here, high water marks were preserved in slim plaques to commemorate Hurricane Isabel's flooding in 2003. Flooding, to a lesser degree, still greeted the street during almost any measure of rain.

At Ego Alley, six groomsmen in their cream-colored suits and flip-flops stood on the seawall, 5-irons in their hands, and pretended to hit golf balls into Annapolis Harbor as a bandana-fitted wedding photographer backed into traffic to get the picture. The tea-colored water teemed with open-bowed pleasure boats, tacking sailboats, and their horny, suspicious relatives from the wrong side of the tracks – speedboats. Dogs crawled all over the place. Some had doggie life jackets, manageable limps, and trigger-happy bladders.

Will watched it all from his bench overlooking the dock – anywhere to keep from bouncing off the walls of his home. For all his complaining and floating, he would miss teaching. Teaching gave him a place to go, something useful to do, a paycheck and what he thought was job security. For each 50-minute class period, no one told him what to do. He was in charge, the captain of his classroom. And while his kids could be aggravating, draining, disappointing and sweaty, other times Will would get one of their jokes or references, and they would get one of his older-than-his-years references (each year, students concurred the man couldn't tell a joke and should never try). Together, they were likable, low-grade dorks.

Will would miss the circadian rhythm of the school year: the rush of fall, taking the wide turn at the holidays, gutting it out until spring break before the big push to June. He would miss the blessed last week of school – teachers collectively relaxing, wearing shorts (who knew they had legs!), splurging on pricey groceries for a change, some would be discovered whistling in their emptying classrooms. He would miss his decoy stapler and even assistant principal Thomas Hull; why, he would not be able to articulate.

He was expecting the numbness of being fired to wear off any day, but it wasn't. After the note had been sent home to parents, they expressed a resounding incuriosity concerning his abrupt departure. He already regretted not having made more of an effort at back-to-school nights. He regretted not having made more of an effort.

Hadn't he been *anyone's* favorite teacher?

The forced-march farewell drinks at the Pasta Trough had been a desultory affair. Will's department head said a few words by way of excusing them all from having to speak (Terri thought about coming but didn't). It wasn't like Will was transferring to a "better" school or leaving for the Peace Corps to teach in Kosovo or Mongolia; the man's criminal resume out-sparkled his academic credentials.

Maybe another school system in Maryland or in another state would hire him. No. Annapolis was his home. *I'm going to muscle through this. One hour at a time. Starting on this bench at Ego Alley.*

On a legal pad, Will wrote "Guiding Principles" while unemployed: Do not drink. Tuck in your shirt. Shave, even for bench sitting. If someone says hello, say hello back but don't go overboard. If you see someone you know, tell them you have the day off from work. If by some particularly cruel twist, you see a former student, be honest with them about what happened. Also, 15-18 minutes is an acceptable amount of time to sit alone on a bench at any one time. Any longer and people might think you have nowhere to go. If you are offered spare change, do not accept. Not just yet anyway.

Next, his blueprint. Having written a few articles for his college news-paper, he remembered an editor telling him to write drafts if you need help getting started. After four drafts, Will stuck with his first:

"Float Plan"

Leave bench, find a job
Prove to Parker I'm not a psycho
Help Mom more
Help Dad more
Go back to the soup kitchen
Learn to start and stop treadmill
Stop hitting things
Follow "Guiding Principles"
PARKER COOL

He re-jiggered the priority of goals three times before leaving for the place that would still have him.

At the Shepherd's Table's volunteer services desk, Will watched as three high school students filled out name tags and received their hairnets. He sympathized with their disorientation. By 10:20, the water and iced tea pitchers were centered on the colorful placemats at the dining tables. The day's menu was baked chicken with mixed vegetables; the vegetarian option was peanut butter and jelly sandwiches. As usual, the desserts were heaping and borderline fresh. Will found Todd in the kitchen.

"Long time no see," Todd said.

"I know. It's been awhile. I was hoping I could volunteer from time to time if you ever need an extra hand."

"We always do."

Todd motioned to the tell-tale cardboard box of hairnets. You know the drill.

"Before I get started, I want to apologize to that man I told to take a seat. Do you know if he's here?"

"He's sitting right over there in the green station," Todd said. "Mr. Bob Eaton. He averaged 22 points a game in 1968 for the Poets of Dunbar High School in Baltimore, won a full scholarship at Morgan State, earned a business degree and ran one of the first black-owned construction companies in Baltimore. He's been unemployed for 17 months."

17 months. Will had been unemployed one month and already wanted to jump off a widow's walk.

"You're Bread Man today," Todd said. "Each guest gets up to seven pieces. Remember, seven."

Will approached the leading scorer for the Poets in 1968. "Excuse me, sir, you probably don't remember me. I met you here about a year ago."

Bob Eaton could not place Will.

"I was rude to you. You asked for some bread, and I told you to take a seat. I don't know why I said that. It was disrespectful, and I'm sorry."

Will tried to remember if he ever told Terri he was sorry for not paying attention to her, for not paying attention to *them*. He should have. And he hoped he could apologize to Parker, her brother, and even that asshole boyfriend.

"Thank you for apologizing, young man," Bob Eaton said. "Wasn't so hard, was it?"

"No sir, it wasn't."

"Easier than having to wear a hairnet."

"True."

"You're a tall fella. Ever play ball?"

"Not basketball. When I was young, I wanted to be a tight end for the Green Bay Packers."

"Why the Packers?"

"My grandfather's team. Lombardi, Bart Starr, Jerry Kramer."

"They won five championships, young man," Bob Eaton said.

Will wanted to thank him for calling him a young man when Todd came over and handed him a basket of bread – white, whole wheat, raisin, potato. A server brought Bob Eaton a warm plate of baked chicken with a slice of pecan pie securely hugging the rim of the plate. Other guests of the

Shepherd's Table were also enjoying the baked chicken. One man pulled from his threadbare L. L. Bean backpack a string-less banjo to rest on his lap. A middle-aged woman with hand-drawn eyebrows, cotton candy blue hair, and a yellow raincoat walked in holding a chain-link leash attached to a studded collar, attached to a young male wearing stick-figure jeans and sporting a Mohawk. The volunteers willed themselves not to stare out of concern the guest might hand-feed her captive companion.

"All God's children," said Bob Eaton. He looked at the name tag on the Bread Guy's apron.

"So, Mr. Will, do you think you could spare a slice or two of your finest potato bread?"

"Absolutely."

For the first time, Will *saw* all the people eating a free, warm meal at dining room tables. They were all country residents like he was. He probably passed them on the street or walked by along City Dock. Some of these people could even be his neighbors. He scanned each table looking for faces he might know when he spotted a kid from Lakeview. Terri had him last year. The kid struggled and barely passed standard English. Now he was at the Shepherd's Table eating chicken casserole with what looked like his parents. Will walked over to offer them whatever bread they wanted. Anything they wanted. No, but thank you very much, they said quietly.

At the end of his meal, Will watched Bob Eaton walk across the hall into the Employment Services Office the facility also headquartered to help the homeless. With the last of the day's guests spilling back out into the streets of Annapolis, Will sat at an empty table and bagged up leftover chicken, casserole and marble cake for himself. Volunteers were invited to have a meal after everyone had been served and fed. He never imagined using a doggy bag. Of course, his parents would help him in every way they could, but his pride was both strident and misguided. Here, in his place of volunteer work, people came to eat their one solid meal for the day with no attorneys in their family to have their backs. The contradiction was not lost on Will, who threw seven pieces of the potato bread into his bag.

"You're still here," he told Bob Eaton, as he walked up to his table.

"I am indeed. I help out at the employment center when I can. Finding work is an equal opportunity pain in the ass."

"I'm finding that out."

Will spared no detail telling Bob Eaton what happened at Red Suit Bash. The man was so easy to talk to, like what Will imagined a priest or pastor would be like. Bob Eaton stopped him only to seek clarification on the red suit but otherwise, he listened to Will unspool the events leading to his arrest, firing, and doggy bag. Will also mentioned the unprovoked gazebo attack, Terri leaving, Dean's heartworms, his father's Alzheimer's, and floating.

"First World problems, I know," Will said. (What was a Second World problem? Will always wondered.)

"Seems like problems in any world."

Will thought on that.

"When did life get so, I don't know, loud?"

Bob Eaton launched a deep-well laugh, a first in months for the man.

"Oh, I like that. When did life get so *loud.*" He laughed again. "It does have a habit of getting loud, doesn't it."

Will laughed and instantly realized he needed to laugh more in this loud life. What better place to start than a soup kitchen.

"You're being tested," Bob Eaton said.

"Any advice?"

"Don't believe in advice," he said, his fingers steepled. "But you're going to be all right, young man."

"But when? When will I be all right?"

"When you don't have to ask that question."

Dinner at home that night was leftover baked chicken, marble cake, and potato bread. It was delicious. Will wanted to tell someone about his talk with Bob Eaton, how they laughed together. He could call his folks, but since his arrest, he had avoided them. Terri? Well, no. He hadn't spoken to her in whenever. It was all so heartbreaking and unfathomable: you meet someone, fall in love, and tell them every silly, serious, random, routine thing, share all your porch-wine ambitions, fears, and fantasies, and then one day have absolutely nothing to say or share with anymore. In the end, the two people can't even stand each other's laugh.

He wanted to tell Parker about his day, but she was done with him or seemed to have made that clear in her phone message. Will checked his Netflix queue but nothing popped out. He checked his mail and was relieved to see no more business envelopes or vaccination reminders for Dean.

He thought about having a drink but didn't.

• • •

On Sunday at 8 a.m., Will arrived at his parents' home bearing gifts. While prowling Ka-Chunk Records on Maryland Avenue, he found a vinyl copy of James Taylor's "JT" – his father's favorite. Will brought the album, along with a baker's dozen of bagels, a book of Philip Larkin's poetry, baseball scoring cards, and a highlighted print-out titled "Home Treatment in the Early Stages of Alzheimer's Disease." He planned to spend the day with his father, while his mother spent the day away from his father. Will forced her hand by buying his mother a gift certificate at a local spa. Barb Larkin, whether she wanted it or not, was entitled to one Swedish massage and a facial. That was her only scheduled event. She had the rest of the day to herself.

"Dear, I appreciate this, but I haven't been to a spa in 30 years. I don't know if I *want* to go to a spa."

"Too late. I paid for it," Will said, stunned over the cost of massages. "Time someone pampers you for a change. Be thankful it's a Swedish massage. I could have signed you up for a fish pedicure down in D.C. where a species of spa people have carp nibble away dead skin on your feet from a bucket. I spared you that treat."

"You know me too well."

"By the way," Will said, "they asked if you wanted a man or woman to give your massage."

She weighed the implications.

"Well?" she said.

"Well, what?" He was enjoying this. It beat listening to her talk about his father's fascination with tits, and it certainly was better than discussing his upcoming assault hearing next month.

"What did you tell them?"

"I told them you want a swarthy, tattooed Wiccan to give you the massage."

"Good Lord."

Will noticed his mother was wearing a new dress, sunnier than usual.

"Are you going on a date?"

"Don't be silly, dear."

"It's a spa, not a block party," Will said. "They'll have the whale music, water fountain with the pebbles in the waiting area, and a mushroom cloud of lavender. I hope they change the sheets and towels."

"Do you *want* to ruin this for me?"

"Now go, run away from home, before dad hollers for you. Don't worry about a thing. Everything is under control. I'll keep him busy and off the streets and away from his car. Maybe he and I will take a 30-minute walk. I read that helps tire the patient and improve communication."

"He's not your patient, dear. He's your father."

"Have you looked into electronic tagging?" Will asked, as his mother found her keys and hitched her purse on her shoulder. There was probably a more dignified way of describing a patient monitoring system.

"Electronic tagging?"

"Some experts like the benefits of tracking an Alzheimer's patient by tagging them with a radio signal."

"Let's not do any tagging. Stop reading health guides and go see him. He's up on the widow's walk. I think he's spying on Mrs. Huber through his binoculars. You have my cell number and his doctor's. Don't use them unless he has escaped and is mounting Mrs. Huber. I can't believe I said that."

"It's the spa talking, Mom."

After she left, Will took bagels and poetry up to the widow's walk, where his father was indeed admiring Mrs. Huber as she knelt in her garden massaging mulch into the topsoil. Bill Larkin was looking through the wrong end of the binoculars, the effect of which greatly minimized the image of the fetching Mrs. Huber. A truly good son would help his father correct the view, but Will decided to end the home invasion of privacy.

"Hey, Dad!" Loudly, as if his father was losing his hearing, which he was not. The man did not move from the railing.

"Dad? Over here."

His father turned slowly and viewed his son through the wrong end of the binoculars.

"What do you got there?"

Bagels and poetry by a guy named Larkin, Will said.

"That's our name."

They sat across from each other in the green Adirondacks. The bay breeze was a familiar stew of salt, speedboat exhaust, and waffle cone. From the widow's walk, they could see traffic running stop-and-go circles around Annapolis' two circles, Church and State. Midshipmen window-shopped, as tourists snapped their pictures. The Larkin men could see the Naval Academy's Bancroft Hall, one of the world's largest dorms and there, the Navy Chapel – where John Paul Jones lies buried in a vault. Now *that* dude was a boater.

Will dressed a poppy-seed bagel in cream cheese and handed it to his father on a napkin.

"Read a poem to me," he said.

When he auditioned Philip Larkin's poems the night before, "This Be the Verse" sounded like a funny poem. Maybe something along the lines of Dr. Seuss. Will didn't bother to read it first. "I got one," he told his father.

"They fuck you up, your mum and dad.
They may not mean to, but they do.
They fill you with the faults they had
And add some extra, just for you…"

Will stopped. He remembered how his father was after the boating accident. The drinking – that ritual of self-medication and retreat – and the chronic moodiness. His father came home after work each night, but he wasn't home. Present but not; with them but not. Will remembered when he was eight, a Monday night in February when his mother asked his father to leave. It was because of his drinking, she told her son many years later. But Will knew that then and had closely watched his father pack one of the good Samsonites and without saying a word, walk out the front door of his own home. He came back some two weeks later, a sober Wednesday, and Will prayed he missed them.

He had tried talking to his father on Horseshoe Island, but his father seemed more confused and more out of element that day on the water. Surely he was relatively calmer and sharper at home.

"Dad, I need you to try and remember something for me." Will's voice was tender as a kindergarten teacher's on the first day of school.

"I remember everything! Don't you worry about that."

"Then you remember taking me boating when I was 6."

"I never took you boating…"

"We were in the creek, Spa Creek, you remember, don't you? We hit something in the water…"

His father's eyes were at a standstill.

"You told me not to tell Mom I fell overboard and almost drowned…"

"I never!"

"We lied to her. I lied to her for you."

Will was standing now, as his father strangled the arms of his favorite chair on his widow's walk. From the widow's walk came faint sounds of sailboat masts clanking in the harbor.

"Liar!"

"That's why you sold your boat. That's why you never went boating again. That's why I never went on the water again. Did you know that? Did you know I've been scared of the water ever since?" And Will realized he had not only been scared of the water ever since the accident. "Dad, do you know that I've been scared of *everything*?"

His father tried to stand but wobbled before folding back into his Adirondack.

"Get out! Get out of my house! Get *out* of my house!"

"You don't mean that," Will said, knowing some part of his father did mean that. He had never seen his father look scared. He must have looked like this as he searched for his son underwater in Spa Creek in those life-long seconds; yes, the man, my father, must have been alone, helpless, and scared to death. There was no point anymore to try and wring an explanation or apology out of him. It would be like trying to kick out the back window of a patrol car. And there was no point in asking his father for legal help. Maybe Leeds Walker could help or maybe Will would have to take his chances in court. His father must never know about his arrest – his mother promised him.

"Do you want to look at Mrs. Huber with me?" Will said.

"Yes!" Bill Larkin said, suddenly energized.

After gazing upon the neighbor woman, his father took to the couch and slept for three hours. Will thought about calling his mother to ask if napping this long was normal, but it was her day off. Let her be. Let him be.

At 5:35 p.m., his father finally woke up. There was wetness around his crotch. The Alzheimer's printout said once a schedule is established, the caregiver should get the person to the bathroom before an incontinent episode. Will did not know what his father's schedule was. He and his mother had not gone over that.

"Dad, we need to change your shorts."

His father didn't move.

"Who are you? What are you doing here?"

Barb Larkin told Will to stay calm when his father was confused or upset. Do not contradict him or attempt to refresh or correct his memory. Remember, she told her son, Alzheimer's patients can become angry, frightened. If you want his attention, gently touch his shoulder or arm and speak in clear, short sentences. Above all, be patient. Will led his father to the shower. His father needed help. And if they didn't fuss around too long in the shower, they could walk up to the widow's walk and take turns at the binoculars. Or they could stay downstairs and watch the Orioles game.

They watched the O's slap the Yankees around, and the Larkin men were overjoyed.

• • •

Steve Cool emerged from one of his signature 10-hour sleeps. He found his sister in the backyard, splayed out in a chaise. Parker's peach-colored tee was rolled up almost to her ears. Wheat thin arm hair. Hint of bicep. Savoring Elizabeth Bishop's "Letter to N.Y." *...taking cabs in the middle of the night, driving as if to save your soul...* Parker ignored her Coke Zero roasting in the heat. She closed her book and eyes and decided to never leave this spot.

"While I have you here," Steve said, "it's time you start thinking about finding your own place."

As sisters go, Parker had been an acceptable house guest. Although she weaseled out of yoga sessions, she was tidy, chipped in with select expenses, restocked the bird feeder without being asked, and never crammed the dishwasher. But the girl was 28 and needed to be on her own – finally.

"You're kicking me out of the nest?"

"Fly away little bird, fly away."

Steve unrolled one of her sleeves, a stunt he pulled when they were kids living across the rock quarry. Parker spent too much time, in her brother's opinion, getting her T-shirt sleeves to stay rolled up, so he'd sneak up behind her on the porch or in her bedroom and thump her sleeve down.

Today in his backyard, Parker tried to slap away Steve's hand but she was woefully late. She was de-rolled again.

"Never forget my superiority over you," he said.

"You'll miss me when I'm gone. Who will stock the bird feeder? Who will make you scrambled eggs on Sunday? Who will kick your ass in handwriting?"

"Handwriting?"

"Oops."

"You got Math Man on the brain."

She hadn't spoken to Will since the Red Suit Bash and didn't plan to.

"Do not have Math Man on brain," Parker said. "And yes, I have to find my own place. You have been patient and kind."

"And generous."

"And generous."

They might have hugged, but it was too sticky, and the Cools were not predisposed to hugging.

"You're kicking me out just when I was on a roll," Parker said. She poured her steaming soda on the grass.

"Not much of a roll, sis," Steve said.

"But I've always lived with someone." Since college, Parker always had a roommate, a record of cohabitation marred by Alex and ending, apparently, with her brother. "What if I get lonely?"

"Get a dog."

Parker reached over to twist her brother's arm hair.

"You can't spend the rest of your life worried that another dog will get run over. And find a boyfriend who isn't a roided-up asshole. Aim higher, which should not be difficult to do."

"Is there anything else, Zen Master Steve?"

"Yeah, give him a call."

"He can call *me*."

"God, straight people are fucked up."

"We try, we try."

That evening, Parker heard a noise outside her open bedroom window. Kids were playing hide-and-seek, and she heard the familiar count up to 10, then *Ready or not, here I come.* Sounded like they were right under her window, but children playing outside on a summer evening always sound that close. It tickled Parker to know hide-and-seek wasn't extinct – that and Hulu-hooping. There should be hula hoops available in vending machines. No better way to relieve stress than hooping. False. There was another way to relieve stress, but she chose not to think about her current sexual hiatus, which left her edgy and destabilized.

When she was at Salisbury University on Maryland's Eastern Shore, junior Parker Cool started a hide-and-seek club that exists to this day. Her stewardship of the campus activity remained a little-known fact owing largely to the founding member's surviving embarrassment. Parker wondered if Dailey would play the game when she got a bit older, wondered if the kids would invite her to play, whether she would always be "It" or become a master hider and seeker.

That night in the Florida Room, Dailey was watching reruns of the classic cartoon, *Johnny Bravo*.

"I asked you not to eat Oreos on the sofa."

"I'm not," Dailey said.

"What do you have in your hand then?"

"An Oreo, but I'm eating it over my *hand,* not over the *sofa.*"

"Dailey, we need to talk about something." The girl responded by building a cushion fort with the sofa cushions, a classic bedtime stalling tactic.

"Uncle Steve has been wonderful to let us live here, but it's time we find our own special place to live. Just the two of us."

Dailey tucked Lambie closer to her chest. The doll looked particularly gamey.

"Is Dad going to live with us?"

Parker steadied herself.

"No, he's not."

Dailey nestled inside her fort and spoke through a crack in her cozy walls.

"He called me his first mate."

"Who did?"

"Mr. Will. When we went boating together. I helped him get that smidge of water out of his boat."

"I know you did. I was very proud of you," Parker said. "So, smidge girl, here's an idea. I don't know if we are going to see Mr. Will again, OK? But if we do, let's ask him if he can take us on the water again but maybe not so far this time. Is that a deal, Neal?"

"That's a deal, Neal."

They toppled the cushion fort together.

Chapter 13

At Buster's, the small army of friends from Lakeview High again assembled for their *Week in Review*. The day manager opened the restaurant's front door and windows to invite in both air and summer customers. Will and Mack took seats at the horseshoe bar and ordered two Coronas and 24 wings. Will breezed over his barren unemployment picture, a duplicate update came from Mack who wore plaid Bermuda shorts, needed a haircut and a shave, particularly on the neck.

"Where's Kyle?" Will asked.

"Couldn't make it. He has Instagram. We might never see him again." Will had neither Instagram, Facebook or Twitter; he suspected he was missing the Sharing chromosome.

"OK."

"OK? Why aren't you cursing him? Not to mention – but I must – you need to shampoo your neck," Will said.

"William, I've been dealt a few setbacks, as have you. I believe a spiritual overhaul is in order."

A crunchy, sprite of a waitress put down two beers.

"And I'm trying not to curse," Mack said.

Will feared his friend had undergone a religious conversation too staggering to classify. But Mack's conversion went deeper. He wasn't talking anymore about hot and cold running broads. He had scraped off his "Follow Me to Hooters" sticker from the bumper of his two-year-old BMW. A new model was not in his future.

"Christina has changed my life."

"Christina? The waitress from here?"

"We're dating."

Mack looked at his Buffalo wings with the bony legs of celery around a pool of bleu cheese. His Corona's feelings looked hurt. He was drinking less these days, too.

"You know we're living together, right?"

"Eh, no. When did that happen?

"I can't say exactly."

"To review," Will said, denuding a Buffalo wing with his teeth, "no more cursing and no more personal grooming. And you're living with a waitress from here. And we're both out of work." The waitress appeared with more napkins. "No wonder we're depressed."

"I'm not depressed. I'm being reflective. Can't I be reflective?"

"No," Will said.

The friends churned up small talk. Will mentioned how looking for jobs on the computer made his eyes sore, so he went to some place called the Kirkwood Dry Eye Center. After four visits and four copays drained from his shrinking savings, the Dry Eye Center specialists confirmed Will had dry eyes. They prescribed special eye drops that when inspected closely resembled Visine. Mack told him he was a lucky fuck for having COBRA and mentioned having to take Tricor for his whopping cholesterol, and lately, his sciatica was bothering him when he lifted anything. On top of those maladies, Mack had become allergic to his deodorant.

"Do you ever feel," Mack said, "that so much of life is spent convincing yourself you're not a total fraud?"

"Yes."

"What did we want to be when we grew up?"

"I thought we pledged to never grow up," Will said. "Obviously we achieved that goal with mixed results."

"Still don't have an attorney?"

"No."

"When's the trial?"

"Oct. 5."

"You know of course that if you Google 'Maryland attorneys' you will be up to your inert johnson in lawyers," Mack said.

"Here's what I remember," Will said, changing course. "You said you wanted to make a lot of money and spend it all on clothes, cars, houses, and hot and cold running broads."

"*You* said you wanted to be a reporter or a teacher and have your weekends free for basketball."

"No, I said I wanted to be a Green Bay Packer."

Bill Larkin didn't want his son playing tackle football. He worried about knee injuries or worse, a neck injury, and the subject was not open for discussion, so Will relegated himself to playing intramural football all through middle and high school and even college. He excelled in punting, an unmarketable skill. Will held a wee grudge against his father for not letting him play football – and for never building him a tree house, which is surprisingly hard to build. In light of the year's events, Will retired the grudges.

Two more beers materialized, which were ignored.

"Life was simpler in high school," Will said.

"No, it wasn't."

"Remember going to Bethany Beach on the weekends?"

When they were old enough to drive, Will, Mack, and Kyle took turns driving to Delaware's Bethany Beach to play basketball on the town's basketball court with the clanky, net-less rims. Kyle would spot Atlantic bottlenose porpoises offshore and point toward those slicing gray dorsals, but Mack never saw anything and swore the dolphins didn't exist. After the missed sightings, they'd bolt into the ocean to play Proof of Purchase. The rule was to swim to the bottom and grab a handful of sand. Whoever swam out farthest and produced a fistful of beach was the winner. "Proof of Purchase!" Mack would holler because he always won. Kyle never went out far; it hurt his ears swimming too deep. Will, who barely left the shallows, was never a factor in the childhood game. At night, they'd return to the basketball court, the games long over. They'd kill three six-packs of Miller Lite and watch tanned girls in flip-flops filter out from the bantam boardwalk.

"Remember that night we met those two girls from Baltimore? You kissed one of them. She had an odd first name. Regina? Catrina?"

"*You* kissed her," Mack said.

"No, I was with the one who went home with her only for her to call her boyfriend. A long-distance call, I should note. There was no kissing. She did have a nice neck, though. I wanted to have a picnic on her neck."

"That probably scared her off."

"Here's to picnicking on necks, beach weekends, and Proof of Purchase," said Will, raising his untouched Corona.

The waitress ducked in with another stack of paper napkins.

"I need some advice," Mack said.

Will waited as his friend stripped the beer label down its perspiring glass. He turned a Buffalo wing over in its peppery soup.

"When did you first know you loved someone? And when," Mack said, "did you know they were going to leave you?"

"I didn't know."

• • •

They had been dating for two months and living together six days. Christina never dated an Irishman before and was bewitched by the prospect. She adopted Guinness as her favorite beer and pledged her allegiance to the Pogues. Mack had never lived with a woman except for his mother. But lots of men lived with women – maybe it wasn't that hard or maybe it was impossible. Either way, Christina was the first in the living-together department. Mack had a nagging sense she liked him.

When he lost his job at a Baltimore brokerage house of regional renown, he believed headhunters would be knocking down his door with offers, so he didn't fuss with his resume and didn't plan on starting. His skills, he felt, were a matter of public record in the financial field. He owned a beach home for fuck sake. But more than a month later, he had no job but a live-in girlfriend who liked everything Christian, which was not the same thing as liking all things Catholic.

In one of her frequent bursts of sharing, Christina outlined plans to start a Christian book club and bounced her club rules off Mack.

"It would be exciting to cultivate a group of people and bring them together to read books that speak to our beliefs," she said. "I'd cultivate – but it wouldn't be a cult!" Christina laughed, as Mack wondered whether she was wearing her red or black thong. Christian girls wore thongs! Mack felt he had uncovered one of life's most beguiling mysteries.

"John, are you listening?"

"Actively, Chris."

He scanned her book club guidelines: No. 7: "Books will be not accepted for consideration that discredit or challenge the spirit of Jesus Christ Our Savior." No. 9: "No books deemed sexually explicit or suggestive will be considered." No. 12: "Membership is a one-time fee of $100."

"You're going to charge people to read?"

The question appeared to sledge-hammer Christina, as did many of Mack's financial queries. Maybe the girl, he conceded, wasn't that bright. Maybe he wasn't that bright. Two not so bright people living together and running, apparently, an expensive book club.

"Let me try and explain something. Generally, you don't charge money for something that people can do for free. People read for free all the time, Chris."

Christine canvassed her boyfriend's face, searching for a clue into what she hoped was his unintentional condescension. Mack sensed a misstep in their conversation.

"People read for free all the time? You don't say," she said. "Thank you for mansplaining that to me."

"Man what?"

"Mansplaining. Look it up, ask around, join our century."

In the prickly days to follow, Mack's unemployment stretched on. With Christina pulling extra shifts at Buster's, he had his days largely to himself. Among other discoveries, he realized he had lived in the same house for eight years but didn't really *know* his home, which made a lot of racket during the day. A man could hardly nap or chart his future with all that creaking and turning off-and-on. He traced the sounds to his basement and a shabby, cramped room where he gazed upon a large, water-bearing canister. He began to suspect his water heater was up to no good during the day. Unnerved, he fled the spider-webbed environs, vowing never to return. Consolation from his increasingly anxious girlfriend was not forthcoming.

"John, you need to stay productive if you're not going to bother to look for work," Christina said.

Mack's productivity had dwindled to re-watching *Wolf of Wall Street* and spending two-plus hours sightseeing on YouTube. He thought about shaving but lost the will.

"You need to get out of the house," she said. "If you sit around here all day, you will go crazy and drive me crazy."

She was right. If he stayed, he would attack the water heater with Will's chainsaw.

"Chris, I need to move out for a little while," he said.

"What?"

"I need to move out."

"But it's your house."

"But you got out of your lease to move in with me. I'm not about to ask you to leave."

"I said you need to get out of the house more. I never said you need to leave. Why does anyone have to *leave?*"

"Because I couldn't stand it if you left me first," he said, "and I was wrong about your book club. What do I know anyway?"

• • •

On Sunday morning, Will was preparing a second bowl of Cap'n Crunch when his cell interrupted his sacred meal.

"William, I need to crash at your place. A few days tops."

Few-days-tops was always a lie. Twenty minutes later, the telltale black BMW appeared in Will's driveway. The driver wore a Springsteen "Magic" T-shirt and carried two boxes with six-packs of Miller Lite balancing atop the possessions.

"Mack, you do know there are now two unemployed people living here, right? By the way, I thought you weren't drinking."

"I'm relapsing – if that's the fucking word for it."

"That would be the word. But I'm cutting back these days, seriously, so I can't join you."

Mack attempted pouting, which was always too much work.

"What's going on? And give me the abridged and sober version."

Leaving his boxes at the front door, Mack walked into the family room. He smelled of high school locker room on a Friday afternoon during a heat wave.

"I need to clean myself."

Splashing hand sanitizer on his face, neck and under his arms had been no substitute for showering. Having abandoned the workman-like act of shaving, Mack's dark reddish beard appeared to be housing juvenile marsupials. Will thought he should say something to Mack about his nose hairs – really just that one, shooting the world a bird.

Mack retrieved a Mars shopping bag from one of the boxes. Inside, his only change of clothes. Mack knew the way to the bathroom. Will heard the door lock behind him. The tub began to fill. Will approached cautiously. There came sounds of light splashing and the squeaky rearranging of a body.

"Mack? Not a bath, please, not that."

One faucet turned off, another one stayed on. Will had a grown man in his bathtub. Through the door, Will heard a bottle lustily squeezed. Mack had brought bath bubbles. A cry for help.

"William, go about your business," Mack said from behind the door. "I'll be awhile. I picked up a new *Maxim*."

"For the love of God, control yourself in there."

What was next – Mac taking a bar of soap and rubbing along those bubble mountains to make them pop? Using a mask and snorkel to stay submerged indefinitely?

"I'm adrift, William."

He's adrift, and I might be going to jail. In the Adrift Competition, it was no contest. Will imagined his house guest thumbing one-handed through *Maxim* amid frothy peaks of bath bubbles.

"We'll talk, promise, but I need to do something."

"What do you need to do?"

"I need to get out of here for awhile."

"Well, I need to shave. So be off," Mack said.

Will was petrified.

"Please, please don't use my razor. I know *where* you shave."

"Just a light pruning of the pubes, William. Women like that."

"Is that even remotely true?"

"How would I know? I'm the one taking a bath for fuck sake."

Chapter 14

He was seven when he ran away from home the first time. Without leaving a ransom or otherwise informational note, he packed up his Legos, O's cap and a fresh box of Cap'n Crunch and headed south. The trip on foot to his back yard was speedy and successful. There, he encamped behind a Carrier air-conditioning unit shrouded in shrubs; the ground at the concrete base was soft sand. The location was, by neighborhood standards, a decent hiding place. But after two hours of crouching and finding the sand *too* soft to erect any Lego masterpiece (plus the ants), Will Larkin felt he had taught his parents a valuable lesson by his fearful disappearance. Gathering his provisions, he headed north in the direction of his kitchen, where he applied the forgotten milk to a bowl of the captain's finest. He read his mother's silence as an apology for somehow being responsible for his father having abruptly moved out those two weeks. She thought her son was merely playing next door with his friend. They both pressed on with their lives.

He was 30 when he ran away from home a second time. Heading east, Will hauled his clanking Honda across the Chesapeake Bay Bridge; just the act of leaving the mainland for the Eastern Shore released toxins in day-tripping runaways. Here were the purifying home movies of passing Mom-and-pop vegetable stands, soy fields, collapsed glorious barns, and imperishable churches with their backyard cemeteries all rooted in Maryland's flatlands. Now in Queen Anne's County, Will took his first left then first right into artsy, antique-rowed Stevensville. Morning traffic and business were light to invisible. He had the town, county, and this shore corner to himself. Back across the bridge, the rest of his life could wait and did.

Will car-crawled along two-lane Main Street until he approached the bridge over Cox Creek, a gangly body of water subject to much environmental concern. Might be relaxing to stop the car, pull over on the gravel shoulder across from the Stevensville Cemetery and take a look at the clay-colored water. But as he drove closer he saw what looked like an olive-black spiked helmet in the road, a very large helmet. The helmet moved, and Will saw the face of the helmet and he was afraid but curious. He pulled over and slowly walked over to the helmet in the middle of Main Street. The helmet hissed, and Will jumped. He had never seen a common Eastern snapping turtle up close, especially one so uncommonly large. The mossy, olive-black beast, all 35 pounds of it, did not appear eager to concede his position. Will feared a car or truck would come along and maul it – a truck, definitely. The thing looked like it could snap a car in two.

The largest freshwater turtle in Maryland, the Eastern snapping turtle holds fort atop its food chain. There is nothing contradictory in its appearance: it looks like a badass and is. Equally armored, it looks like a pet descendent of the Stegosaurus. The turtle's neck can extend two-thirds the length of its broad carapace and swivel as if exorcized. They are roundly considered dangerous given their vice-like jaws, quick strikes, temperament and the whole neck thing. Unlike his TV knowledge of warthogs, Will had not seen a nature special on the Eastern snapping turtle. Introductory information would have been useful.

The turtle was not budging, so a good deed was necessary to prevent it from becoming a whole lot of mashed road kill. Will considered strategies for moving or, better yet, telepathically suggesting the turtle exit the road on its own safe accord. For his first attempt, he tip-toed up to the reptile chieftain and marveled at the knobby, spiked legs (paws? hooves?) and alligator-like head. Its tail was also spikey, gnarled and prehistoric. When alarmed, Eastern snapping turtles face their prey head-on. The turtle remained unalarmed.

Maybe the sound of car keys would rattle the turtle enough to send it back to swampy safety. Moving closer, Will jangled his car keys above the turtle's snout. No reaction. Inching closer, he rattled his keys six inches above the specimen, which slowly faced Will and emitted a guttural hiss that almost sent Will back to Annapolis. But he stood his ground – and the turtle's lightning strike nearly cost Will his thumb and forefinger. He backed away to re-assess.

Six cars passed both man and turtle, making a wide sweep of them there in the road. "That's a snapping turtle," a man called out from his Dodge Ram. "They're nasty fellas. Want me to shoot him?" No thanks, Will said. I'll take care of him. "Sure you don't want me to shoot it for you?" No, but thanks, really. No further roadside assistance was offered, although motorists did get some good cell phone pics.

Will stood guard over the turtle, even directed traffic around it. The turtle was not going to be harmed – not today and not on his watch. Three teens ambled by and one threw a rock at the turtle, while the others scratched around for sticks for shit-brained poking and harassing. Will left his post and walked across the street to address the boys. He told them it was time for them to move along. He said it once, and they understood and kept walking. "Go ahead and fuck your turtle, you turtle fucker," the rock thrower said by way of elegant goodbye.

The day stoked up, insects from the creek buzzed his face and snipped at his arms and legs. Will opened his trunk looking for anything to nudge the turtle under the guardrail and back into the water. Not a man to carry a lot or any tools in his car, he picked up the umbrella Terri had accidentally left. It was her favorite, a Barnes & Noble number wall-papered infamous lines from famous books. *I sing the body electric. I am Oz, the great and terrible. Call me Ishmael.* Will walked toward his own white whale armed with his own harpoon. The turtle stared ahead blankly as if pondering moving at some point this month. Will snuck up behind it and tapped its massive shell with the umbrella tip. Nothing. He tapped again. Nothing. Was it possible turtles had no feeling in their shells? Will poked one of the turtle's front legs, which looked like a bear paw.

He never heard the hiss.

• • •

Given how explosive umbrellas can be (they spring open at uninvited times), Will was astonished to witness a 35-pound, helmet-faced snapping turtle gracefully exit a roadway with the umbrella gripped in its jaw. The strike caught Will so off-guard he found himself momentarily dragged along with the umbrella since he hadn't time to let go. In those few seconds, he imagined again falling into a muddy creek and being dragged under. But he did let go and watched in admiration as the Eastern snapping turtle stole his ex-wife's favorite umbrella. Safe steps behind, he trailed the turtle as it lumbered across the gravel shoulder, under the guardrail and down into Cox Creek with its slender, wrapped prey.

Will walked on the bridge to see the turtle float away, but there was no sign of it or even a sinking quote from *Moby-Dick*, not even trace bubbles. He hoped the umbrella wouldn't suddenly open up on the turtle. Don't care who or what you are, it's a pain in the ass when umbrellas pull that stunt.

The runaway ex-teacher looked out over the winding, unspectacular creek and became overcome by laughter. He hadn't laughed so hard since the soup kitchen with Bob Eaton, and the laughing again felt cathartic. He didn't think he could lose anything more this year but found a way to lose an umbrella, too.

Saved a turtle, killed an umbrella. He'd take that deal any day. And the day had been startling and fun and loud.

A victory.

Chapter 15

Parker Cool was in the backyard watching a goldfinch balance on the feeder. Goldfinches were her favorite birds because how could they not be anyone's favorite bird? Her pants legs were rolled up in makeshift shorts. She wore a Kiawah Island white T-shirt with the sleeves also rolled up. She heard Will's car, still a noisy thing. She heard his footsteps to the front door, heard her brother answer the door. Finding an affordable apartment for her and Dailey in Eastport had proved elusive so far, so Steve cut her some slack and extended his home invite.

She tiptoed to the front of the fence closest to the front door. The fence was high enough for concealment, as a crouching Parker eavesdropped.

"What are you doing here?" Steve said, in what Parker thought was a decent badass voice.

"I need to talk to Parker."

"What if I call the cops?"

Will didn't budge.

"Do what you got to do. But I need to talk to your sister."

Will heard a slight movement behind the fence and the sound of someone trying to breathe quietly. He heard two knuckles crack before addressing the fence.

"I'm sorry I scared you and Dailey. I'm sorry I ruined the party. But I'm not sorry I punched him. I lost my job. I lost you. And I'll probably go to jail. Not probably, *will* go to jail if there isn't some kind of miracle. But no one should treat you that way, Parker. No one should ever lay a hand on you. I know you don't need me or anyone to protect you. I just like you. I like you a lot. That's all."

Will turned and walked to his car. Backing out of Steve's driveway, Will's Honda emitted a more pained sound having been ordered to accelerate. Parker emerged from her observation post.

"That wasn't an altogether bad apology," Steve said.

"Not altogether."

That night Parker opened a bottle of merlot and dabbed at the floating cork crumbs in the flickering wine. Upstairs, Dailey was asleep or should have been. It was after 10. There is no quiet like the quiet after a child falls asleep or even pretends to be asleep. Wrapped in an afghan on her brother's sofa, Parker drank her wine, cork crumbs and all. Tucked behind her husband's pillow, her cell's ringtone went off, a tinny version of Rick Astley's "Never Gonna Give You Up." The earworm song reminded her of Alex in better days, all six, seven of them. Any number of friends, associates, toddlers, prison inmates, or species of coral could instruct her how to change her ringtone, but she never got around to it.

"Parker?

The math man.

"So, I was talking to a fence today, a nice fence but it was a one-sided conversation. I'm going to assume you picked up your phone because I'm incredibly intuitive. I'm also going to assume you have again chosen against direct communication."

Will had never been this chatty with a phone.

"I have a humble proposal. I want to take you and Dailey to lunch. Just a simple lunch. Your choice of fine eateries and expense is no concern – unless it's expensive."

Parker cupped her cell to conceal a giggle for she prided herself on never giggling.

"You both can leave after five minutes if you want, although there is nothing sadder than a 30-year-old former teacher eating lunch alone. Wait – that's what I did at school every day."

That *almost* jarred a word from Parker.

"If you're interested, tell me what restaurant and I'll meet you there. I'll count to 10 and if I don't hear anything, I'll hang up and never contact you again. What's more likely is I'll count to 100. Then a 1000 and really, who has time for all that nonsense?"

Parker's defenses in proud tatters.

"Applebee's," came a faint voice.

"Where?" Will said.

"Applebee's!"

• • •

Three weeks before his hearing, Will met Parker and Dailey at the Applebee's on Rowe Boulevard. Will hadn't been to an Applebee's in 15 years and never with a 6-year-old girl. He made a last-minute wardrobe change and switched out of his Rehoboth Beach T-shirt and into a maroon Polo. He was 10 minutes early and waited by the "Please Wait to Be Seated" sign. He snagged a toothpick, rolled it in his fingers, snapped the toothpick, and looked for a place to trash the pieces. Applebee's front door opened and blew warm air over Will's back. He turned to see Parker and below, a stern-faced girl holding Lambie, her stuffed animal.

"Dailey, it's nice to see you again," Will said. The girl looked up at the tall man and not so much smiled as leveled daggers at his skull.

"Thanks for coming," he said to them both.

They sat in a high-backed booth and shared two glossy menus that were slightly less wordy than the Torah. Parker and Dailey on one side, Will the other. Amid the thick silence, he realized Parker was not going to bail him out in the conversation department.

Meanwhile, the girl studied Will's neck.

"Is that a wart?"

Will touched his neck.

"No, I don't think so."

"It looks like a wart." Dailey's voice was not as childlike as Will remembered from the Red Suit Bash. She sounded 25.

"It's not a wart," said Will, who was having his own doubts.

The Applebee's waitress, a girl named Ashley (Will taught her last year – nice girl, wore too much eye shadow; mysteriously missed most of March;

obviously didn't remember her algebra teacher), said she would be their server, and asked if they want to start with some appetizers. Parker ordered beef nachos, mozzarella sticks, and a Sprite for the young lady. Will sat across from them folding a cloth napkin lengthwise until he couldn't roll it anymore. He unrolled and started over.

"If it's not a wart," said Dailey, "what is it?"

A mole, a harmless mole, adults were loaded with them. Instead, Will said: "You're right. It's a wart, a very special wart." Parker might have smirked.

"Dailey, have you ever heard of a warthog?"

She shook her head. Obviously, her TV travels hadn't exposed her to a nature show about *P. africanus*, the wild pig of Africa, the warthog. During one of his sleepless jags, Will stumbled on the National Geographic Channel and a special about warthogs. Warthogs can grow up to 330 pounds and will feast on anything from roots, berries, and tree bark to dead animals, eggs, and birds. Known for their protruding tusks, warthogs are fast runners and skilled jumpers. They are, in short, wild pigs that can eat small villages.

Ashley the waitress returned with the appetizers and Sprite. She scooped up the menus and made room for three plates on the center of the table. Dailey looked at the nachos – the seasoned beef, the cheese, and jalapeños on every chip, the pico de gallo and sour cream – and pictured a warthog grunting and belching and rubbing his whole warthoggy head into their nachos. She picked up a mozzarella stick.

"Dailey, what you see on my neck is a warthog *seed*."

She learned all about bean seeds in kindergarten, but her teacher didn't mention anything about warthog seeds. The girl took a one-inch bite of her cheese stick. Under the table, she searched for Lambie's paw, a loving, limp connection.

"If I don't get to a doctor and I mean fast, a baby warthog will grow out of my neck. It starts with the tusks. They break out of the wart, like a baby bird cracking out of its shell. After the tusks come out, the baby warthog face appears. Before you know it, I have a baby warthog to take care of."

Dailey was almost positive there was no such thing. She put the rest of the cheese stick in her mouth, too much for one bite.

"Is it a friendly baby warthog?"

"Absolutely," Will said. "Except on Sundays."

"Why isn't it friendly on Sundays?"

Dailey jerked away from holding her mother's hand under the table. Will hoped Dailey would find his story funny, but she looked frightened.

"I was just kidding. It's a harmless mole. See, look closely. Touch it if you want. Just a mole. No tusks."

Dailey was speechless.

"Honestly, a warthog seed is not growing out of my neck. You're safe."

Dailey began to gasp. The color in her cheeks was changing from pink to red, her eyes watering and bulging. Her gasping became louder, then a horrible lack of sound.

"Oh, God!" Parker screamed.

Will knew the signs. He spent three summers as a camp counselor and saw campers choke on one thing or another, three times he swept their mouths with his finger, and once, Will gave two mouth-to-mouth breaths into a 5-year-old named Jennifer, and that was enough first aid for a lifetime. Until today.

He spun around toward Dailey's side of the booth. Her face had lost color. This wasn't a car accident or some horrible man in the neighborhood. Just as a stupid cheese stick. Dailey wasn't making a sound now. Will looked at Parker and saw in her eyes a terror he remembered in his father's eyes when he almost lost his son. Will dropped to his knees and scooted the girl to the ledge of the booth. The waitress ran for her manager. Two families on either aside abandoned their booths to huddle by Parker. Will opened Dailey's mouth and moved her tongue down with his index finger. The light was lousy. He tilted Dailey's head slightly to the right to horde natural light from the window. Will swept Dailey's mouth with his finger and felt something sticky and wet. He yanked out a mangled fragment of a cheese stick, as hungry breathing was followed by coughing and sobbing. Will was still on his knees when Dailey reached for him. The girl smelled like bile and cheese stick sauce. She cried into his neck.

"Hey, you're going to water my warthog seed with all those tears, and then it will grow too big for me to keep as a pet."

A raspy giggle.

After assuring six diners that Dailey was all right, Parker swooped up her daughter and carried her outside to her car. There was no check because the restaurant manager was more than happy to cover their meal.

• • •

Will marveled at how he had not received an interesting piece of mail since 2012, and that was a Maryland tax refund for $32.85 (he celebrated the largesse by paying his cable bill). Two days after Applebee's, he shucked the week's postal take: *Pennysaver,* Harry & David catalog (he never found himself in the market for a chocolate gift tower), and a dental flier promising virtual smile makeovers. A letter was tucked in the rubber-banded batch and addressed in Parker's superior handwriting. Inside, a note was taped to a folded piece of construction paper.

"Dailey drew this for you. She said it was her best drawing EVER. Display prominently. And thank you, Will."

The fragile crayon drawing showed a smiling warthog-like figure sharing a fluffy pillow with what appeared to be a lamb. Judging by the animal's expression, it wasn't clear whether it enjoyed sharing the pillow, but the warthog looked happy. The rendering of the tusks was both simple and bold. The artist added a giant sun with yellow spokes radiating from its center. Will used his refrigerator magnets to hold up the artwork. Someone could write a children's story based on Dailey's picture.

After addressing an envelope to Miss Dailey (was her last name Cool? Unsure, Will skipped the surname), he jotted down a brief note to the artist:

Thank you for the extra-wonderful warthog drawing. I'd like to repay you with a real outing. Would you and your mother like to go on a REAL outing with me? Your friend, Will.

Chapter 16

She hadn't spoken to Alex since the golf range and her second dramatic exit from the relationship. But she needed a favor or rather Will did. It suddenly felt like the same thing.

"Would you do something for me?" she asked Alex on the phone.

"Why should I? Your boyfriend sucker punched me, and then you ran away *again* from me."

"I need your help, Alex." And the way she asked reminded him of when they met and all that spark and softness. "I'm listening."

Parker told him about the trip to Applebee's, about seeing Will again, the harder part about Dailey choking on a cheese stick, and Will's quick actions to save the girl's life, their daughter's life.

"So, we owe him. I still don't know what you want from me."

Parker took a deep breath and exhaled.

"Do you think we owe him enough to keep him from going to jail?"

Parker's cell buzzed in her ear. Damn call waiting. Damn call didn't want to wait.

"Shit, Alex. I better take this. I'll call you back."

She took her other call.

"Come home," Steve Cool said.

"Home?"

"Church Lane. Come home. Now."

Three days later, strange cars were bunched outside the two-story home across Deerco Road from the rock quarry. Cradling tuna casserole in their chubby hands, two neighbors in their Sunday best clacked up the drive. Their husbands, hands dug in their pockets, took their time walking behind them. Someone forgot to close the home's front door or it was purposively left open. The kitchen was overrun with other women making room on the counter for other casseroles and pies; pitchers of iced tea were loaded into the refrigerator, along with enough Coke, Diet Coke and Baptist ice to out-fit a multi-state Fourth of July picnic. Someone was running the dishwasher in the middle of the day. On the over-taxed refrigerator, a Scotch-taped pic-ture was crookedly displayed. Dailey's crayon portrait of her grandparents on their front stoop was widely praised for the beaming-sunshine smiles she assigned Richard and Grace Cool, who never failed to babysit at a moment's notice.

Steve Cool wanted a beer by IV if necessary. Instead, he found the iced tea, salads, and soda, Christ, so much soda. All they needed was a Moonbounce and a rental clown. Steve couldn't ask people to leave his par-ents' home, although he wished they would think of it themselves. He feared they might stay the summer.

Parker found her brother in the backyard hiding behind a brick barbe-cue grill their father built four years ago. She sat on the grass next to him. A ladybug fluttered onto her right knee. Parker watched it bee-line off her knee and in the direction of her upper thigh. Not so fast, ladybug.

"I want these people to leave," Parker said.

"Me, too, but they're here for Mom."

"Can they be somewhere else for Mom?"

Steve reached up and touched the brick backside of his father's grill, a solid thing.

"Want to eat something? God knows there's food," Steve said. "What is that mound of goo in Mom's big Tupperware bowl?"

"It's ambrosia."

"Is it multiplying?"

"Not if someone doesn't take it out back and shoot it first."

"I'll do it, I'll do it!"

Parker pledged to scavenge for beer.

"Failure is not an option," Steve said.

She got up, brushed off her black dress (arguably a tad short for the occasion), and walked through the back porch and into the kitchen. She checked in on Dailey in the living room; Parker didn't feel completely right leaving her with two aunts during some of the wake but she wanted to have some time alone with her brother. Behind the casseroles, a tub of ambrosia, and an open box of baking soda, two Pabst Blue Ribbons listed in the corner of the fridge. Parker confiscated the beers and avoided eye contact with four women she didn't know. She almost escaped the kitchen before a neighbor seized her arm.

"I'm so sorry about your father," she said. "My father died of a heart attack. He was 65 – three years younger than your dad."

Parker didn't know what to say. Margaret Griffin clearly had the better heart attack story.

"Take comfort in knowing your father has been promoted from labor to reward," Mrs. Griffin said.

"Will you excuse me," Parker said. "I'm going to promote myself from labor to beer."

The Cool children drank their father's favorite beer behind his home-made grill. They poured out some of the beer and watched it bubble into the grass. They whispered so not to be discovered by the grown-ups.

"Dad did like his Pabst," Parker said.

"So do hipsters," Steve said.

"You would know."

"Hey, remember our vacation in Ocean City in that rental house that smelled like rotten Campbell's soup?"

"Dad joined us a few days later. All the houses looked the same, and we watched him pull up into the neighbor's driveway," Parker said.

"He walked right in, sat right down and started talking to them. Dawned on him he was in the wrong house."

"Took him awhile."

"What did he ask them again?" Steve said.

"*So, where's the rest of the gang?*"

They choked up laughing before crying, as they heard and felt the noon-time detonations from Lone Star's quarry rumbling through their wake.

"Dad could talk the ear off a phone solicitor."

"Sometimes did," Parker added. And she remembered, always would, her father cradling the broken body of her childhood dog and promising to turn the rock quarry into a dog park. Broken promises are also prizes.

"Whose idea was it to have the wake *before* the service?" Steve said, swishing his warm Pabst.

"Dad's."

Richard Cool's will, updated in 2010, included four requests: 1. "Any wake should occur BEFORE any cemetery service so folks can eat/drink before heading out to the cemetery. Then they can drive home and be finished with the damn thing." 2. "Would not object to a simple cremation with my ashes placed in a Pabst Blue Ribbon can. If this offends my family, forget it." 3. "Someone read a good poem but make it short." 4. Along with my surviving wife and children, my granddaughter Dailey Grace Cavanaugh will be financially provided for by any and all means." His family would accommodate three of his wishes.

An hour later, Parker was riding in the front seat of a Cadillac hearse, as it crawled along Padonia Road to Parkview Memorial Gardens. She noticed the driver's shoes. They needed buffing. There was no excuse for scuffed shoes on the job. Parker wanted Steve to see them and silently confer, but he was in the back seat with their mother. The hearse was followed by an obedient train of cars passing single-file by the pet memorials, "Fresh Flowers Are Always Welcome" sign, and graves of fallen police officers and firefighters. Twenty-two cars eventually parked along the cemetery's back road adjacent to the eighth hole of a golf course. The driver of the nineteenth car in the procession locked his car for some reason. He stepped out, straightened his tie from Target in the reflection of the driver's side window, and took two deep breaths. His tie still leaned right despite his prep work.

Will saw the canopy, the fresh mound of dirt, other men in suits, the mahogany coffin. He snaked his way through graves marked Walker, Hart, Geppi, Roberts. A squirrel shredded his nut lunch atop the Hart tombstone.

On the back lot of Parkview Memorial Gardens, services began for Richard E. Cool, 68, of Cockeysville, MD. Grace Cool, Parker's mother, stood by the casket in a trance. Parker and Steve stood by her side, as the minister spoke generically about Mr. Cool. The minister offered no recognizable measure of the man. Wobbly but determined, Parker powered through a reading of Tennyson's "Crossing the Bar." ... *I hope to see my Pilot face to face when I have crost the bar.*

When the service ended, Parker hugged her mother, muttered thanks to the others for coming, and excused herself. Parker crossed six rows of graves until she found a marble boulder by the cemetery's duck pond. A spouting fountain pushed the algae away from the center of the pond. A bluegill flapped the water surface, and in the reeds, a bullfrog tried to turn over its engine. Only a doorknob of a city water tower marred the view. Three mallards moved in front of the fountain, which sent ripples against the bows of the ducks. Parker kicked off her black heels. Behind her at the grave site, fresh dirt was heaped high to withstand immediate erosion until sod could be planted. The canopy would be left up until tomorrow. Tripods of flower bouquets ringed Parkview's newest gravesite. Parker watched the ducks coast. She never saw him coming.

"Hey."

Will sat next to her on the marble boulder, quarried just four miles away.

"What are you doing here?"

"Your brother called me."

Will noticed Parker's hair had given up its blonde crusade and gone to the dark side. Close by, a golfer cursed his putter. Will looked over at the fresh flowers on Richard Cool's grave.

"I'm so sorry, Parker." He had never abruptly lost a parent but was losing slowly one, which might have been close to the same thing.

"Do you want to take a walk?"

She stood, straightened her black dress, and walked toward the pond. She was still barefoot. Will walked alongside her.

"I had my first beer on that boulder over there. First beer and first French kiss. Jim Vaughn felt me up over that hill on the right. God, why did I say that? What's wrong with me?" Parker said. In an emergency pivot, "My grandfather is buried there. There's a bench with his name on it, although they screwed up his middle initial."

They watched the last of the cars snake out of Parkview Memorial Gardens.

"Have you ever seen a rock quarry?" Parker said.

"Well, no."

"Today is your lucky day."

They walked to his noisy Honda. Will threw his tie into his backseat and brushed MapQuest directions to the cemetery off the passenger seat. He opened the car door for Parker, who, from an intimate location, felt an object in the shape of a small hard ball. She removed the golf ball from under her startled rump.

"I found it in the cemetery," Will said. During the service, he had spotted a golf ball buried like an Easter egg inch from his left foot. It was a Titleist, No. 4 with a golfer's black dot over the number. Although he hated golf, Will couldn't resist swiping lost golf balls. He told Parker at least he waited for the service to end before adding to his collection.

"I wouldn't have cared if you took that ball during the service. My dad would have done the same thing," she said. "He collected golf balls in shoe boxes. Must have had two hundred golf balls. I guess he wanted to be ready if he was ever overcome with the sudden urge to golf."

They both did a practice chuckle.

"I wish I could have met him. You met my dad, but it isn't the same thing."

"Don't say that. Your father is your father."

"True, but your dad didn't spend his days talking about tits, did he?"

"Probably did."

Parker told Will to take the right at Beaver Dam Road, the quarry would be on his left. There was a service road winding along the eastern rim of the engineered pit. A picnic table remained in this private place, which provided a panoramic view of the 500-foot deep hole in the earth. Will parked near the picnic table. There was no railing or fence. Sagging, thick trees encircled them. They sat on the picnic table, a rotting wooden thing. Parker gave the golf ball to Will.

"Think I can reach it?"

150

"If you do, you win a Grand Prize," Parker said.

He threw long and deep and swore saw the ball bounce along the shaved bottom of the quarry.

"What do I win?"

• • •

"Here?"

"Yes."

Parker sat atop the bleached, crippled picnic table.

"I'll get splinters."

"Why did you tell me about Jim Vaughn?"

"No reason. Maybe I went a little insane."

Will, standing, facing her, moved closer, her dress an open tent, partially.

"How did it feel?"

"Jim?"

"Yes, how did that feel the first time?" Will said.

"I was just…"

Both of Will's hands holding her knees.

"…making a little…"

Letting go of her knees, smoothing her dress, un-smoothing, a slight arch of her back, hands gripping an edge.

"…a little insane post-funeral conversation…"

Will bunched up her funeral dress up by her hips, scooting to the very edge of the picnic.

"Tell me, how did it feel, his hands. Did they feel like this?"

He softly rolled her breasts, as her hands moved between his legs, rubbing the seam of his charcoal funeral pants.

"I wanted…"

"You wanted Jim to do more to you on that boulder there where your grandfather is buried. You wanted his cock."

"I…did."

Her hand unbuckling his belt, unzipping.

"You wanted Jim to fuck you."

On schedule, a quarry detonation, rumbling the picnic table. Will slipped aside her Candy Apple thong, clearing away the slight fabric. He pushed inside her. Electric.

"I'll get splinters…"

"Yes, you will."

Chapter 17

During a lingering squall of guilt, Parker opened a bottle of Saint Clair pinot noir, a high-end number someone brought to her father's wake. As inexplicably, Parker had been rude to guests and far more astonishing, she and Will had christened a picnic table 25 minutes after the last shovel of dirt sealed in her father. What if her mother had stumbled upon them or that Margaret Griffin woman with the better heart attack story? Worse, worse, worse: what if her father's spirit dropped by at that moment? *So, where's the rest of the gang?*

"I'm sorry everyone," Parker said to no one.

She flipped through an IKEA catalog the size of a small, ignored phone book. "Textiles: Be brave. Be smart. Be you." Parker didn't know how to feel about textiles; generally, she had a problem with commitment regarding smart and brave IKEA items. Turning to a Grace Paley anthology, Parker landed on a short story, but her mind floated off. She found a yellow legal pad and unloaded:

I want to go back to school to become a vet
Math man.
Bring fresh flowers to cemetery
Visit mom more
W.P.L.
Call Alex back.
Start novel.
William P. Larkin

Besides wanting to be a vet – or a drummer – Parker wanted to be a novelist but her work in the field had resulted only in titles: *Old Souls. Stay in Your Lane. Gym Rat. Kiss Me Sober. Good Luck Road. Hard Candy.* And of this morning, *Splinter Girl.* A self-identified word nerd, she wondered if she had the bravery and stamina to write a book. Hadn't Mrs. Chisholm loved her essays in high school? "On the level of the sentence, you are a fine writer," she told Parker junior year. The teenager didn't know what that sentence meant, but it sounded writerly and made her feel like a writer. Then the days like rolling pins flattened out the years and there was a half-baked relationship, a career in domesticated animals, life with Dailey. Parker wondered if she had the bravery and stamina to book-dream anymore. Her body of literary work consisted of book titles, a dormant dog blog, and Post-Its that said things like "An impatient writer is a rejected writer" and "Writing is an act of faith – not a trick of grammar." All she wanted was to tell one beautiful story in her life. Or live one.

Her cell's ringtone erupted. She looked at the number.

"Hi."

"Hi."

Parker poured herself more Saint Clair.

"I still have a splinter."

"Is that a good or bad thing?" Will said.

"It's a splinter."

"Can I say something?"

"Please do," Parker said. "Wait, I know what you are going to say. You were feeling sorry for me. It was a mistake. It was one of those life and death insane moments where we both went crazy. But you still need to find out if you love your ex-wife."

"Wow. That was not at all what I was going to say. I wasn't feeling sorry for you. I was feeling something *for* you. I always have."

Parker felt the rare urge to shut up.

"I was feeling something unexpected. Something real." He remembered one other time with one other person answering a question so confidently. He had spent most of his life walking back emotions. Not now. "Shouldn't life…be arousing?"

Yes, it should be, she said to herself.

"And there's one more thing, for what it's worth."

Will told her he had been reading poetry and found a line he liked from an Italian poet named Pavese.

"The only joy in the world is to begin."

Not a sound from the other end of the phone, not even heavy poetry-loving breathing.

"Listen," Parker finally said, "I'm reading a Grace Paley short story and am in the middle of a sentence, but I would consider concluding the sentence another time if you would care to come over."

"I care to, very much."

"Bring poetry. Leave the golf balls."

She gave Will her address where 25 minutes later he arrived. Having moved out of her brother's house, Parker had found a funky apartment in Eastport enough blocks away (many blocks) from the million-dollar-plus waterfront homes at Horn Point. While tiny, Dailey's bedroom was cozy and outfitted in a My Little Pony motif. Her mother had made sure to bring the night light from her bedroom at Steve's, where Dailey was sleeping over tonight.

Will and Parker sat in her kitchen at opposite ends of an Ikea kitchen table featuring a Manny Machado Bobblehead as a centerpiece. The apartment was decorated in Christopher Guest movie posters, Santa Fe-looking pottery, enough poetry books to suffocate an English department, a mint condition 1955 Smith-Corona typewriter (with original case), and a sparkling new dog dish.

"Meet Dusty."

From around the corner wiggled in a dachshund named Dusty, who head-butted Will's hand to indicate he was required to pet the dog for an excessive period of time. Dusty conveyed this also by plopping her svelte rump on Will's sneakered foot.

"Where did you find this gorgeous girl?"

"She was brought to the office last week, a little banged-up, a little scared."

"You caved."

"Completely."

The three of them adjourned to Parker's sofa. She kicked off her shoes with a certitude that suggested bare feet were a house rule. Will took off his Nikes.

"Tell me about your marriage. We've never talked about that," Parker said.

Will sipped a glass of his wine, trusting himself more with wine these days. Wine minus the Nyquil.

"Our marriage became a routine. Marriages don't survive on routine, I learned."

The dachshund emitted a sound they both hoped was a tummy rumble. It was not.

"Dusty!"

An acidic ice-breaker. Will and Parker backed away slowly. To the sofa, to the sofa!

"Your turn," Will said.

"I met Alex junior year in high school English. He was a wrestler." Mentioned his sport as if it alone explained her first serious boy crush.

"And?"

"Things kind of snowballed from there. Meeting up a few years later. Dating. Living together...Dailey."

Will put his wine down. Not his thing, expensive or not, red or not.

"Can we not talk about this now?" Parker said. "Raise your hand if you're in favor of no more talking."

Both hands shot up.

• • •

Will woke to a paralyzed left arm cradling Parker's head. He was parched and in need of a light snack or TV break – maybe a hit of *Autopsy: The Last Hours of Karen Carpenter* or another savory viewing of *Behind the Candelabra*. But he didn't see Parker's remote. Will worried the candle on top of her dresser had burned through to the wood. The bedroom might soon be engulfed in flames, her smoke detectors put to the test. At the least, Will wished he could make a bathroom run.

Wake up, Parker.

He had severe breakfast needs (Will heard of a restaurant in Baltimore where they specialized in French toast made with Cap'n Crunch. Worth checking out one day). Come on Parker, up. How could a woman *never* change positions when sleeping? And the firmness of her mattress! Why not sleep tied to the mast of a sailboat?

The alarm clock's numbers blinked 5:58. Will remembered shedding his clothes five hours ago but had no recollection of putting his boxers back on. He traced his finger along the back of her upper arm and found a slight crater. With Houdianian agility, Will contorted himself whereby he could plant a minor kiss on what he believed was Parker's smallpox vaccination scar, which, while not a traditional erogenous zone, might work in a pinch. She stirred.

"Hey you," he whispered into the webbing of her ear. Parker stretched like a Lab waking from a cat nap, limbs at shaky attention then relaxing, eyes unshuttering.

"Well, hi," Parker said. "Is your arm OK?" She raised her head off the lifeless extremity. Will estimated full use of his arm by next Wednesday.

"How long have you been up?"

"Long enough to pay tribute to your scar," he said.

"My what?

"Your vaccination scar."

"Sorry, buckaroo. I'm far too young to have one."

Will goosed her under her arms.

"So, what was that deformity I was probing?"

"Look at you, Math Man with the vocabulary. The scar, if you must know, is from where I fell off my bike when I was a kid. I was riding on a dirt road inside the rock quarry."

Will's finger found the scar again.

"My, my, someone has a scar *and* picnic table kink."

In slow motion, Parker flipped over on Will's stomach and chest. She noted he was in his boxers, the navy blue numbers as he called them. He bought them in a pack of three that promised: "The Fly Will Not Gap." A man's fly must never gap.

"Still tired?"

"Oh, I'm awake," said Parker, her chin parked on his upper chest.

Having sensation back in his arm, his hand strolled over to her back then lower back and lower still. Soft, stringed fabric at hand, Will gently kneaded. Parker did not *purr* – she hated it when writers claimed women purr; cats *purr*, women make other noises – but she did emit an ultrasound that vibrated into Wills' chest. Parker kissed him there and started to move her hips. Will's fingers found the mini waistband to her red thong and peeled it a quarter down off her hip. Still too dark to detect even the faintest of a tan line. Parker shimmied out of her thong, and Will did the same with his boxers, the blue numbers. Her queen bed proved the creakiest thing on four legs. Maybe a blast of WD-40 would quiet the bastard as he thought and thought about the O's record weird losing streak on Sundays until, blessedly, Will didn't have to think anymore as they both shuddered and clutched, both slightly slick with perspiration.

She slowly ejected herself from her seat on Will's lap and swung over on her back. He draped his leg over hers. Her thong was balled on the floor.

"Hungry?"

"Ravenous," she said.

Will kicked off the sheet. Parker sat on her side of the bed and began re-assembling some kind of outfit for the day. She flipped Will his boxers with the fly that did not gap.

"I know a place," he said.

At Chick & Ruth's on Main Street, Parker ordered a Belgium Waffle with homemade strawberry topping, and Will committed to the Annapolis Cheese Steak Omelet – and from the menu's "Go Withs" section, two bagels with cream cheese, plus coffee, waters, and two pulpy OJs. Known for naming sandwiches after state politicians, this being a capital city, another Chick & Ruth's tradition was the standing for the morning "Pledge of Allegiance." Parker and Will stood to be respectful.

Will tipped the right amount for breakfast, and they walked out of the diner turned right toward Compromise Street. They stopped at the seawall.

"I want to talk about Alex. You have a child together. That's a pretty big deal, Parker."

"About the biggest."

"So, you two are together, not together, all three together, or just go golfing together?"

In a familiar pang, Parker felt cornered and defensive, as if she had done something wrong trying to raise a daughter alone as if *accused*.

"I don't think this is any of your business, Will."

"Not my business? After last night? After your father's funeral? After you helped me with my dying dog and my father? After …Applebee's?" He was looking deep enough into Parker's eyes to spot an auburn speck on her left iris.

"He's Dailey's father."

"And I'm going to go to jail because of him."

"Because of *him?*"

"No, not because of him. Because of me…"

But Parker had already stood up and walked off toward home and looked back only once.

• • •

She called Alex two days later, which should have given him enough time to pitch her idea to his lawyer. It had to be enough time since Will's hearing was next week. Why she was helping Will Larkin was beyond her. Well, not quite.

"Any news?"

"Don't you even say hi anymore?"

"I'm sorry, hi."

Alex explained that, according to his lawyer, no one person can drop criminal charges against a defendant. Once Will was officially charged with second-degree assault, the State of Maryland was in control, as in, The State of Maryland vs. William P. Larkin. A lawyer could meet with the State

Attorney's Office and communicate his client's desire to drop the charges, but it was the state's decision not to prosecute.

"So did your attorney talk to the State Attorney's Office?" Parker said.

"He did."

"And?"

"And what?"

She refrained from assaulting him herself, preferably with a deluxe vacuum cleaner to his groin.

"Please, Alex."

"Fear not, Park. Your boyfriend ain't going to the slammer. His virginity is safe thanks to me."

Alex, ever the poetic legal crusader, told Parker if she didn't believe him, just ask her boyfriend when he hears from his public defender, which should be any day now.

"I believe you," she said.

"About time I did right by you, eh? Plus, any dude who hits that fucking hard must really care about you."

"Thank you, Alex. From both of us."

"Just from you will do."

Chapter 18

The tipping point was the sloth.

Will returned home from getting OJ and Drano from the Safeway and found a shirtless Mack on his couch, a bag of UTZ barbecue chips between his legs, and a Resurrection Ale in his palm. In fairness, he paid for the provisions and the light bill and three-quarters of the rent. Still, the man looked homeless and a bit dangerous.

Kyle had come by to watch the Ravens-Bengals game on the NFL Network – a replay from two years ago. He and Mack looked like they hadn't moved since middle school. Two pizza boxes were on the sofa, and a smeared pizza wheel poked out from a seat cushion. It was 10:30 in the morning.

"I might be going to jail and this is what I come home to? Maybe I do need a little time away." Usually sarcasm, self-deprecation, or alcohol could deflect his anxiety and fears. But the *usual* wasn't working anymore, and Mack knew this before Will did.

"William, we're just trying to cheer you up. Get your mind off things," he said. "Answer me this, Riddler. Do you think as guys get older their earlobes get bigger?"

"My grandfather lived to be about 92, and his earlobes were enormous. You could paddle board on them," Kyle said.

Mack extended the thought. "Do men lose the hair on their legs when they get older? I see older dudes on the beach and their legs are hairless. I've studied it, and it scares the living fuck out of me."

Earlobes, old man leg hair. Will picked up a sofa cushion to smother himself. Kyle brought him a beer, which he waved off. Kyle turned to his chief source of information and entertainment, but Google could not render an instantaneous verdict regarding the effects of aging on male earlobes and leg hair. It was a shame to waste a search opportunity, though.

"Whatever happened to Ted Williams' head?" Mack said. "Google that head!"

Kyle typed in "Ted Williams' Head" and 5,400 searches came up. A daughter and son of Ted Williams, the famous Boston Red Sox, had their father's body cryonically frozen rather than have his ashes scattered off the Florida Keys as another daughter claimed her father desired. It was a scurvy piece of family business.

"Ted Williams rests suspended in two places," Kyle read aloud (he did have a good broadcasting voice). "The body stands upright in a 9-foot-tall cylindrical steel tank, while the head is stored in a steel can also fill with liquid nitrogen."

Eight minutes and three time-outs later, the NFL rerun was over. The Bengals beat the Ravens, again. But for those eight minutes, Will did manage to forget about his day of judgment.

"One more for the ditch?" Mack said.

"The bar is closed," Will said. "What happened to your job search?"

Mack informed his grumpy landlord he uploaded his resume on three job search sites. Listings for "Hot Projects recently added in your area" were e-mailed to Mack, who grew more despondent with each listing: ColdFusion Web Developer, ePublish Specialist, Front End Web Developer, Web Content Manager, Web Project Manager. Mack again kicked himself for not pursuing "The Real Housewives of Anne Arundel County," a porn site that stalled in its developmental stage. Will and Kyle had been standoffish about the project.

Mack reminded them he did have a stint as the sole employee of the Hertz rental location on West Street. He served two customers: One was under-aged and ineligible for Hertz's array of car rental services; the other customer robbed him (Mack gave him the keys to a Prius, but the armed man took Mack's wallet instead.) Mack was relieved of his position by the regional office in Glen Burnie, which cited the employee's unorthodox business hours – Mon-Wed. 1-3 p.m. – as the primary reason for termination, security concerns aside.

"What's your plan?"

"My plan is to escape the clutches of adulthood, William."

Kyle stood to tidy. He found a Hefty bag for the empties and pizza boxes. He fished around the kitchen for something to get pizza stain out of Will's only sofa.

"Drinking in the morning, frozen heads, old men's earlobes, hairless legs. This isn't helping, Mack."

"But you haven't seen the Big Reveal!"

Mack read about a B-list pop star renting a two-toed sloth for her boyfriend's birthday party. Weeks ago, he followed a Google trail to Slothville, the headquarters for a sloth appreciation society. After consuming three videos and buying a sloth calendar, Mack was determined to rent a sloth for Will's home. Trouble was he couldn't find an outfit to rent him one. He'd have to go all in. For $7,200, an exotic pets supply company in Florida (the state teemed with them) promised delivery of a "healthy" two-toed sloth to anywhere in the United States. Prohibitive state laws involving exotic pets did not appear to be a sales impediment.

Despite its adorable appearance and Internet popularity, a sloth – and to a larger degree an Eastern snapping turtle – is not an ideal house pet given its dietary, environmental and clinical needs. Their stomachs can be a tad sensitive. The slowest of mammals, they are also unparalleled sleepers. When not foraging or making little sloths, the two-toed sloth can spend the other 20 hours of the day hanging upside down motionless from a tree branch. They can also bite when threatened. Threats include, but are not limited to, living unexpectedly in someone's home.

"William, if you would follow me," Mack said. Kyle stayed behind. He felt lousy enough helping Mack de-crate the sloth when Will was at Parker's for the night.

Off the kitchen, 13 steps led down to Will's unfinished basement. At step two, Will encountered the sloth by its rank, earthen smell, like a rainforest way past its expiration date. Mack had set the basement's thermostat at 90 to create what he hoped was a suitably warm and humid climate for the new roommate. At the bottom of the stairs, Will witnessed in the darkened makeshift solarium a jungle gym with ropes, platforms, and a slide. Leaves, twigs, tree limbs and branches had been carefully organized on, through and around the outdoor playhouse relocated to his basement. His punching bag and stand had been pushed into a corner. Clinging from one of the thick ropes, the sloth slept as if positioned by a bored taxidermist. Will was at a loss to compare with any conviction the mammal to another animal (a cross between a seal and a depressed raccoon?) but did feel the grinning creature resembled his mother's great uncle Oscar.

Mack felt his friend didn't look well, so he slowly – sloth-like, one could say – explained how the sloth came to be living in the basement and how Mack would assume total care and maintenance of the exotic.

"You don't have to worry about a thing. I'm taking care of it. Bought it dog chow, yogurt, and mealworms. Someone was throwing out a jungle gym on your street so I scarfed that baby up. I put newspapers down and everything. I think a sloth really cheers the place up. It's been too goddamn depressing around here. Want to pet it?"

"Fuck no I don't want to pet it," Will said, keeping his distance and noting the thorny length of the sloth's two toes. He already had his brush with nature in Stevensville. "Have you finally lost your mind?"

"But look how cute it looks," Mack said.

"Is it alive?"

"I believe so, yes."

"I can't do this anymore, Mack. Anything of this. You need to move out."

Mack reached out to pet the sloth but it actually moved, so he quickly withdrew his hand. He turned to his friend.

"I guess you forgot your promise."

They had met in middle school and became friends from gym class those first few weeks of sixth grade. By virtue of the alphabet, their gym coach joined Will Larkin and John McGuire at the hip for any and all team selections. The first thing Will noticed was what the rest of the boys in gym noticed about John McGuire: his family must be poor. The kid wore the same green, no-name Polo and same blue, no-name jeans every day to school. He didn't look *clean*. In particular, his hair was stringy and greasy. Will, whose parents were what people called "well-off," guessed John's folks didn't have enough money to buy him shampoo much less new school clothes.

Dressing out for gym became John McGuire's daily nightmare, the exposing ritual shrinking his size and spirit. His one set of clothes became more obvious as was his lack of hygiene. The boys in the locker room didn't bother to learn his name. They started calling him *Hey, Mack*, and soon their taunts adopted the moniker. *Hey, Mack* when are you going to wash that greasy shit mop of hair? *Hey, Mack* when are you going to clean our jocks? *Hey, Mack* if you don't take a fucking shower and clean that hair we'll do it for you. The bullying continued for three weeks interrupted only by the four days the boy stayed home pretending to have pneumonia.

Then one Friday in gym, after Larkin and McGuire managed to win a two-on-two basketball game, the other boys had enough of *Hey, Mack*. He couldn't fend them off with his fortressed humor anymore. While Will got dressed after showering, three boys dragged John McGuire, in his only set of school clothes, into the tiled far corner of the showers. Two boys held his head under the cold water as a third boy doused his hair with an open bottle of shampoo. Expecting to go eat lunch in the cafeteria with his friend, Will scanned the locker room but didn't see John.

He heard him.

He heard him screaming and cursing, a cursing so advanced, so infused with *fuck* that even a middle school boys' locker room blushed. Will raced to the corner of the showers where he saw his friend, on his knees, his eyes blinking shampoo. Something inside of him detonated. Eleven-year-old Will Larkin hurled himself into the scrum, throwing and landing punches to their backs, faces, heads, kidneys, groins. Stunned, the boys fell away and off their soaked prey. Will dragged him back to his locker, grabbing three clean white towels along the way. Trying not to cry – anything but that

– John McGuire cried, as Will helped him get the shampoo out of his eyes. They sat on the bench by their lockers to catch their breath.

"Looks like you're stuck with me," Will said.

"Promise?"

"Promise, John."

"Call me Mack. You're the only one I'm going to let call me that from now on. Now let's get some fucking lunch."

Will never told a soul.

"Yes, I remember," he told his friend now. "You can stay. But the sloth has to go."

"Understood. Now let's get the fuck out of the basement. It stinks like a locker room in here."

Upstairs, Mack asked Will about any updates on Parker as he set out to somehow return a sloth to Florida (the return policy was fuzzy). Knowing his friend's capacity for retaining personal information, Will gave Mack a *Reader's Digest* condensed version of his hurtful exchange with Parker and how something or someone always seemed to be working against them.

"So, what's your plan?"

"I plan to be with her," Will said. "But first I need a job."

• • •

He had forgotten about vespers until his mother brought it up on the phone.

"Would you come with me this evening? I know you have a lot on your mind, dear. But I have something important to discuss with you." Me, too, but Will decided not to tell his mother about the hearing tomorrow. His father's worsening condition was enough worry and heartache. Soon enough he wouldn't have a choice but to tell her, but not today. (The public defender called Will twice to remind him of the court date and time and to say their request for a bench trial was granted; a judge would decide his fate.)

His mother's church, St. Gregory's, held the evening prayer service at 5:30 p.m. The literature said nothing about a homily, guitar mass or shaking hands with the man next to you in the pew. Vespers, Will hoped, didn't

166

involve any personal interaction. At 5 p.m., Will picked up his mother and they drove three miles to the church. She couldn't leave her husband alone, so a neighbor stayed with Bill.

At the church, Will opened the heavy, street-side door. St. Gregory's, deep and chilled, had that new church smell. There was a comforting shabbiness to the church illuminated now by long-stemmed candles placed on the ground at every seventh pew and on the altar. Five people sat as far as five people can sit from each other in a church. Will and his mother chose the sixth pew from the back. Will was not a church-faring man and had no talent for praying. The few times he had gone to church he feared knocking something over – a candle, a cross, a nun.

An older man, in his Sunday best and relying on a cane, came in behind them – his dress shoes squeaking on the floor. In his jeans and University of Maryland sweatshirt, Will felt woefully underdressed for the world of ancient chant and incense. In this cave of silence, he stared at the ceiling, then at the stained-glass windows. The wooden pews were unforgiving. After ten minutes of silence, Will hoped either the chanting would come to life or the sensation in the left quadrant of his ass. A mother and two girls, maybe eight or nine each, sat four pews in front of him.

"You are a prayer hog!" one girl whispered to the other in the cave of silence. "Mom! Lily called me a prayer hog!" Whispers do carry in a church.

Seven robed figures, moving at break-monk pace, entered the church stage right. They bowed before the altar then disappeared into an anteroom. A voice was heard clearing and another. Will heard his mother's breathing. On silent cue, the bells of St. Gregory's North Tower chimed, and the Vespers Schola began chanting. Will managed to make out the outline of the Lord's Prayer. The prayer hogs were quiet. Incense, released somewhere behind them, scented the church, like the faint smell of a gift shop in Maine.

"Your father came once."

"You're kidding."

"I liked him being with me here," she whispered. "It was very hard to get your father to try anything new."

Will didn't believe in miracles and he was pretty sure he didn't believe in God, but he felt overcome by the spiritual setting. He knelt on the carpeted pew below and asked above for another chance.

At 5:00, the chanting stopped and the hooded singers walked out followed by the handful of congregates after offering a few dollars and change to St. Gregory's for the pleasure of its vespers.

"I owe you dinner," his mother said.

They walked three blocks down Bay Bridge Road to McDougals, a popular Irish bar, and restaurant known for being popular. The Larkins ordered water, one New Castle beer, the shepherd's pie, and the bangers and mash. Ancestral Irish murals, pennants, and flags were the interior decoration. County Kerry, County Limerick, County Cork, County Tipperary.

"Where was your side of the family from again?"

"County Baltimore," his mother said, forging a smile.

Finishing her beer, she noticed her son wasn't drinking – no need to stick a neon sign on it. The shepherd's pie, and bangers and mash arrived, and they wondered how people could stomach Irish food at first sight. The meal was delicious.

"I made a decision," she said. "We both know your father is worse. I'm afraid the next time he walks out of the house, he'll hurt himself or... I don't want to think about it. I can't take care of him by myself anymore, dear. I can't give him the help he needs anymore."

For her husband, every day at home was new and every experience and object: his morning bowl of Honey Nut Cheerios; his faded green Adirondack chair on the widow's walk; his binoculars; the view of the harbor; the feel of tepid bath water on his toes; the wonder of radio; the comfort of long memory. As his mind failed, his spirits appeared unmarred. His wife read about the curious development in David Shenk's book *The Forgetting*. "Ever-freshness," Shenk said, "may be considered an Alzheimer's consolation prize."

Will angled his chair to face her.

"He talks about dying."

"What does he say?"

"He talks about what he'll miss."

"What will he miss?"

"He says he'll miss the smell of bacon and wood smoke."

She told Will she called the Somerset Assisted Living & Alzheimer's Care facility and told them she had made a decision. They were abundantly sympathetic, and too-soon the paperwork was done. Money, mercifully, was not an issue.

"When do you want to do this?"

"Within the month. They have an opening... of course, they have an opening. The staff seems very professional and friendly. Your father will have his own room. TV. Bathroom. Even a small balcony. Like a widow's walk but with guardrails."

"A month?" Will imagined the unimaginable: stuck in jail and not being able to help her move his father.

"We'll take him together, Mom," Will said, quieting her shaking shoulders with his arms. Barb Larkin righted herself and dabbed her face with the corner of her napkin. She reached into her purse and handed Will three folded $20 bills. Just a little pin money. No, I'm good Mom, really. She tucked the money in his hand anyway.

"Do you want to hear a joke?" she said.

Her people, who did trace their roots to County Baltimore 40 miles upstate, were not known for their jokes. In point of family fact, Will never heard his mother or father tell a joke. He knew of none himself.

"What's Irish Alzheimer's?"

"I don't know. What's Irish Alzheimer's?" Will said.

"It's when you forget everything but your grudges."

The people at a nearby four-top looked at the Larkins as if they had never heard people laughing at an Irish restaurant before.

• • •

The week before his hearing and after scouring journalismjobs.com and other such websites, Will nearly gave up finding an entry-level job in journalism until Kyle told him about an opening at the weekly in Eastport. The offices of *The Eastporter* were in a three-story row house on Chester Avenue. To prepare for his interview, he channeled one of his father's favorite movies, "Kramer vs. Kramer," where Dustin Hoffman's character absolutely must get a job to keep custody of his son. Will needed a job in the desperate hope of convincing the State of Maryland he deserved another chance.

He unearthed his resume, injected it with trumped-up claims of vast experience writing for his college newspaper, *The Diamondback.* A journalism major (briefly) at the University of Maryland, Will did write two articles that were published, including one on the fitness regime of the Lady Terrapins who won the National Championship that year. He brought his thin resume – including references from three Lakeview teachers including Terri – to his first newspaper interview.

"May I help you?" asked the woman in the homey lobby of *The Eastporter.* She bore a disquieting resemblance to Kathy Bates in "Misery," but Will was often prone to snap movie comparisons.

"Yes, I'm here to see..." he said, before channeling Hoffman, "I need a job, and I need a job today."

"Do you have an appointment?"

"No, but I am here."

"I am here, too," the Bates woman said.

Two people, very much there.

"I need a job. It's important," he blurted.

"We already have four reporters." The Bates woman made *four* sound like they were overstocked with reporters, a regular Sam's Club of a newspaper.

"May I speak with your managing editor?"

"My what?"

"Your managing editor? The person in charge." (Kyle provided Will a basic outline of a newsroom's organizational chart complete with job titles and enough journalese to get him through the interview, they both hoped.)

"I'll see if Ms. Thompson is *here."*

Will took a seat in a floral, puffy couch and flipped through several "Best Of" issues of *Annapolis Style* magazine: Best Doctors, Best Places to Meet Singles, Best Lawyers, Best Crab Cakes. If pressed, what would be his best "Best of" story pitch? For some reason, Will thought of Best Classroom Dissections. He remembered dissecting owl pellets in high school biology. When dissected, the pellets revealed treasure troves of rodent and small bird skeletons and other bony remains of really dead things. Owl pellet dissection was generally preferred over, say, pigeon dissection. He wrote "Owl Pellets?" in his first reporter's notebook, another gift from Kyle on the occasion of this hopeful day.

"Hello, I'm Ms. Thompson. Can I help you?"

Ms. Thompson – perhaps 5'11, 45-50 years of age, freckly nose, a whiff of a Baltimore accent, wearer of Ann Taylor Loft – did not resemble Kathy Bates.

"My name is Will Larkin, and I understand you have a job opening. I am here to interview for it."

Ms. Thompson confirmed the job vacancy; one of her part-timers had left to take a job in PR at St. John's College.

"Have you worked in journalism?"

His voice cracking, Will said his experience was limited to writing articles for his college newspaper, but journalism had always been an interest, which was remotely accurate.

"I'll keep you mind. Thank you for taking time out of your day to stop by."

Failing to achieve Hoffman-like results, Will found his way out. Walking back across Spa Creek Bridge from Eastport to downtown, he bought a pretzel and lemonade, found a bench, and watched a water taxi bob in Ego Alley. He called Kyle and told him things had not gone well. By noon, he couldn't stand sitting on a bench a second longer and walked home.

• • •

The Men's Warehouse charcoal suit, his only suit, was snug in the waist. He figured he'd leave an hour early to give himself plenty of time to get to Annapolis District Court out on Rowe Boulevard. Never be on time – always be early, Bill Larkin always preached. Will wished he had his father at his side.

Having parked at the nearby Naval Academy parking lot and with 40 minutes to spare, he sat on the brick steps of the courthouse waiting for his public defender. The lawyer said Will wouldn't have to address the court. Will hadn't prepared to say anything; no, that wasn't true. After four drafts, Will abandoned his effort to write a heartfelt response and explanation for his crime. The words sounded flimsy and warped by desperation.

The courthouse grounds overlooking the bulbous Navy water tower featured a landing pad of rolling greenery with benches for those needing to collect their thoughts and gird themselves for the business awaiting them inside. The centerpieces of the natural waiting room were free-standing, classical columns. The eight structures, named for architect Benjamin Henry Latrobe, appeared sown from the ground beneath them. Will walked in between them as if playing hide-and-seek in slow motion. A ground-level plaque said the columns were made from Italian marble. Will felt the cool strength of a column and imagined it quarried Cockeysville marble from Parker's old neighborhood.

"There you are! I've been looking for you," said a voice behind him. His public defender was out of breath and sweating. "Good news, Will. Very good news." Will's legs began to wobble so he gripped one of Latrobe's columns.

"*Nonolle prosequi.*"

"What?"

"You're not being prosecuted for assault. The State's Attorney's Office dismissed the charge."

"I don't understand."

"His attorney requested the State's Attorney's drop the charges based on his client's wishes. Apparently, Mr. Alex Cavanaugh had a change of heart."

Fearing no column could hold him and rather than collapse in a fetal ball of exoneration, Will sat down among the marble pillars of justice.

"Thank you."

"Don't thank me," the public defender said. "Thank *him.*"

Three times Will stopped by Gold's Gym in hopes of finding manager and personal trainer Alex Cavanaugh to thank him, but he was out each time. Twice he drove to the Annapolis Animal Hospital in hopes of finding Parker. Only Parker, he imagined, knew Alex's heart well enough to change it. But she wasn't working either when he came by. Had their deal – could it be that? – brought them back together? A fresh start? Leaving unreturned phone messages didn't alleviate Will's creeping suspicion.

Had he lost any chance with Parker in the deal?

Chapter 19

Barb Larkin was distracted when Will gave her the news about the charges being dropped. It had been two weeks and none of it had sunk in.

"Well, that's nice dear," she said, distantly. "Today is the day."

He had nearly forgotten.

He called Parker but still no answer. He hadn't spoken to Terri since his father went missing, but she deserved to know.

"It's Dad."

"What's wrong? Tell me. I can be there in 20 minutes."

"You don't have to, Terri. I just thought you should know we're moving him today."

"Twenty minutes."

She beat Will to the house by 10 minutes, as Barb Larkin watched from her kitchen window. She went out to the driveway to hug her.

"You came, dear."

"Of course," Terri said.

"Until Will gets here and we're all ready to go, could you please go inside and turn on the baseball game for Bill?"

Bill Larkin was out on his widow's walk looking through the wrong end of his binoculars. The sky was a cue chalk blue with winds pushing out of the northwest. From a neighbor's tulip poplar, starlings shot out like a cannon and assumed a defensive formation. The harbor water was tea-colored, as usual. Terri turned on the O's game in the family room, as Will's Honda announced its arrival.

He had been spared the packing. His mother selected the clothes her husband needed. Given the one bedroom, there was surprisingly little to bring, which didn't seem right. The man should have his old books and

James Taylor records, but the staff assured her Somerset had an extensive book and music library. She did pack her husband's completed and blank baseball scorecards – and his binoculars. Most of the man's clothes were left in his closet, including his London Fog overcoat with the missing middle button. The *Playboys* could stay.

Two framed photos were chosen for the move: Will, as a young boy, holding a fish, and a 1978 photograph of Bill and Barb Larkin at a forgettable block party. He hated block parties, but a neighbor's camera candidly caught him smiling at something she said. He kept the picture on his dresser for 38 years.

Will and Terri followed his mother's car eight miles out of Annapolis. Somerset Assisted Living was easy to find; it was the only gated, country-club-looking building off Sweet Air Road. An orphaned golf course had been converted into walking trails for residents, and a re-purposed putting green fronted the entrance. On the grounds, an osprey nested atop one of the telephone poles. Four staff members greeted Mrs. Larkin as she opened the passenger side door for her husband, who wore a new Polo shirt and khakis. She had helped him on with the clothes because he should look presentable. Will's car swooped in behind her car and then Terri's. They all walked in together.

His private room overlooked a small courtyard with shrubs and two garden benches. Inside the room, the single bed looked stunted, as if a bed for a circus acrobat or young boy. The bathroom was fitted with handles in the shower; the toilet was raised and surrounded by a rubber railing; a single deep sink. She unpacked her husband's few things and fit them into the four-drawer dresser. The photographs sat on his new dresser. Will put his father's scorecards on the night table along with his binoculars and his visor from Harris' Crab House.

After settling in (if settling in was possible), Will's mother led her husband to the community room to meet more staff and the other residents. *Your husband will meet new and interesting people here*, a staffer named Bonnie had told his wife.

"Here we go," Will told Terri.

They followed his parents into an ample yellow room encircled with windows and fitted with card tables, L-shaped sofas and a flat-screen TV set on a low volume. Ansel Adams prints hung on the walls. A cart rolled by filled with pens, pencils, poker chips, chalk, large pieces of colored paper and sponge watercolors. Another floater, Will thought. By an upright piano, a Somerset volunteer in her early 60s led a sing-along.

"Mom, do you recognize the tune?"

Barb Larkin watched her husband sit at one of the card tables. Someone shuffled and dealt a deck of shiny red Bicycle cards.

"'A Pretty Girl Is Like a Melody.' My dad used to sing it to me at bedtime."

Terri walked to the card table. Bill Larkin said he couldn't talk because he was in the middle of a hand, but she could join them later if she wanted. His former daughter-in-law laid her hand on his right forearm and said thanks, but she wanted to say hello before she left. Come back and see me, he said.

Leeds Walker arrived 20 minutes later. He hugged Barb and shook Will's hand. They agreed the place seemed fine.

"Will, I bought a Zodiac to knock around in. If you ever want to take it out, just ask. My only condition is to have Marcus or me go over a few basics with you first."

"Like a float plan?"

"And a tide chart," Leeds Walker said.

Will almost laughed but caught himself. Leeds Walker excused himself to say hello to his old friend. He wasn't gone long. Another round of cards was underway. Leeds Walker didn't look up until he was out of the community room.

"All right, then. Barb, I'll be back to visit. Will, take care of yourself and your mother."

"Yes, sir."

He hugged them both before walking out.

"Dear, if you could say your goodbyes now. I'm going to stay with your father awhile longer."

The sing-along group chose for its next tune, "There's No Business Like Show Business." The selection caught Will off-guard and he couldn't stop himself this time. A staff member touched his arm and told him it was all right to laugh here. Laughter was healthy. They wanted Somerset to be a happy place for the residents.

"Does your father have a favorite song we could sing?"

"Do they know any James Taylor?"

The woman said she could ask. Terri released Will's hand (how long had she been holding it?) and said she'd wait in the lobby. He walked to the poker table where his father was collecting his cards. Will touched his shoulder to get his attention. Bill Larkin looked up.

"Do you want us to deal you in?"

"Not today, next time. Or maybe I can come and watch an Orioles game with you."

"Oh, do you like baseball?"

"It's the thinking man's game," Will said.

Tears wobbled down his cheek and chin before settling on his collar. His father thanked him for coming, but he wanted to get back to his card game. Will kissed the top of his head.

"I'll see you soon, Dad."

Bill Larkin didn't look up from his game. In the corner of the community room, residents stood around the piano and sang "Happy Days Are Here Again." They remembered every word. In the lobby, Terri took Will's hand again. They walked out to the newly paved visitors' parking lot. Overhead, two turkey vultures tilted in what could pass as a western sky. A dusty black BMW was parked in the lot.

"Terri called. Said you'd be here," Mack said. Christina sat on the passenger side.

"We're going to the beach house while I still have it," he said. "Oh, here's your house key. I moved out." There went half the rent.

"William, I highly recommend you reconsider the merits of baths."

"Maybe I will, Mack. A man can change."

"How's your dad?"

"Winning at poker, but everyone here wins at poker. Looks like he has made friends already. Mom is still in there."

"Hang in there, buddy."

"I'm a fighter, remember?"

Will looked beyond Somerset's parking lot to what was once a fairway. Long lost golf balls were out there waiting to be hoarded. Terri walked up and smiled at Mack, who was making the slow trip in his pocket for his car keys.

"Have fun at the beach," Terri said.

"Don't talk about earlobes and frozen heads and don't go buying a sloth."

"William, a man can change."

They watched Mack drive off from the Somerset Assisted Living facility. They felt their hands drop away from each other.

"Thank you for coming."

"What are ex-wives for?" Terri said, weakly chuckling. "Actually, I thought she'd be here."

"I haven't talked to her lately."

Will stood as if posing for a White House portrait.

"So…?"

Still like pulling cemented wisdom teeth with this guy, this aggravating, sweet man.

"Christ, Will, just give me the outline."

An outline he could manage.

"Parker is a vet tech. I met her when I brought in Dean for the last time. She helped me with him. She has a little daughter. I got drunk and scared them both. I got arrested *again*. Lost my teaching job, as you know. But I kind of saved her daughter's life. And I almost went to jail but didn't. I almost lost everything."

"But not her."

"I hope not," Will said. "She likes poetry."

"You don't say."

The stab of details didn't roll off Terri but didn't crush her either. She surprised herself by feeling proud of the first man she ever loved and knowing, hoping, not the last.

"Can I ask you something?"

"Of course," she said.

"Why did you leave me?"

"I needed someone to care and pay attention just a little more. I think I needed a grown-up."

"Yeah, I've heard about those grown-ups. They're everywhere."

Terri smiled.

"I'm looking at one. Oh, the irony."

Irony must be one of those English teacher things. Will smelled her hair and felt the small of her back and wondered if she still crab-picked through the *Times* on Sundays, still preferred poppy seed bagels, and still loved New York City and rollercoasters.

"I'm sorry."

"For what?"

"For Dean, for us, for everything."

He took her in his arms.

"Is this our goodbye hug?"

"It is, Terri Morrow, first girl I ever loved."

Will kissed her briefly, softly.

"You go find the second girl you ever loved. Promise?"

Will nodded and stepped back. "Promise you won't wear a Red Sox jersey to Camden Yards ever again. I'm extremely serious."

"A woman can change," Terri said.

• • •

After up-ending eight shoeboxes in his closet, Will found the photograph. It was his only fish picture, and it had never been to a fish picture party.

Summer, 1995. Great Smoky Mountains National Park. L.G. Mills Fish Camp. Will caught six rainbow trout. The pond was over-stocked and given the odds against the stock, successful fishing was guaranteed; that, and no casting or other discernable angling skill set was required. Like his father taught him, the boy used his thumb to hold one of the fish under its gill plate. It wasn't hard or gross. Will, in a white T-shirt and over-sized sunglasses and shorts that went up to his belly button, held the trout away from his body as his father snapped a picture from his Kodak. They ate the fish for dinner and no meal tasted as sweet since.

Will taped the fish picture to the refrigerator along with his "Float Plan" and a magnificent drawing of a warthog.

Chapter 20

She finally picked up.

"Hi."

"Hi."

Will resisted asking where she had been trusting instead to read the tone of her voice.

"I still owe you a better outing. Actually, I owe you everything."

"Don't mention it. And by that I mean, of course, mention it often as you like," Parker said, laughing. She accounted for her spot absences at work and radio silence between them. She needed time alone to try and calm *her* jittery soul.

"I tried to find Alex to thank him. Do you know where he is?"

"Don't have a clue."

Will thought he would split open from missing her.

"I missed you, math man. So, what kind of outing?"

"It's a surprise."

Not a Zodiac ride, please God.

"For the two of us?"

"The three of us. I want Dailey to come. Please."

• • •

The boating forecast for Saturday called for 72 degrees, winds out of the north-northwest at 8 mph. with possible gusts, fog, and rain – visibility four miles. At 12:45 p.m., 26 people stepped off the dock behind the Annapolis Waterfront Hotel and onto the Schooner *Woodwind*. High school crew members Sam and Hannah told folks to sit anywhere except beyond the rope in the bow. The captain, a solidly-tanned woman named Sandy, launched her thrice-daily lecture on the inherent frailties of the sailboat's electrical head. Sam and Hannah ran down the beer and wine for sale. Soda was free.

The captain left the dock under power and after the sailboat emitted a prolonged horn blast that made one passenger, a 6-year-old girl lacquered in Coppertone SPF 30 and wearing crooked Ray-Bans, nearly jump out of her sensible boat shoes. Will checked on Parker who looked sensational.

As they moved away further from the dock, Will explained to Dailey that boats blow their horn to talk to other boats. Like drivers honk their car horns. She appeared to accept the explanation but did not like her mother coating her ears with more sunblock.

"Ears aren't that important," she declared.

"Sorry pal, we got to get every nook and cranny."

"What's a cranny?"

"Sailor talk for ears."

They sat midship, starboard side, with Dailey on the other side of them. Parker and Will held hands, a first. How they could have waited so long to hold hands stumped and shocked them, but there they were, holding hands on a schooner. Parker noticed Will's ring finger was bare, as the *Woodwind's* horn blew. Dailey nearly jettisoned over the State House dome as the colonial Annapolis skyline grew smaller.

"Are they going to blow their horn again?" Dailey asked.

"When we come back, but I'll warn you," Will said.

Parker reiterated to her daughter the absolute fact sea monsters – notably the Loch Ness monster – did not frequent these bay waters. They would probably see osprey nests on harbor buoys or maybe, if they were blessed, they'd see a bald eagle, but no Nessie. *The Woodwind* eased out of the harbor past a colony of moored boats.

"Want to play a game?" Will said.

"What game?" Dailey said.

"It's called I Spy Boat Names. Only special people who know their alphabet can play along. If you can't read the name on the boat, read the letters. Who wants to go first?"

"I will," Parker said.

She stood and held tight to the rope railing.

"I spy… *Rock Quarry.*"

A gust of wind almost knocked Dailey's floppy pink hat into the bay. Parker adjusted the hat's wind cord.

Will scanned the moored boats.

"My turn," he said. "I spy… *Picnic Bench.*"

Flirting via phony boat names – now *their* thing.

Dailey tried standing but felt the boat move under her feet, so she plunked back down. She kept her eye peeled for boat names. The captain turned off the engine, and *The Woodwind* was under sail and quiet as a church before vespers. The crew helped volunteers raise the mainsail, its red and green telltales gauging the wind coming across the sail. A brief lecture on the boom was delivered, as the schooner prepared to tack. As the aluminum boom passed overhead, the wooden craft creaked and shifted its thick weight.

Dailey straightened her mother's hand-me-down Ray-Bans and watched the boats bounce and juke by. The boats were too fast, so she set her sights on a white sailboat slowly cutting across their bow. Sandy and her crew waved and yelled something to the sailors, who laughed. Dailey didn't see people in the fast boats waving or talking to people in other fast boats. Sailors seemed nicer.

"I spy… the letter W," Dailey said.

Will looked at Parker, who shook her head.

"Sailor girl, you need to give us more clues than that."

"W…A…R…T."

Will and Parker smiled, as a lull in the wind kept the shadowing sailboat close to the schooner.

"I'm still stumped, sailor girl," Parker said.

"H…O…G."

"Will, I don't spy any boat with those letters. Do you think someone is playing a trick on us?" Parker said.

They looked at Dailey, whose nose was shading pink.

"Do you both give up?"

They said they did.

"It spells WARTHOG. I spy a boat called WARTHOG!"

"Give that girl a free soda," Will said, hailing Sam who went below deck to snag a Pepsi and two more sodas for the grown-ups.

The Woodwind passed a buoy as it cut toward the opening of Whitehall Bay. Atop the buoy, a mother osprey fidgeted in her sticky nest of twigs. She was a radiant dark brown with a white head, black eye stripe, and a dark-spotted necklace. The schooner passed by her and her two hungry chicks.

"Where's the dad?" Dailey asked.

"Oh, he's flying around here somewhere looking for food. He'll catch a fish and bring it back for them all to have lunch," Will said.

"What if he doesn't come back?"

"Then he's a stupid head," Parker said. "And we sail on without him."

• • •

The great schooner approached the spans of the Bay Bridge, the captain asked for volunteers. Parker took her iPhone out of her backpack and prodded Will and Dailey take a turn at the mammoth wheel.

"Go on," Parker said. "I know you two aren't nervous about steering this itty-bitty sailboat with all these people watching you. Go on. I'll take your picture. I heard a rumor Uncle Steve is planning another party – a Sailboat Picture Party."

Clutching the rope railings and ever-mindful of the fickle boom, Will and Dailey made their way to the stern where, without much ado and less instruction, the captain handed the boat over to them.

"Where do I… aim?"

"Do you see the middle span of the bridge?" the captain said.

"Yes," Will said.

"Aim for that."

Will took the wheel, and the schooner acted accordingly. With one hand steady on the wheel, Will used his free hand to tug Dailey into position. She was sandwiched between the wheel and Will, as Parker steadied herself on a life vest locker to take pictures.

"Take the wheel, Dailey."

She reached up to grip two of varnished wooden spokes of the wheel. Parker took eight pics, three of which showed a man smiling as he stood directly behind the girl with the pink nose. Fifteen minutes from City Dock and back under the captain's control, *The Woodwind* trimmed its sails, and the boat was under power again. Boat traffic thickened as the schooner glided into Annapolis Harbor.

"Get ready," Will told Dailey. "Here comes the horn blast."

The girl took the blast in stride.

After crew members tied off at the dock, the captain cut the engine. There had been no emergencies with the electrical head. No one marooned on an island. No one decapitated by the boom. Some passengers played I Spy Boat Names and steered and saw an osprey nest. A girl in crooked Ray-Bans was seen resting her head in her mother's lap. And not one sea monster was spotted – just a sailboat allegedly named WARTHOG.

Chapter 21

At an Eastport seafood restaurant called Catch and Release, they sat by the window under a jaundiced sailfish hanging from the ceiling. Red lights were strung along the ceiling where mounted tarnished trombones and tubas formed a sad *Music Man* tableau. An inscription on a napkin was framed on the wall: "I promise to be good," the pledge from a quarrelsome regular. Near the bathrooms, a pock-marked bulletin board showcased bumper stickers – "WRNR," "There is no life west of the Chesapeake Bay" – and posters of the bar's occasional entertainment: the Eastport Oyster Boys and guitarist Jonathan Stone.

Ms. Thompson ordered the mussel chowder and shrimp salad sandwich. Will, who copycatted her order, wasn't planning to pay for lunch because he wasn't planning to have lunch with a newspaper editor, who shocked him by calling him. He knew he should tell her about his arrest and termination from the Anne Arundel County School system, but he didn't.

"Thank you for seeing me again. I came on a little strong the first time. Nerves and frustration, I guess."

The editor squeezed lemon into her iced tea. If a lemon could say ouch.

"A friend of yours called me since you and I last spoke. He also happens to be a friend of mine."

"Kyle Dixon?"

"The very one."

The chowder arrived. Oyster crackers were noticeably absent.

"Kyle vouched for you," said Ms. Thompson, who did not volunteer information on how she knew his friend. He wondered how much Kyle had told the editor; he wondered how soon lunch would take before he could thank his friend.

"If I were to give you a chance, you'd have a 6-month probationary period. You would write a variety of stories from news to features and event listings. You would have to work some weekends and fill in for staff members when they're on vacation. It's not glamorous, but it's community journalism, and it's important."

"It sounds great," said Will, who was familiar with the concept of probation.

"Good. Now how do you feel about grown men and women racing each other with cups of green beer in their hands?" Ms. Thompson said, introducing her smile. Eastport's Green Beer Races were a fabled yearly custom.

"I'd like to try it."

"Not the beer. We cover the race – rather, you would be covering it."

The shrimp salad sandwiches arrived. Will hoped the restaurant had doggy bags.

"Also, as you might know, every 17 years cicadas descend on Maryland," she said. Will had no idea when cicadas last infested Annapolis, but their timing appeared germane. "You would be writing about cicada recipes."

"And green beer races."

"And green beer races," she said.

Will inhaled his shrimp salad sandwich. Ms. Thompson hardly touched hers.

"The work is part-time. 6-month probation, as I mentioned. Monday-through-Wednesday. We publish on Thursday. The job pays $18,500 with medical and dental. Vision, too."

Out of habit, Will reached for his wallet when the bill came and struggled to dislodge his last twenty trapped in a coal mine of wounded singles. The bill was $27.32.

"Can you start next Wednesday?"

"I can absolutely start Wednesday. Thank you. You don't know what this means to me."

"I just might," Ms. Thompson said. In another act of compassion, she remarked how the cicadas were particularly abundant last year; her new reporter had a 16-year reprieve on the recipe story.

"Consider it a signing bonus," she said, before putting down her Visa and asking that her sandwich be wrapped to go.

Will thanked her twice more for the job and twice for her wrapped sandwich.

As a reporter newbie, he made every conceivable mistake – even the nightmarish typo of leaving the "l" out of "public" when writing a brief about the public being invited to the Green Beer Races. But Ms. Thompson, the four full-timers, and even Kathy Bates were patient in their mentoring. And in discovering Annapolis through stories, he was discovering his home for the first time; his small town had become a new world. He met people he never would have met and rather than spending the day teaching 15-year-olds and hiding his good stapler, he had adult conversations with adults at work. Will even had his own desk and had not been asked to float even once.

• • •

He called his mother more often, even though she didn't have much to report. He came by more often, even though she hadn't cooked enough for two and, frankly, was hoping to have a night by herself. He offered to drive her to Somerset every Saturday, even though she wasn't planning to go *every* Saturday. It might be a Sunday or a Tuesday or she might skip a week or three. Barb Larkin didn't want to hurt her son's feelings, but she needed some space and told him so.

"Does this mean I can't mooch dinner off you?" Will said.

"Of course not. But I wouldn't mind the occasional dinner out with you and Parker."

With delicacy, she declined Will's offer to come over.

"How are you?" she said. (The universal question to stump all universal answers.) "Do you need a certificate for a spa? A lifetime pass to vespers?"

Will chuckled.

"I'm good," he said, realizing that was true. "He's let go of us, hasn't he? I know he has. I know I have to let him go."

"When did you get so smart?"

"It's been a hard year, Mom."

Will thought about his father's wallet and the photograph of the unknown family. If needed, he could be the son in the picture.

"I'm still going to watch O's game with him."

"And you should," she said. "Most of your father's clothes are still at the house. I want you to have his London Fog overcoat. You're bigger than he is, but it will still fit."

"I love that coat."

"Then it's yours."

"One more thing for today," his mother said. "Your father's grill, the Weber. It's yours, too."

"But Mom I don't grill."

"Learn."

• • •

By late October, they shrink wrap boats in cocoons again until next April. The bigger boats head south to Florida or Bermuda. *The Woodwind* takes the winter off for repairs and maintenance. The harbor water taxis keep working, but they have Ego Alley mainly to themselves. The small inlet, so compressed during the season by watercraft, is downright spacious. The locals get their town back, day by day – at least until January when state lawmakers descend on Annapolis like pin-striped cicadas.

The locals ordered two coffees at Starbucks that were either Grande or Venti. Will and Parker perched their drinks on the seawall by the Alex Haley statue, currently unmarred by fallen ice cream.

"I spy… *Reporter Man,*" she said, lying, giggling.

"You giggled."

"I did not. I have not giggled since 2011," Parker said.

"Own the giggle."

"I will not own the giggle because I didn't giggle. Now on with the game. It's your turn."

"I spy… *The Lying Giggler.*"

"Liar!"

"Giggler!"

"Do you dare challenge me in a rematch of our handwriting contest?" Parker said.

"I dare not."

She put down her coffee and reached into her handbag and pulled out Jerry Kramer's *Instant Replay*. She could have gift- or even shrink-wrapped it, but any true Green Bay Packer fan wouldn't complain about receiving such a prize unwrapped. Will held the new hardback like it was a cold-case DNA sample. Without inhibition, he caressed its cover and thanked Parker three times until she asked him to stop. The man might weep. Will put the book on the seawall – too risky – he put the book on the bench.

"Darlin', you're so damn sweet..." Will crooned, having committed to memory Bambi Lee Savage's song upon an earlier recommendation. *"... Don't forget the milk..."* Parker crooned in return.

"Seriously, how did you know I wanted a new copy?"

In an awkward courtesy, Parker had reached out to Terri not so much to ask for approval but to let her know her feelings for Will. She didn't know how things would turn out. No one ever does, Terri said, before gifting her the idea to get Will his favorite book.

"It's a mystery," was all Parker said.

"You know what this means."

"What?"

"We're betrothed?"

"Not so fast, buckaroo. Betrothing is serious business. For adults only, I hear."

"We might qualify – barely."

Will reached into the Barnes & Noble bag he had been carting. He handed Parker a book of poetry by Elizabeth Bishop.

"I meant to give you this at the Red Suit Bash but some crazy dude got in a fight and ruined the party."

"I wondered whatever happened to him."

"Institutionalized, sadly."

He also gave Parker three large Moleskin notebooks. To take notes, he said. For your novel. "The first time we really talked you said you wanted to be a novelist. So, start noveling. But first, walk down the dock with me."

In the red brick square at the end of City Dock, "See you next Spring!" signs were posted at the vacant slips. They reached the encased yellow life rings attached to the cone-headed pilings. It was clear enough to see the Tinker-Toy spans of the great bridge. As a south-bound yacht left Ego Alley for the season, Will thought about Dean the perfect dog, and he thought about Terri and her kindnesses, old Bob Eaton at the soup kitchen, and even that damn gazebo. If he had his father's binoculars, Will could spy on their home off Compromise Street and see the empty widow's walk with his mother gardening below. Farther away, his father was winning at poker with new friends, all of them singing about those happy days again.

Will and Parker stood by the life ring, neither quite ready to leave. Clouds like animal crackers marched in front of the noon sun then back out.

"Now what?" Parker said.

Will Larkin stared into the harbor water, which, for a change, looked blue.

"We begin."

12 years later

Chapter 22

After years of living in Sarasota, Teresa Morrow was still staggered by the volume of grapefruits produced by a single grapefruit tree in her verdant yard. She acquired a love of grapefruit juice but didn't need a distillery of the stuff. More astonishing was the number of grapefruits that plunked in her pool after the routine thunderstorms, which were so rare in Maryland. It's like bobbing for mutant pink apples, Terri told her ex-husband on the phone. They managed to catch up a few times a year.

"Beyond the surplus citrus, how's life in God's waiting room?" he said.

"That's St. Pete. Sarasota is God's back yard. And life is good."

She moved to Florida's west coast to be close – but not too close – to her convalescing parents up in St. Petersburg. Also, a job had dislodged her from Maryland. She was head of the English department at Sarasota High School and had found a ranch house in a cozy enclave on Wood Duck Lane near placid Sarasota Bay (her three built-in bookcases were nearing capacity). She was amused by the absence of a single duck on Wood Duck Lane and attributed their absence in her yard to Lila, her 12-year-old Black lab and a 10-year-old gift from her ex-husband. No dog could replace Dean, but the kindness of the gesture survived.

Terri came to learn Florida's mild weather mood swings and its other *ways*. Restaurants weren't stocked with Old Bay, but the stone crabs were ambrosial, football, not lacrosse, was the big deal, politics leaned un-blue, and the O's Bird was a superior mascot to Raymond, a furry seadog employed by the Tampa Bay Rays. Fortunately, the Orioles' spring training was in Sarasota, so she got her required dose of Baltimore baseball in March, and she never once wore a Red Sox jersey to a game. Terri did not miss shoveling snow or raking leaves and developed a fascination with the horseshoe crabs skating in the bay shallows near her home. Running an English department wasn't unlike coaching girls; sometimes she wanted to bop teachers with a lacrosse stick, too.

Many evenings Terri planted herself in her back yard and ignored the bobbing grapefruits and scolded Lila for digging up or eating something she shouldn't. On her reversed, adopted coast, she scooted, turned, re-scooted in her Adirondack to watch the day go down before she stopped chasing the sun. A gin and tonic was optional company, but she was seldom in a hurry to get up and fix just herself a drink. Neighbors remarked on seeing Terri sitting alone for hours, seemingly content in her gazebo.

• • •

Kyle Dixon never returned to the barren field of radio broadcast journalism. An unrepentant dreamer, he moved to Napa and became an organic farmer and took up the ukulele with uncanny success. A living wage, however, still eluded him. He felt compelled to seek part-time work at any of the many area vineyards. Responding to an ad for a Tasting Room Specialist Associate, he found himself interviewed by Black Tie Vineyard's co-owner one delicious afternoon in Northern California. Kyle stated he could speak knowledgeably about wine, varietals, and viticulture in general.

"No, you can't," the co-owner said. His eyes, Kyle noticed, seemed like blue swinging kitchen doors. He wanted to walk through them.

"No, I can't," he said. "I don't know anything about wine."

The vineyard's co-owner grinned.

"Do you know how to drive a fork lift?"

"Not in my wildest dreams."

"Good. We'll start you on the fork lift."

Six months later, Kyle was still driving the vineyard's lone fork lift, but on-site collisions had tapered to a workable 1, 2 incidents a month involving the dedicated driver. More rewarding but professionally tricky, he and the vineyard's co-owner were dating. He shared his news with his best friends on the East Coast in an emergency *Week in Review* meeting by conference call.

Kyle was nervous about declaring his affections for a man. It was all very shocking and wonderful.

"I'm happy for you."

"Thanks, Will. Who knew, eh? I guess I'm what they call 'sexually fluid.'"

Mack rose up.

"Sexual fluids? I don't care who you bang, but do we have to hear about your sexual fluids? Have some fucking mercy on us."

Kyle attempted to clarify his statement, but Will urged them off the topic. He asked Kyle if he could recommend a good Cab or Merlot.

"Oh, don't get me started."

• • •

Annapolis attorney William P. Larkin Jr., 72, died peacefully in his sleep at the Somerset Assisted Living facility in Anne Arundel County (when told, Kyle wondered why they always say people died *peacefully*. "Why can't anyone die *jauntily* or *angrily*?") William Larkin's iron-clad will stipulated, among more standard directives, that a live version of "Country Road" be played at his non-denominational service. His son, who inherited his father's 12 James Taylor compact discs, chose a suitable live version and played it on a yeoman-like CD player at Somerset's chapel, where friends and family gathered. The deceased's surviving wife, Barbara Larkin, asked their son to read a poem. William P. Larkin, 42, also of Annapolis, read a Donald Justice poem and stopped only twice to steel himself. He added that his father once said he would miss the smell of bacon and wood smoke. Then Will was finished talking.

In the ensuing years, Barb Larkin remained in the home on Compromise Street overlooking Annapolis Harbor. She converted her husband's "man cave" on the widow's walk into her "woman cave," as she joked. Removed were the *Playboys* and *Reader's Digests* and Igloo cooler once outlawed with beer. She found a nice throw rug from Home Depot and hung a Bar Harbor Buoy Bell wind chime. Having to cut back on her gardening, she did maintain four potted plants on the widow's walk, where she strolled looking out toward the gray-blue water off her town's shore.

She attended vespers at St. Gregory's on four more occasions and was accompanied each time by her son, who bought dinner twice.

• • •

The beach house two blocks from Bethany Beach's bantam boardwalk was upgraded with central air and heat – no more overworked, underperforming wall units. The two bathrooms and master bedroom were remodeled at intervals of unforeseen expense at the primary residence. But money was not an issue. Mack had re-entered the world of personal investment services after failing to secure a license to open a medical marijuana dispensary at outlet malls and select Wawa stores in Maryland. He stayed long enough to make enough money to again leave the world of personal investment services. The details were beyond his friends, who probably still believed in certificates of deposit and the earning power of savings accounts, as he feared.

Three years ago, Mack sunk his wealth into acquiring a deserted neighborhood bar. The buying was remarkably easy; the operating revealed itself as a ball-busting, around-the-clock enterprise guaranteed to lose copious amounts of money, a sweaty horror interrupted occasionally by moments of relief bordering on morsels of satisfaction.

"I don't care what you say. I love this place," Christina said. "I love everything about it."

Throughout their marriage – 9 years now – Mack came to accept and find security in the fact he and his wife agreed on virtually nothing. He breathed cursing; she did not and instituted a swear jar that required constant emptying. Mack wanted to take another stab at owning a sloth, and rented one, despite furious and well-founded opposition from Christina. For the sloth bit the index finger of their exterminator, who while spraying for silverfish in their basement, thought it wise to fondle one of the sloth's elongated toes. The ensuing Urgent Care visit prompted Mack to both cancel his exterminator's contract and consult an attorney regarding potential liability.

In lesser disagreements, he wanted to call their bar *The Drunk Penguin*. The name failed to gain traction on the home front. He proposed *Hot and*

Cold and Running Beer, which was also roundly dismissed by Christina, the head bartender and often only bartender at the Bethany speakeasy. The name was too long and didn't make any sense. Hot beer? Let's name it after that bar you and your buddies hung out in back in the day. *Buster's*, they both agreed, was a fine name. They also disagreed on the name of their son. Mack liked the name Vaughn in honor of Vince Vaughn, but Christina nudged him off the corner of that idea. Why not William, she said. Why not name our son after your best friend? Can we call him Willie? Only when he is young, they both said.

When they were able to hire reliable help at Buster's, Mack and Christina had more time for their young family. In the early mornings, they walked along the beach before the crowds materialized. Willie collected shells but only to hold and pretend-polish before returning his *treasures* back to the sand. Ghost crabs poked up and skittered to other crab caves. No one played beach golf or Proof of Purchase anymore. Perpetually on dolphin look-out, Christina pointed out to her husband the dorsals of cruising Atlantic bottle-nose porpoises. Mack couldn't see a damn one of them and still denied their existence. He finally agreed to get his eyes checked and joined the rest of the world paying too much for frames.

"Chris, I should have invested in Ray-Bans years ago. Holy sweet fuck there's a fortune in frames."

"Hush," she said, taking his hand one morning on the beach. "Be grateful for what you have and if you love me, look to where I am pointing. Look. Look hard. Now, wait. Wait for it… see?"

And John McGuire saw his first Atlantic bottlenose.

• • •

"Come on, let's go, buckaroo," Will told the back of the bathroom door. "We're going to be late."

"Let her be. We're not going to be late," Parker said.

"Why do women take forever to get ready?"

"First, we don't. That's a stereotype. Second, if some of us do occasionally take longer, it's because we have more to get ready."

"You never see me late."

"You were almost too late asking me to marry you."

"That is true, Dr. Cool."

Parker was still getting used to being called Dr. Cool, but that was her title having become a veterinarian. Her two associates, one vet tech, and assorted pet owners often remarked hers was absolutely the greatest vet doctor name of all time. There was nothing to refute.

Re-tucking his dress shirt, Will checked the time and emotionally paced. Finally, his 18-year-old stepdaughter emerged from the bathroom. Dailey suddenly looked younger and older, a child and an adult, simultaneously, miraculously both on the verge of high school graduation. Her grades had been exemplary except for one blemish: Dailey received her only C of high school in freshmen algebra, believing her teacher had been unnecessarily demanding.

"I don't change my grades," he had told her in a tense dinner conversation that year. "You got a C because you earned a C." Dailey bolted from the table and didn't speak to him for two days. She received, in her opinion, insufficient sympathy from her mother. Even Uncle Steve was no help, telling her he would have sold his body parts *and* hers for a C in algebra.

During graduation in Lakeview High's new auditorium, Will held Parker's hand for the two and a half hours. Given he was a member of the faculty, he had the option of being on stage to personally deliver Dailey her slightly-blemished diploma, but he wanted to watch from the stands with every other parent. After the ceremony, Dailey had four post-graduation parties to attend, her father estimated. He promised he would treat them all to Applebee's next weekend, a family tradition still involving a group toast to the appetizer that brought them together.

With Parker having to work most Saturdays at the animal hospital, Will used the time as Volunteer Services Coordinator at the Shepherd's Table. Thanks to the expansion of its dining room, more than 600 guests could be served lunch daily. Will often scheduled and directed as many as 30 volunteers a shift. If the crew was short, he'd don a hairnet and apron and be Dessert Guy on the floor or work on the line dishing out the day's donated casserole. When in a real jam, he'd enlist Dailey who insisted on gender-neutral names and when assigned the job was indeed addressed as Bread Person. He and Bob Eaton kept a standing after-lunch lunch date every month.

Developing an unexpected zeal for journalism, Will became an editor of *The Capital,* Annapolis' hometown paper; and when the time came he would assign the newest reporter to cover Eastport's Green Beer Races. He kept in touch with Ms. Thompson, who playfully threatened him with having to write her a cicada recipe story when the time came. The insects were due back in five years.

Will and Parker became keepers of each other's stories and holders of their history through the dark and light shading of their marriage. Brief but healing chapters of marriage counseling were far outnumbered by passages of comforting routine all in the making of what Parker called their *Book of Us.*

"We need to highlight the chapter on how I converted you to Triscuits," Will said.

She was finally weaned off Wheat Thins in favor of Triscuits. But Parker believed he inflated her snack food conversion for the purposes of punching up the story among friends; she enjoyed *his* conversion: when her husband drank he drank small and they drank together. A case of Merlot would occasionally be shipped to their home from Black Tie Vineyards in Napa Valley, and the case lasted a good long while.

Boat ownership was not in their future, but a dog was. They picked out a short-haired, dusky dachshund they named Typo. Along with an undiplomatic bladder and diabolical resistance to house training, Typo was territorial. She didn't like Will and Parker sitting together on the sofa during movie night, so she wiggled her way between them. But more often, as the Larkins watched another viewing of "Annie Hall" or "Apollo 13," Typo would snuggle into Dailey's lap for the duration.

While another dog was predictable, Will's latent adventure streak was not. He surprised Parker by buying them paddleboard lessons on Spa Creek, where they spent Sundays exploring and "getting a good work-out" (he deserted his punching bag after developing chronic plantar fasciitis).

Carrying an extra 12 pounds since his wedding day, Will stuck with the strenuous paddle boarding and when he took a tumble or two into the murky creek, he easily righted himself. Will claimed his core was stronger, but when questioned could not define or locate his core.

More recently he surprised Parker with spontaneous long weekends to Mack's beach house when those two were away and once, a parasailing trip off and over nearby Ocean City. Parker thought her husband had lost his mind. Last spring break came a surprise week in Key West and snorkeling in the Dry Tortugas, a tour of the Hemingway House and afternoon beers at the Green Parrot. They fantasized about one day retiring there until they perused Key West real estate prices and promptly renewed their vows to Maryland. At Christmas Will bought Fodor's guidebooks to Greece and Spain and wrapped them to look like real books under the tree.

"What are you up to, newspaper man?" Parker said, easily disrobing his shoddy wrap job.

"We're going to be empty nesters in the fall. Time to think big on the vacation front."

"I have no problem with that at all."

"Because we're betrothed."

"Yes, we are."

• • •

On the rare nights she couldn't sleep, Parker walked to the marina to listen to baby waves slap against the docked sailboats. The briny air was limitless and embracing. She felt her foot steadier on the ladder of years and didn't mind her hands were still crossed with cat scars, her tattoos of labor, her hard candy. She thought about her parents, gone, and their family home across the rock quarry, sold and felt pangs of loss encircled by a tide of gratitude, love, and memory. A friend told her 40 was the new 30, which was so ridiculous Parker practiced believing it.

Will tip-toed outside to the backyard and sat on the hood of their picnic table when he was restless at night. The picnic table had not been intimately christened, but it served for writing when his wife opened her laptop to record book titles (she had amassed enough titles to make a fun book, he mentioned twice). Dozens of hand-me-down Chinese lanterns, strung in the trees, appeared as light-less, papered apparitions. A pastry of a cloud sometimes slipped across the moon. From a nearby marina, the same sailboat masts whined in night-call.

They are more fathers than sons themselves now, Will remembered from the poem he read at his father's funeral. *Something is filling them, something...*

When they went back inside on their separate nights, they walked upstairs to their bedroom where the other would be awaiting their return.

Epilogue

When I say publishing fiction was a lifelong dream of Rob's, I mean it. On July 23, 1989, he wrote about it in the journal he kept for our then infant son Ben. "This preoccupation of mine to be a novelist haunts me," he said in the first of several journal entries about his goal. "It preys on my insecurities as a writer."

Although Rob confessed in that journal to Ben that he worried about not having the self-discipline to finish a book, his actions prove that fear unfounded. He crafted *Float Plan* by writing at night and on weekends, and he spent years attempting to perfect his creation. What's more, Rob thought deeply about his characters. I see proof in the notations about Parker Cool and Will Larkin left behind in the moleskin notebooks he parked on his nightstand, in his car, and in his briefcase.

As bittersweet as it is to see *Float Plan* published posthumously, our family is pleased that readers will get to experience this comic tale of a mid-life crisis set in Rob's beloved Annapolis. We take great pride and joy in seeing the fulfillment of Rob's dream – and our dream for him.

— *Maria Hiaasen, August 2018*

About the Author

A native of Ft. Lauderdale, FL, Hiaasen lived in Maryland for almost 25 years, where he wrote for *The Baltimore Sun* for much of that time. More recently he was an award-winning columnist and editor at *The Capital* in Annapolis. His published fiction is a short story in the mystery anthology, *Baltimore Noir* (Akashic Press). Hiaasen's journalism has also appeared in *The Washington Post Sunday Magazine* and *The Los Angeles Times*.

Benefitting Organization
Everytown for Gun Safety

At the request of Rob Hiaasen's wife, Maria, Apprentice House Press will be making a contribution to Everytown for Gun Safety Support Fund.

Everytown is a movement of Americans working together to end gun violence and build safer communities. Gun violence touches every town in America. For too long, change has been thwarted by the Washington gun lobby and by leaders who refuse to take common-sense steps that will save lives.

But something is changing. Nearly 5 million mayors, moms, cops, teachers, survivors, gun owners, and everyday Americans have come together to make their own communities safer. Together, we are fighting for the changes that we know will save lives.

Everytown starts with you, and it starts in your town.

Learn more: www.everytown.org

Apprentice House is the country's only campus-based, student-staffed book publishing company. Directed by professors and industry professionals, it is a nonprofit activity of the Communication Department at Loyola University Maryland.

Using state-of-the-art technology and an experiential learning model of education, Apprentice House publishes books in untraditional ways. This dual responsibility as publishers and educators creates an unprecedented collaborative environment among faculty and students, while teaching tomorrow's editors, designers, and marketers.

Outside of class, progress on book projects is carried forth by the AH Book Publishing Club, a co-curricular campus organization supported by Loyola University Maryland's Office of Student Activities.

Eclectic and provocative, Apprentice House titles intend to entertain as well as spark dialogue on a variety of topics. Financial contributions to sustain the press's work are welcomed. Contributions are tax deductible to the fullest extent allowed by the IRS.

To learn more about Apprentice House books or to obtain submission guidelines, please visit www.apprenticehouse.com.

Apprentice House
Communication Department
Loyola University Maryland
4501 N. Charles Street
Baltimore, MD 21210
Ph: 410-617-5265 • Fax: 410-617-2198
info@apprenticehouse.com•www.apprenticehouse.com

CPSIA information can be obtained
at www.ICGtesting.com
Printed in the USA
LVHW020923091118
596394LV00007B/82/P